Burned

A PRETTY LITTLE LIARS NOVEL

SARA SHEPARD

Hanna glanced at the photo, then did a double-take. Even though she'd seen the girl for only one night, the face was unforgettable. It was like a ghost staring back at her.

She backed away, tripping over an upended suitcase and nearly falling on her butt. As she righted herself, her hands were suddenly shaking so badly she had to shove them into the folds of her dress. The room felt hot and close, and so many people were staring at her.

"Um, I have to ... " Hanna fumbled past everyone to the door.

Beep.

It was Hanna's phone. She pulled it out of her purse, figuring it was Mike. But then she looked at the screen. *One new text message from Anonymous.*

"No," she whispered, scanning the dark courtyard. Then she looked down at the screen. With shaking fingers, she pressed READ.

Be careful who you hit and run, jailbird. See you on the Fiesta Deck! —A

Burned

A PRETTY LITTLE LIARS NOVEL

SARA SHEPARD

www.atombooks.net

ATOM

First published in the United States in 2012 by HarperTeen
First published in Great Britain in 2012 by Atom

Copyright © 2012 by Alloy Entertainment and Sara Shepard

alloyentertainment

Produced by Alloy Entertainment
151 West 26th Street, New York, NY 10001

The moral right of the author has been asserted.

A CIP catalogue record for this book
is available from the British Library.

ISBN 978-1-907411-95-3

Typeset in Sabon by M Rules
Printed and bound in Great Britain by
Clays Ltd, St Ives plc

Papers used by Atom are from well-managed forests
and other responsible sources.

MIX
Paper from
responsible sources
FSC® C104740

Atom
An imprint of
Little, Brown Book Group
100 Victoria Embankment
London EC4Y 0DY

An Hachette UK Company
www.hachette.co.uk

www.atombooks.net

To Colleen

Loose lips sink ships.

– American idiom

Hit and Run

Ever told a lie to save yourself? Maybe you blamed the dent in your parents' Mercedes on your brother so you could still go to the spring formal. Maybe you told your Algebra teacher you weren't part of the group of kids who cheated on the midterm, even though you were the one who stole the answer key from her desk. You aren't normally a dishonest person, of course. But desperate times call for desperate measures.

Four pretty girls in Rosewood told some very dark lies to protect themselves. One of those lies even involved walking away from a crime just miles from their home. Even though they hated themselves for leaving the scene, they thought no one would ever know about it.

Guess what. They were wrong.

It had been raining for eight days straight at the end of June in Rosewood, Pennsylvania, a wealthy, idyllic suburb about twenty miles from Philadelphia, and everyone was beyond fed up. The rain had drowned perfectly manicured lawns and the first blooms in organic vegetable gardens, turning everything to mud. It had waterlogged golf course sand traps, Little League baseball fields, and the Rosewood Peach Orchard, which had been ramping up for its beginning-of-summer bash. The first sidewalk chalk drawings of the season swirled down the gutter, LOST DOG signs turned to pulp, and a single wilted bouquet on the cemetery plot containing the remains of a certain beautiful girl everyone *thought* was named Alison DiLaurentis washed away. People said such biblical rain would surely bring bad luck in the coming year. That wasn't welcome news for Spencer Hastings, Aria Montgomery, Emily Fields, and Hanna Marin, who'd already had more bad luck than they could handle.

No matter how fast the windshield wipers on Aria's Subaru swept across the glass, they couldn't brush off the driving rain quickly enough. Aria squinted through the windshield as she headed down Reeds Lane, a twisty road that bordered thick, dark woods and the Morrell Stream— a bubbling creek that would most likely flood within the hour. Even though there were upscale developments a stone's throw away over the hill, this road was pitch-black, without a single streetlight to guide them.

Then Spencer pointed at something ahead. "Is that it?"

Aria hit the brakes and nearly hydroplaned into a speed limit sign. Emily, who looked tired—she was getting ready to start a summer program at Temple—peered through the window. "Where? I don't see anything."

"There are lights near the creek." Spencer was already unbuckling her seat belt and springing out of the car. The rain soaked her immediately, and she wished she'd worn something warmer than a tank top and workout shorts.

Before Aria had picked her up, she'd been running on the treadmill in preparation for this year's field hockey season—she hoped she'd be an early decision shoo-in for Princeton after completing the five AP classes she was set to start taking at Penn, but she also wanted to be Rosewood Day's star field hockey player to get that extra edge.

Spencer climbed over the guardrail and peered down the hill. When she let out a little scream, Aria and Emily looked at each other, then bounded out of the car, too. They pulled their raincoat hoods over their heads and followed Spencer down the embankment.

Yellow headlights shone over the raging creek. A BMW station wagon was T-boned into a tree. The front end was smashed and the airbag dangled limply on the passenger side, but the engine was still humming. Windshield glass littered the forest floor, and the odor of gasoline eclipsed the smell of mud and wet leaves. Near the headlights was a slight, auburn-haired figure staring dazedly around as though she had no idea how she'd gotten there.

"Hanna!" Aria yelled. She ran down the slope to her. Hanna had called them all in a panic just a half hour before, saying she'd been in a crash and needed their help.

"Are you hurt?" Emily touched Hanna's arm. Her bare skin was slick with rain and covered in tiny shards of glass from the windshield.

"I think I'm okay." Hanna wiped the rain from her eyes. "It all happened so fast. This car came out of nowhere, knocking me out of the lane. But I don't know about . . . *her*."

Her gaze drifted to the car. There was a girl slumped in

3

the passenger seat. Her eyes were closed, and her body was motionless. She had clear skin, high cheekbones, and long eyelashes. Her lips were pretty and bow-shaped, and there was a small mole on her chin.

"Who *is* that?" Spencer asked cautiously. Hanna hadn't mentioned that anyone was with her.

"Her name's Madison," Hanna answered, brushing off a wet leaf that had just blown against her cheek. She had to scream over the sound of the pounding rain, which was so violent it was almost like hail. "I just met her tonight—this is her car. She was really drunk, and I offered to drive her home. She lives somewhere around here, I guess—she gave me directions piecemeal, and she seemed really out of it. Does she look familiar to any of you?"

Everyone shook their heads, slack-jawed.

Then Aria frowned. "*Where* did you meet her?"

Hanna lowered her eyes. "The Cabana." She sounded sheepish. "It's a bar on South Street."

The others exchanged a surprised look. Hanna wasn't one to turn down a cosmopolitan at a party, but she wasn't the type to go to a dive bar alone. Then again, they all needed to blow off some steam. Not only had they been tortured the previous year by two stalkers using the alias *A*—first Mona Vanderwaal, Hanna's best friend, and then the real Alison DiLaurentis—but they were also sharing a terrible secret from spring break a few months before. They'd all thought Real Ali had died in a fire in the Poconos, but then she'd appeared in Jamaica to kill them once and for all. The girls had confronted her on the roof deck at the resort, and when Ali had lunged at Hanna, Aria had stepped forward and pushed her over the side.

4

When they ran to the beach to find her body, it was gone. The memory haunted each of them every day.

Hanna wrenched the passenger door open. "I used her phone to call for an ambulance—it'll be here soon. You guys have to help me move her to the driver's seat."

Emily stepped back and raised her eyebrows. "Wait. *What?*"

"Hanna, we can't do that," Spencer said at the same time.

Hanna's eyes flashed. "Look, this wasn't my fault. I wasn't drunk, but I did nurse a drink all night. If I stay here and admit I was driving, I'll definitely get arrested. I might have gotten away with stealing and crashing a car once, but the cops won't go easy on me a second time." Last year, she'd drunkenly stolen her old boyfriend Sean Ackard's car and smashed it into a tree. Mr. Ackard had decided not to press charges, and Hanna had done community service instead.

"I could go to *jail*," Hanna went on. "Don't you realize how that would look? My dad's campaign will be ruined before it even begins." Hanna's father was running for senator in the fall; his campaign was already all over the news. "I can't let him down again."

The rain fell relentlessly. Spencer let out an awkward cough. Aria chewed on her lip, her eyes drifting to the motionless girl. Emily shifted her weight. "But what if she's really hurt? What if moving her makes things worse?"

"And then what do we do?" Aria added. "Just ... *abandon* her? That seems so ... *wrong*."

Hanna stared at them in disbelief. Then, setting her

jaw, she turned back to the girl. "It's not like we're leaving her here for days. And I don't think she's hurt at all—it seems like she's just passed-out drunk. But if you don't want to help me, I'll just do it myself."

She squatted down and tried to lift the girl by the armpits. The girl's body tilted awkwardly to the side like a heavy sack of flour, but she still didn't stir. Grunting, Hanna planted her feet and hoisted the girl upright again. Then she began to shift her across the center console and into the driver's seat.

"Don't do it like that," Emily blurted, stepping forward. "We have to keep her neck stable, in case there's any damage to her spine. We need to find a blanket or a towel, something to keep her neck steady."

Hanna eased the girl back down into the seat, then peered into the back of the station wagon. There was a towel in the footwell. She grabbed it, rolled it up, and wound it around the girl's neck like a scarf. For a moment, Hanna looked up. The moon had drifted out from behind a cloud and momentarily lit up the road, and the whole forest was alive with movement. The trees swayed violently in the wind. As a flash of lightning turned the sky white, all of them swore they saw something move near the creek bed. An animal, maybe.

"It will probably be easier for us to carry her around the outside of the car instead of trying to shift her from the inside," Emily said. "Han, you take her under the arms, and I'll take her feet."

Spencer stepped forward. "I'll get her around the middle."

Aria reluctantly peered into the car, then grabbed an

umbrella from the backseat. "She probably shouldn't get wet."

Hanna looked at all of them gratefully. "Thank you."

Together, Hanna, Spencer, and Emily lifted the girl out of the passenger side of the car and slowly shuffled her around the back and toward the driver's seat. Aria held an umbrella over the girl's body so that not a drop of rain hit her skin. They could barely see through the driving storm, having to blink every few seconds to keep the rain out of their eyes.

And then, halfway around the back, it happened: Spencer's feet slipped in the quicksandlike mud and she lost her grip on the girl. Madison tilted violently inward, her head banging against the bumper. There was a *snap*— maybe of a tree limb, but maybe of bone. Emily tried to bear the brunt of Madison's weight, but she slipped, too, jostling Madison's limp, fragile body even more.

"Jesus!" Hanna screamed. "Hold her up!"

Aria's hands wobbled as she tried to hold the umbrella steady. "Is she okay?"

"I-I don't know," Emily gasped. She glared at Spencer. "Weren't you watching where you were going?"

"It's not like I meant to do it!" Spencer stared into Madison's face. That *snap* resonated in her mind. Was the girl's neck now tilting at an unnatural angle?

An ambulance wailed in the distance. The girls stared at one another in horror, then started shuffling faster. Aria yanked the driver's-side door open. The key was still in the ignition, and the left-turn signal was blinking. Hanna, Spencer, and Emily moved the airbag aside and set the girl down in the buttery leather seat behind the wheel. Her

7

body listed to the right. Her eyes were still sealed shut, and the expression on her face was placid.

Emily let out a whimper. "Maybe we should stay here."

"*No!*" Hanna screamed. "What if we *did* hurt her? We look even guiltier now!"

The sirens grew louder. "Hurry!" Hanna grabbed her purse from the backseat and slammed the driver's-side door hard. Spencer shut the passenger door. They scrambled up the hill and dove into Aria's car just as the ambulance appeared on the ridge. Emily got in the car last.

"Go!" Hanna screamed.

Aria jammed her key in the Subaru's ignition, and the car sputtered to life. She did a quick three-point turn and sped away.

"Oh my God, oh my God," Emily sobbed.

"Keep driving," Spencer growled, peering out the back window at the whirling lights on top of the ambulance. Two EMTs jumped out of the ambulance and carefully maneuvered down the hill. "We can't let them see us."

Hanna swiveled around and stared out the window. All kinds of emotions knifed through her. Relief, definitely— at least Madison would get help. But the regret was like a vise around her throat. Had moving Madison made her worse? What had just *happened*?

A low sob burst from her lips. She put her head in her hands and felt the tears come.

Emily started crying, too. So did Aria.

"Stop it, guys," Spencer snapped, though tears were running down her cheeks as well. "The EMTs will take care of her. She's probably fine."

"But what if she's *not* fine?" Aria cried. "What if we *paralyzed* her?"

"I was just trying to do the right thing by driving her home!" Hanna moaned.

"We know." Emily hugged her tight. "We know."

As the Subaru wound around the hairpin turns, there was something else everyone wanted to say but didn't dare: *At least no one will know about this*. The accident had happened on a desolate stretch of road. They'd gotten away from the accident before anyone had seen.

They were safe.

The girls waited for the accident to hit the news: CAR CAREENS OFF EMBANKMENT ON REEDS LANE, they imagined the headlines would read. The story might recount the girl's high blood-alcohol level and how badly the car had been smashed up. But what else would the reporters say? What if Madison *was* paralyzed? What if she remembered she hadn't been driving, or even remembered the girls moving her?

All the next day, each of them sat by the TV, checked their phones for breaking news, and kept the radio on low, on alert. But no news came.

A day passed, and then another. Still nothing. It was like the crash had never happened. On the third morning, Hanna got in her car and drove slowly down Reeds Lane, wondering if she'd imagined the whole thing. But no, there was the bent guardrail. There were the skid marks in the mud and a few shards of glass on the forest floor.

"Maybe her family was really embarrassed about what happened and made a deal with the cops to keep it quiet,"

Spencer suggested when Hanna called her to express her uneasiness at the lack of news. "Remember Nadine Rupert, Melissa's friend? One night, when they were seniors, Nadine got drunk and wrapped her car around a tree. She was fine, but her family begged the cops to keep the DUI a secret, and they did. Nadine was out of school for a month getting rehab, but she told everyone she was at a spa retreat instead. Later, though, she got drunk again and told Melissa the truth."

"I just wish I knew if she's hurt," Hanna said in a small voice.

"I know." Spencer sounded worried. "Let's call the hospital."

They did, on three-way, but since Hanna didn't know Madison's last name, the nurses couldn't give them any information. Hanna hung up the phone, staring into space. Then she went on the website for Penn State—which was the school Madison said she attended—and did a search for her, hoping she'd find her last name that way. But there were quite a few Madisons in the sophomore class, way too many to go through one by one.

Would she feel better if she came forward and confessed? But even if she explained that another car had come out of nowhere, knocking her off the road, no one would believe her—they'd assume she'd been as wasted as Madison. The cops wouldn't congratulate her for being honest, either—they'd haul her off to jail. They'd also realize that she'd needed help moving Madison and had had to recruit her friends. They'd be in trouble, too.

Stop thinking about it, Hanna decided resolutely. *Her family wanted to make it go away, and you should do the same*. So she went to the mall. She tanned poolside at the country club. She avoided her stepsister, Kate, and was a bridesmaid in her father's wedding to Isabel, wearing a hideous green dress. Eventually, she stopped thinking about Madison and the accident every second of the day. The crash hadn't been her fault, after all, and Madison was probably fine. It wasn't like she *knew* Madison, anyway. She'd probably never see her again.

Little did Hanna know that Madison was connected to someone they all knew very well—someone who hated them, in fact. And if that someone knew what they all had done, terrible things might happen. Acts of retribution. Revenge. Torture. That very person might take it upon himself—or herself—to become the very thing all four girls feared most.

A new—and far more frightening—A.

1
Beware, Ye Liars

On a blustery Monday morning in late March, Spencer Hastings stared into the vintage Louis Vuitton trunk on her queen-sized bed. It was packed full of things for her upcoming journey on the Rosewood Day Prep Eco Cruise to the Caribbean, a combination of class trip and environmental-science seminar. Using the trunk was a long-standing good-luck tradition: It had once belonged to Regina Hastings, Spencer's great-great-grandmother. Regina had bought a first-class reservation on the *Titanic* but decided to stay in Southampton for a few extra weeks and take the next steamer out.

As Spencer tossed a third bottle of sunscreen onto the top of the pile, her phone let out a *bloop*. A text bubble appeared on the screen from Reefer Fredericks. *Hey buddy*, it said. *What are you up to?*

Spencer found Reefer's number in her contacts list and dialed it. "I'm packing for the trip," she said when he answered on the first ring. "You?"

"Just putting some last-minute things together,"

Reefer answered. "But I'm bummed. I can't find my Speedo."

"Oh, please," Spencer teased, curling a tendril of honey-blond hair around her finger. "You don't own a Speedo."

"You got me." Reefer chuckled. "But I really *can't* find my trunks."

Spencer's heart did a flip as she thought about Reefer in swim trunks—she could tell through his T-shirt that he was toned. His school was going on the cruise, too, along with several other private schools in the tristate area.

She'd met Reefer at a Princeton Early Admission dinner a few weeks earlier, and although she hadn't been into his hippy, pothead vibe at first, he ended up being the best thing she got out of her disastrous pre-frosh weekend on campus.

Since she'd returned to Rosewood, they'd been texting and calling each other ... a *lot*. During a *Dr. Who* marathon on BBC America, they'd called one another during the commercial breaks to discuss the doctor's bizarre alien adversaries. Spencer introduced Reefer to Mumford & Sons, and Reefer schooled her on the Grateful Dead, Phish, and other jam bands, and before she knew it, she had developed a massive crush on him. He was fun, clever, and more than that, nothing seemed to shake him. He was the human equivalent of a hot-stone massage—just the type of guy Spencer needed right now.

She hoped that something would happen between them on the trip. The top deck of the cruise ship seemed like the perfect setting for a first kiss, the tropical sunset like a huge bonfire all around them. Or maybe their kiss would

14

happen on a dive—they were both taking a scuba class together. Maybe they'd be swimming around a crop of neon-pink coral, and suddenly their hands would touch under the water, and they'd swim to the surface, pull off their masks, and then ...

Reefer coughed on the other end, and Spencer blushed as if she'd voiced the thoughts aloud. In actuality, she wasn't sure what Reefer thought about her—he'd been flirty at Princeton, but for all she knew, he was like that with all girls.

Suddenly, a banner on her TV caught her eye. DEATH IN JAMAICA: MURDERED GIRL INVESTIGATION BEGINS. A familiar blond girl's picture flashed on screen. TABITHA CLARK, a caption read.

"Uh, Reefer?" Spencer said abruptly. "I have to go."

Spencer hung up and stared at the TV. A stern-looking gray-haired man appeared next. MICHAEL PAULSON, FBI, said a caption under his face. "We're beginning to put together the pieces of what might have caused Ms. Clark's death," he said to a group of reporters. "Apparently, Ms. Clark traveled to Jamaica alone, but we're trying to re-create a timeline of where she was and who she was with that day."

After that, the news shifted to a story about a murder in Fishtown. Suddenly, the cheerful, colorful resort-wear folded neatly in the steamer trunk looked perverse and ridiculous. The smiling sun on the sunscreen bottle seemed to be sneering at her. It was ridiculous to be jetting off on a tropical trip like nothing was wrong. *Everything* was wrong. She was a coldhearted killer, and the cops were narrowing in on her fast.

Ever since Spencer and her friends discovered that they'd killed Tabitha Clark—not the real Alison DiLaurentis, as they'd all thought—Spencer hadn't been able to draw in a full breath. At first the cops had thought Tabitha had accidentally drowned, but now they knew she'd been murdered. And the police weren't the only ones.

New A knew, too.

Spencer had no idea who New A, the insidious text messenger who knew everything about their lives, might be. First, she and the others had thought it was Real Ali— maybe she'd survived the fall off the roof deck and was after them once and for all. But then the authorities identified the washed-up remains as Tabitha's, and they realized how crazy they'd been to even consider that Ali had survived the fire in the Poconos. Her bones might not have been found, but she'd been inside the house when it exploded. There was no way she could have gotten out, even though Emily still clung to that theory.

Next, the girls had thought A might be Kelsey Pierce, whom Spencer had framed for drug possession the previous summer. Kelsey made sense: Not only had Spencer wronged her, but Kelsey had also been in Jamaica at the same time the girls were.

But that turned out to be a dead end. Next they had thought A was Gayle Riggs, the woman to whom Emily had promised—and then unpromised—her unborn baby, and who happened to be Tabitha's stepmom. But that theory fell through when Gayle ended up dead in her driveway. Even more chilling? They were pretty sure New A had killed her.

16

Which was baffling—and terrifying. Did Gayle know something she shouldn't have? Or had A meant to kill Spencer and the others instead? And A knew *everything*. Not only had A sent pictures of the girls talking to Tabitha during dinner the night they'd killed her, but the girls had also received a picture of Tabitha's broken body on the sand. It was like A had been poised and ready on the beach, camera in hand, predicting the fall before it happened. There was another weird twist, too: Tabitha had been a patient at the Preserve at Addison-Stevens, a mental hospital, at the same time Real Ali had been there. Had they been friends? Was that why Tabitha acted so much like Ali in Jamaica?

Spencer's phone bleated again, and she jumped. Aria Montgomery's name flashed on the screen. "You're watching the news, aren't you?" Spencer said when she answered.

"Yeah." Aria sounded distraught. "Emily and Hanna are on the line, too."

"You guys, what are we going to *do*?" Hanna Marin said shrilly. "Should we tell the cops we were at the resort, or should we keep quiet? But if we *do* keep quiet, and then someone *else* tells the cops we were there, we'll look guilty, right?"

"Calm down." Spencer eyed the news again. Tabitha's father, who was also Gayle's husband, was on the screen now. He looked exhausted—as he should. Both his wife and his daughter had been murdered in the span of a year.

"Maybe we should just turn ourselves in," Aria suggested.

"Are you crazy?" Emily Fields whispered.

"Okay, maybe *I* should turn myself in." Aria backtracked. "I was the one who pushed her. I'm the guiltiest."

"That's ridiculous," Spencer said quickly, lowering her voice. "We *all* did it, not just you. And no one is turning themselves in, okay?"

A tiny movement outside caught her eye, but when she went to the window, she didn't see anything suspicious. Her mother's fiancé, Mr. Pennythistle, had parked his enormous SUV in the driveway. The new woman who'd moved into the Cavanaugh house across the street was kneeling in the flower bed, weeding. And to the left, Spencer could just make out Alison DiLaurentis's old bedroom window. When Ali had lived there, the pink curtains were always flung open, but the room's new owner, Maya St. Germain, always kept the wooden blinds twisted closed.

Spencer sat down on the bed. "Maybe it doesn't matter that the cops figured out Tabitha was killed. There's still no way they can trace the murder back to us."

"Unless A talks," Emily warned. "And who knows what A is capable of—A might not stop at blaming Tabitha's murder on us. A could frame us for killing Gayle, too. We were there."

"Has anyone heard from A?" Aria asked. "It's weird that A's been quiet since Gayle's funeral." The funeral had been almost a week ago.

"I haven't," Spencer said.

"Me neither," Emily piped up.

"A's probably planning the next big attack." Hanna sounded worried.

"We need to stop it before it happens," Spencer said.

18

Hanna snorted. "How are we going to do *that*?"

Spencer walked over to her bed and nervously fingered the gold latch on the steamer trunk. She didn't even have the beginning of an answer. Whoever New A was, New A was *crazy*. How could she anticipate a lunatic's next move?

"A killed Gayle," Spencer said after a moment. "If we figure out who A is, we can go to the cops."

"Yeah, and then A will turn around and tell the cops about *us*," Hanna pointed out.

"Maybe the cops wouldn't believe a murderer," Spencer said.

"Yeah, but A has *pictures* to prove it," Aria hissed.

"Not of us specifically," Spencer said. "And anyway, if we figure out who A is, maybe we could find them and delete them."

Aria sniffed. "That all sounds great if we were, like, James Bond. Right now we don't know who A *is*."

"You know, it's good we're going on this trip," Hanna said after a moment. "It'll give us time to think."

Aria scoffed. "You really think A is going to leave us alone?"

Hanna breathed in. "Are you saying A might *come*?"

"I hope not," Aria said, "but I'm not holding my breath."

"Me neither," Spencer said. She'd considered the possibility of A being on board, too. The idea of being trapped in the middle of the ocean with a psycho was chilling.

"How do you guys feel about going back to the Caribbean?" Emily asked nervously. "I feel like it will remind me of ... everything."

Aria moaned.

"At least we aren't going to *Jamaica*," Hanna said. The cruise ship was stopping in St. Martin, Puerto Rico, and Bermuda.

Spencer shut her eyes and thought about how excited she'd been to go to Jamaica last spring break. They had all planned to put Real Ali, the evil A notes they'd received from her, and their near-death in the Poconos behind them. She'd packed bikinis, T-shirts, and the same Neutrogena sunscreen she'd plopped in the steamer trunk, hope rising in her chest. *It's all over,* she'd kept thinking. *My life is going to be great now.*

She glanced at the clock on her bedside table. "Guys, it's ten. We'd better go." They were supposed to be at the boat docks in Newark, New Jersey, a little after noon.

"*Shit,*" Hanna said.

"See ya there," Aria answered.

Everyone hung up. Spencer dropped her phone in her canvas beach bag, then hefted it onto her shoulder and righted the steamer trunk on its wheelie-board. When she was almost to the door, something out the window caught her attention once more.

She walked over to the window again and stared out at the DiLaurentises' yard. At first, she wasn't sure what was different. The tennis courts, which the new family had built over the half-dug hole where the workers had found Courtney DiLaurentis's body, were empty. The wooden blinds at Ali's old window were still shut. The multilevel deck at the back, where the girls used to hold court, gossiping and boy-rating, was swept clean of leaves. But then she saw it: There was a child-sized life preserver in the

20

middle of Ali's yard. It was red-and-white striped, like a candy cane, and had large, curly, piratelike script across the bottom that read DEAD MEN TELL NO TALES.

Acid rose in Spencer's throat. Even though there was no one around, it still felt like the preserver was a message expressly from A. *Better hang on to this for dear life*, A seemed to be saying, *because I might just make you walk the plank*.

2
Emily's Little Mermaid

The road leading up to the Newark shipyards was a nondescript two-lane highway with generic-looking office complexes, gas stations, and seedy bars. But when Emily Fields and her father took a sharp left and pulled onto the waterfront, the sky opened up, the scent of salt hung heavy in the air, and the enormous Celebrity cruise ship rose before her like a giant, many-tiered wedding cake.

"Whoa," Emily breathed. The ship stretched several city blocks, and there were more circular portholes on each level than she could count. Emily had read in the Eco Cruise brochure that the vessel contained a theater, a casino, a gym with nineteen treadmills, a yoga studio, a hair salon and spa, thirteen restaurants, eleven lounges, a rock-climbing wall, and a wave pool.

Mr. Fields pulled into an available parking space near a big tent with a banner that read PASSENGERS, CHECK IN HERE! There was a line of thirty or so kids with suitcases and duffels. After he cut the engine, he sat staring straight ahead. Seagulls circled the sky. Two girls squealed excitedly when they saw each other.

Emily cleared her throat awkwardly. "Thanks for the ride."

Mr. Fields turned abruptly and looked at her hard. His eyes were iron-cold, and two curved lines accentuated his mouth like parentheses.

"Dad ... " Emily's stomach started to hurt. "Can we talk about this?"

Mr. Fields set his jaw and faced front. Then he turned up the radio. They'd been listening to a New York news station for the second half of the drive; now a reporter was droning on about someone nicknamed the Preppy Thief who'd escaped from a New Jersey holding cell that morning. "Ms. Katherine DeLong might be armed and dangerous," the reporter was saying. "And now, on to weather ... "

Emily twisted the volume down again. "Dad?"

But her father didn't pay any attention. Emily's jaw wobbled. Last week, she'd broken down and told her parents that she'd secretly had a baby girl over the summer and had given her up for adoption shortly after she was born. She'd omitted a few of the more sordid details, like accepting money from Gayle Riggs, a wealthy woman who'd wanted the baby, and then changing her mind and returning the payment, which A had intercepted. But she'd told them a lot. How she'd hid in her sister Carolyn's dorm room in Philadelphia during the third trimester. How she had seen an ob-gyn in the city and had a scheduled C-section at Jefferson Hospital.

Emily's mom hadn't blinked through the whole story.

23

After Emily had finished, Mrs. Fields took a long sip of her tea and thanked Emily for being honest. She even asked Emily if she was okay.

The clouds had parted in Emily's mind. Her mom was being *normal*—cool, even! "I'm holding up," she'd answered. "The baby is with a really great family—I saw them the other day. They named her Violet. She's seven months now."

Then a muscle in Mrs. Fields's cheek twitched. "Seven months?"

"Yep," Emily said. "She smiles. And waves. They're wonderful parents."

And then, like a light switch abruptly flipped on, reality hit Emily's mom at full force. She blindly groped for her husband's hand as though she were on a sinking ice floe. After letting out a squeak, she leapt up and ran to the bathroom.

Mr. Fields sat, stunned, for a moment. Then he turned to Emily. "Did you say your sister knew about this, too?"

"Yes, but please don't be mad at her," Emily said in a small voice.

Since that day, Emily's mom had barely come out of her bedroom. Mr. Fields handled the chores, making dinner, signing Emily's permission slips, and doing the laundry. Every time Emily tried to broach the subject with him, her dad shut her down. And forget about talking to her mom: Whenever Emily even got near her parents' bedroom, her father appeared, seemingly out of nowhere, like a rabid, protective guard dog, shooing her away.

Emily had no idea what to do. She would have preferred her parents send her to reform school or to live with her über-religious relatives in Iowa, like they'd done when they were mad at her in the past. Maybe she shouldn't have told her parents about the baby, but she didn't want them to find out from someone else—like New A. The Rosewood PD knew, too, as well as Isaac, the baby's father, and Mr. Clark, Gayle's husband.

Amazingly, the news about the baby hadn't made its way around Rosewood Day, but it didn't matter—Emily still felt like a pariah. Add in the fact that she'd witnessed a murder two weeks prior and that the police were now investigating Tabitha's death, and most days she could barely hold it together. She was also more certain than ever that A was Real Ali—that she'd survived the fire in the Poconos and was out to get them once and for all. Real Ali had framed Kelsey Pierce, driving Emily to almost kill her at Floating Man Quarry. Then she'd thrown suspicion on Gayle, shooting her when she got in the way. Emily shivered. What would she do next?

A loud horn on the boat roused her from her thoughts. "Well, I guess I should go," Emily said softly, glancing at her dad again. "Thanks for, um, still letting me go on this."

Mr. Fields took a sip from his water bottle. "Thank the teacher who nominated you for the scholarship. And Father Fleming. I still don't think you *should* go."

Emily fiddled with the University of North Carolina ball cap in her lap. Her parents didn't have money to send their kids on frivolous class trips, but she'd won a scholarship through her botany class. After her parents had found out about the baby, Mr. Fields had gone to Father Fleming, their priest, to ask if they should still let her attend. Father Fleming had said they should—it would give them time to process what had happened and figure out their feelings.

There was nothing left for Emily to do but open the door, grab her bags, and start toward the check-in tent. She hadn't walked but three steps when her dad gunned the engine and took off down the road, not even staying to see the boat off as most parents were. She blinked back tears, trying hard not to cry.

As she joined the line, a twentysomething guy wearing a pair of red, star-shaped sunglasses bounded up to her. "I'm on to you!" he said, wagging a finger.

Tabitha's face flashed in Emily's mind. "W-what?" she croaked.

"You're totally a secret Cirque du Soleil fan!" The guy stuck out his hand. "The name's Jeremy. I'm your cruise director this week. How would you like to be a guest in tonight's kickoff Cirque du Soleil performance in the theater? The show's theme is Mother Earth, in honor of this being an Eco Cruise and all."

Several kids nearby stopped and smirked. "I think I'll pass," Emily mumbled, scurrying forward.

She flashed her passport to the check-in girl and was given a key to her cabin, a meal card and daily menu, and a map of the boat. Last but not least, she received a pamphlet that listed the various classes, activities, seminars, group meetings, and volunteer opportunities for the week—students were required to participate in one for-credit class and volunteer in the ship's "community," helping to clean, cook, plan events, or take care of the ship's enormous endangered-fish aquarium, and so on.

The volunteer spots were on a first-come, first-served basis; Emily had already signed up for lifeguard duty at the main pool. She still didn't know which class she'd take, though, so she scanned the list quickly. There was Exploring the Reefs Responsibly, Hunt for Sunken (Eco)Treasure, Clean Up the Tide Pools in a Kayak. She decided on a course called Caribbean Bird-Watching.

She boarded an elevator that would take her to her room. A calypso band played loudly on an upper deck, the bass thudding through the walls. A few girls were talking about a great bar in St. Martin they'd heard about. Two guys chattered about kiteboarding in Puerto Rico. Everyone was dressed in shorts and flip-flops, even though it was forty-five degrees outside.

Emily envied their carefree excitement—she couldn't even coax the corners of her lips to bend into a smile. All she could think about was her mother's vacant eyes, her dad's punishing scowl, the hatred in their hearts. The FBI agent on the news this morning. Gayle's dead body. Tabitha's face just as she realized she was falling. A lurking in the darkness, laughing, ready to hurt her for real.

She thought about Ali, too—Real Ali *and* Their Ali. All this time, Emily had been hiding a secret: In the Poconos, the girls had escaped the house just before it blew up, with Real Ali still inside. What the others didn't know, however, was that Emily had left the cabin door open so that Real Ali could escape, too. She'd told everyone she'd closed it tight. And when the cops didn't find her body, Emily was positive Real Ali *had* gotten out and was still alive.

For many, many months, Emily had hoped that Real

27

Ali would come to her senses and apologize to all of them for being A. Emily would be the first one to forgive her, of course. After all, she'd loved Ali—*both* Alis. She'd kissed both of them, Their Ali in her tree house in seventh grade, and Real Ali last year.

But that was before Real Ali messed with her daughter. Some of the notes from A threatened Violet's life. It was then that she realized Real Ali was beyond the pale. Real Ali didn't care for Emily at all, and she certainly had no intention of trying to make things right. She was just . . . *evil*. Almost immediately, the hope and love Emily had felt withered away, leaving a huge hole in her heart.

The elevator dinged, and an automated voice announced that they were on the Sunshine deck. A bunch of kids marched down the long, garishly carpeted hall to find their rooms. Not wanting to get stuck behind them, Emily turned toward the sliding-glass door that led to a small patio overlooking the water instead. She stepped through it and let the chilly sea air fill her lungs.

Gulls called overhead. Traffic swished in the distance. The waves had foamy white tops, and a lifeboat bobbed seven decks below. Then Emily heard a cough and jumped. A girl with olive skin and long, chestnut-colored hair stood at the far end of the balcony. She wore dark sunglasses, a white eyelet dress, and ballet flats with pink-and-white grosgrain ribbon trim.

Emily didn't speak at first. The girl was so ethereal and quiet that she thought she might be a ghost.

But then the girl turned and smiled. "Hey."

"Oh!" Emily said, stepping back. "Y-you scared me. I wasn't sure you were real."

28

The corners of the girl's mouth turned up. "Do you *often* see people that aren't real?"

"Never anyone like *you*," Emily blurted, and then clamped her mouth shut. Why had she just said that?

The girl raised her eyebrows, taking her sunglasses off. And then she strolled over. Up close, Emily could see the dimples on her cheeks. Her arresting green eyes sparkled, and she smelled so fragrantly of jasmine perfume that Emily felt a little light-headed.

"Maybe I *am* a ghost," the girl whispered. "Or a mermaid. We *are* at sea, after all."

Then she touched the tip of Emily's nose, turned around, and disappeared through the sliding door. Emily remained in a cloud of jasmine, her mouth hanging open, the tip of her nose tingling. She wasn't sure what had just happened, but she definitely liked it. For one fleeting second, the ghost—or mermaid, or whatever she was— had made her forget absolutely everything wrong with her life.

3

The Best Couples Always Compromise

"Welcome to the Activity and Volunteer Fair!" a sandy-haired guy said to Aria Montgomery and her boyfriend, Noel Kahn, as they walked up to the ship's casino. "Aren't you *so* psyched to be here?"

"Uh, sure," Noel said, looking at the guy warily.

"Awesome!" the guy said. Aria was almost positive she'd owned an identical version of the star-shaped sunglasses he was wearing when she was six. He stood uncomfortably close to her when he talked.

"The name's Jeremy. I'm your cruise director for the week," he went on. "And we're going to have fun, fun, fun! We have the best shows on the sea—and the funniest comedian in Lou the Earth Crusader. You'll laugh—*and* learn how to save the planet!" He ushered them inside. "Walk around! Make new friends! And don't forget to choose an activity and a volunteer task!"

Aria looked around. Humming slot machines, green-felt poker and blackjack tables, and a curved, marble-topped bar stretched as far as the eye could see. But there were no

30

liquor bottles behind the bar, no cards sitting on the tables, and when Noel pressed a button on the slot machine, a message came up that said TRY AGAIN LATER.

Noel glanced at another cruise worker, a glossy-lipped woman in a white suit. "Can we gamble?"

"Oh, yes, on casino night!" The woman had a glazed-over, Barbie-doll expression on her face. "You don't win real money, though—you get these cute little dolphin coins you can take home as souvenirs! They're made by tribal women in South Africa from 100 percent recycled wool!"

Noel wrinkled his nose. Aria nudged him in the ribs. "It's probably a good thing we can't play for money, you know. Remember that time we played blackjack and you tried to count cards? I whipped your butt."

"You did not," Noel said gruffly.

"Did too!"

"Well, I demand a rematch. Even if it's for recycled dolphin tokens." One corner of Noel's mouth rose.

Aria smiled happily. It felt so good to be getting along with Noel again. They'd been fighting a lot recently, first because Aria was sure that Noel had a crush on his family's exchange student, Klaudia, who luckily was having visa issues and couldn't come on the cruise. Then Aria had discovered a secret about Noel's father, which had led to more trouble between them. But they'd reconciled about everything, and now they were great.

They moved deeper into the casino, looking at activity booths for hiking expeditions, art walks, and mandatory for-credit classes like Convert Your Vehicle to Corn Power! Then Noel squeezed her arm.

31

"Are you sure it was okay that I took that lesson this morning?" he asked.

"Of course," Aria answered in a mature voice. The ship had disembarked a few hours earlier, and Noel had almost immediately abandoned Aria to surf with an ex-pro in the wave pool. Now he smelled overpoweringly like chlorine, and his eyes were a little droopy, the way they always got when he'd had a hard workout.

"Come on," Noel urged. "Tell the truth."

Aria sighed. "Okay, maybe I'm a *little* disappointed we didn't spend the first few hours together. Especially when the boat sailed out of the harbor. They played 'Over the Rainbow!' It was really cute and romantic. But we'll have lots of time to spend together, right?"

"Of course." Noel took Aria's face in his hands. "You know, I really like this new let's-always-be-honest policy."

"Me too," Aria said, but then fiddled with the ties on her sailboat-printed blouse. She and Noel were really trying to stick to an honesty-is-the-best-policy rule, telling each other the truth about everything. When Aria didn't want to watch *Game of Thrones* on HBO *again*, she said so. When Noel really, *really* wanted McDonald's drive-thru instead of another dinner at Aria's favorite vegan restaurant, he made it clear.

It was liberating, but Aria also felt like a fraud because she still hadn't told him her *big* secrets, like what had happened in Iceland last summer—only one person knew about that. He didn't know that there was a new A in town, either, or that she and her friends had done something terrible in Jamaica.

Worse, now that Tabitha's death had been deemed a

murder, Noel was suddenly interested in the story. While the two of them were hanging out at his house a few days earlier, a CNN report about Tabitha had popped on the screen. Noel had paused and squinted at Tabitha's picture. "She looks really familiar," he'd murmured.

Aria had quickly changed the channel, but she could feel Noel's mind working. He'd taken note of Tabitha while in Jamaica. When would he make the connection? Once he did, he'd likely tell the police everything he remembered about her from the trip. He'd tell them that Aria had been with him in Jamaica, too, and then the police would ask *her* questions.

On the phone with the girls, she'd mentioned an idea that had been brewing in her mind all week: turning herself in. On one hand, it would be a huge relief—she wouldn't have to hide anymore. On the other, her life would be over. Did she really want that?

Aria had hoped to use the time on this cruise to really figure out what she wanted to do, but she worried about the police investigation. What if the cops figured it out before she'd decided? What if A gave them a clue they didn't even know A *had* yet? Aria would rather the confession be on *her* terms, *her* decision, but it felt like she was running out of time.

Now they passed a bunch of booths offering sign-ups for short-fiction workshops, pottery classes, and an eco-tour sponsored by Greenpeace. Then Aria spied a sign that said SCAVENGER HUNT! Next to it were pictures of kids looking at clues, riding down zip-lines, and trekking through the rain forest. EXPLORE THE ISLANDS! a sign read. MAKE AN ENVIRONMENTAL DIFFERENCE! WIN BIG PRIZES!

33

"Cool." Aria grabbed a flyer.

A pudgy strawberry-blonde with a name tag that said GRETCHEN stepped forward, a big smile on her freckly face. "Interested?" she asked. "We give you clues that send you all around the three islands. There's some research involved, so it would meet your for-credit class requirement. It'll be a lot of fun, too."

"That sounds great." Aria could easily imagine hunting for clues and exploring the islands with Noel. But when she looked at Noel for his opinion, he was talking to a tall guy with sunburned cheeks at another table. BECOME A CHAMPION SURFER IN SEVEN DAYS, read a banner over Sunburned Guy's head. Amazingly, it was a for-credit class, too, the cruise ship's version of PE.

"Dude, sign me up," Noel said excitedly, grabbing a pen from a cup with a surfer on the front.

"Noel, wait." Aria caught his arm. "Doesn't this look like it could be fun for both of us?" She pointed to the scavenger hunt sign.

Noel frowned. "Let's surf instead."

Aria turned to Sunburned Guy, who was presumably the instructor. "Is it okay that I'm not a strong swimmer?"

He wrinkled his freckled nose. "Can you do the crawl?"

"I can dog-paddle," she said optimistically. She had never technically learned how to swim—there were so many other more interesting activities she'd wanted to try out when she was little instead. Cliff-diving in Jamaica had terrified her half to death. She'd always made Emily stay very close to where she landed so she could rescue her if she needed it.

The instructor looked skeptical. "Surfers need to be able to paddle through some pretty tough waves. I don't think you'd be able to handle it."

Noel looked crushed. Aria smiled at him. "Take the surf lessons anyway."

"No!" he said quickly.

"It's okay." Aria squeezed his hands. "Who cares if we don't do the same activity? We could do the same volunteer job, maybe. Or hang out at other times."

"Are you sure?" Noel's voice wavered.

"Absolutely." Aria kissed his nose. "I want us both to be happy."

Noel wrapped his arms around her and lifted her off the ground. "You're the sweetest person in the world."

He put her down, and for a moment, Aria *did* feel pretty sweet. But then the back of her neck prickled, and she sensed someone's presence behind her. She peered through the crowd of kids, the activity booths, and the blinking slot machines. There was a big banner over an empty table that read PROTECT THE SEAS. SAVE THE PLANET. LIVE LIFE TO THE FULLEST. A shadow moved behind it, and then a door marked STAFF ONLY eased shut. Aria's heart jumped, and she stared hard at the door, willing whoever it was to return.

The door remained shut. And yet, drifting over the sound of the slot machines, the whoops of the activity leaders, and the chattering of all of the kids stuffed into the room, there was a thin, eerie laugh. Aria's heart dropped to her feet. Whenever she heard that laugh, whether by coincidence or not, someone was always close.

A.

4
Hello, Roomie!

Later that night, Hanna Marin sat with her boyfriend, Mike Montgomery, in a plush booth at Café Moonlight, an al fresco restaurant on the top deck of the boat. Bright, twinkling stars served as the ceiling, and a light, salty-smelling breeze occasionally blew out the candles on the tables. Waiters dashed to and fro delivering big salads featuring organic vegetables, jerk-seasoned free-range chicken, and the best organic sweet-potato fries Hanna had ever tasted. A reggae band played a Bob Marley song, the musicians dressed up in tropical-print garb.

When the song ended, the cruise director, whom Hanna had started calling "Creepy Jeremy" because of how close he stood to people when he spoke and the weird smile that seemed to be tattooed across his face, grabbed the microphone. "These guys are amazing, huh? But if you think *you're* better, show off your skills at the *America's Got Talent* extravaganza on Sunday night! Start working on your act now, guys! First prize is a Vespa scooter!"

Mike crossed his arms over his chest. "Noel and I are going to do a hip-hop act."

Hanna gave him a crazy look. "You're actually going to *participate* in the talent show?"

Mike shrugged. "Didn't you hear him? First prize is a Vespa. And Noel and I put together some sick rhymes in Jamaica."

Hanna nearly choked on a fry. The last thing she wanted to do was reminisce about Jamaica. But everything today had reminded her of that awful trip: The artificial strawberry smell of someone's spray-on sunscreen, the brand of orange drink sold in one of the cafés, a boy's T-shirt that said JAMAICAN ME CRAZY! There was a Jamaican-themed party planned for two days from now, which didn't even make sense since they weren't going to Jamaica on this cruise.

She grabbed another fry and stuffed it into her mouth, resolving not to think about Jamaica on this trip—or any of the other shitty things that had happened. Like the fact that she'd recently witnessed a murder. And, oh yeah, that *she* was the intended target. Or that the cops were *this* close to figuring out what they did to Tabitha. What would happen when they did? Her family would be disgraced, of course. Her dad's senatorial campaign would be ruined. Hanna would have a long life in prison to look forward to.

James Freed, a friend of Mike's, appeared at their table. "Dude." He sank into a seat. "Did you hear about the Catholic girls' school that's here? They are *H-O-T*." He whispered the letters dramatically. "Apparently they're dying for some."

37

"*Hello*, James?" Hanna leveled a stare at him, reminding him she was Mike's girlfriend.

James looked at Hanna apathetically. "Hey." Then he turned back to Mike. "Some of the beaches in St. Martin allow nudity. Wanna help convince the Catholic girls to take a little trek with us?"

"Definitely." Mike practically began to drool.

Hanna pinched his arm. "Like hell you will!"

"Just kidding," Mike said quickly, then leaned toward her. "Unless you want to make it a threesome."

Hanna pinched him again. Then she flicked a lock of auburn hair over her shoulder and peered at James. "What Catholic school are you talking about?"

Again, James looked at Hanna like she was one of the pesky horseflies that had buzzed around them during the ship's departure. "I don't know. Villa ... something."

"Villa Louisa?" Hanna spat.

"I think that's it." James squinted at her. "Why, are you thinking of stalking them?"

Hanna pressed her nails into the heel of her hand. "Very funny." Two weeks ago, she'd won Mike away from what she now called his "mistake," Colleen Bebris, despite the fact that A had sent the entire school an embarrassing video montage of Hanna trying to dig up something naughty about Colleen by stalking her. Though Mike seemed to have forgotten the video, no one else had. Girls from Rosewood Day and some of the other private schools nudged each other and giggled at her as she'd boarded this morning. When she'd tried to take a spin class this afternoon, a not-even-that-cute-or-thin girl from the Quaker school had quickly set her water bottle on a free bike, saying it was saved. Hanna felt like she had a big sign on her back that said LOSER and just didn't know about it.

Hanna knew *of* the Villa Louisa girls, but she didn't know any personally. People from other schools called them Villa Gorillas. They pranced around the King James Mall wearing their plaid jumpers and naughty-girl kneesocks like they were *sooo* sexy, making eyes at every available (and unavailable) guy. Every Gorilla was thinner and blonder and more beautiful than the next, and the rumor was that they were all incredibly sexually talented. A lot of people had theories as to why: The holy water the nuns blessed them with actually contained an ancient aphrodisiac. Their uniforms were too tight in all the right places. They all had über-strict parents who forbade them to speak to any boy, anytime, and they were dying for male interaction. Apparently, Kate, Hanna's stepsister, knew a few girls from the school, but Kate had decided to stay home to do a community service project with her boyfriend, Sean Ackard, instead of going on the cruise.

"Hey!" Mike looked excited as he nudged Hanna. "Maybe your roommate is someone from Villa Louisa!"

"Then you're never coming in my room," Hanna joked. But she felt a little worried. Everyone on the cruise had been assigned roommates randomly—Jeremy had boasted that he'd personally pulled names out of a captain's hat. No one had known who they'd be stuck with until they got on the ship. There had been no sign of Hanna's roommate when she'd put her stuff down this morning.

39

Rooming with a Villa Gorilla was a terrible possibility. Hanna couldn't be the *uglier* roommate. And she felt like she was skating on thin ice with popularity-hungry Mike, anyway, what with everyone snubbing her.

The conversation between Mike and James moved from the Villa girls to the fact that several people had already had things stolen from their rooms. "It's not iPads or cell phones, either," James said. "It's random crap like shampoo and socks."

"Dude, I'd better hide my boxers," Mike joked.

Then James pulled a flask out of his bag. "Want some?" he asked, pushing it toward Mike, though not Hanna. When he unscrewed the cap, the scent of freshly squeezed limes wafted out.

Hanna inhaled the fragrant limes of the margarita—it was one of her favorite aromas, though it had been ages since she'd smelled it. Suddenly, a memory of the last time she really remembered the scent wriggled its way into her mind. The memory was about the other secret she was keeping, the one about Madison last summer.

She'd been in Philly with her dad that day to attend a political rally for one of his cronies—her dad's campaign hadn't really ramped up yet, but he'd done his fair share of handshaking and drumming up financial support. Afterward, when her dad had gone to a fancy dinner at the Four Seasons, Hanna had wandered over to South Street, wanting to get lost in the crowd of sightseers. Even though she was psyched that her dad was running for office, the secret from spring break weighed heavily on her. What if someone found out about it?

She'd noticed someone smiling at her from one of the

side streets and saw an attractive guy standing in front of a bar called the Cabana. He was cute in that clean-cut, interchangeable-frat-boy way.

"Drinks are half-off right now," he said, pointing to the bar. "Come in for happy hour."

"Uh, I have a boyfriend," Hanna said quickly.

One corner of the guy's mouth turned up. "I'm the bartender. I'm just on a break right now. I'm not trying to hit on you."

Hanna peered into the bar. It wasn't really her type of place—there was an outdated Phillies schedule in the window, a naked girl–silhouette doormat at the front door, and the smell of stale beer and cigarettes. But there was an old-timey jukebox in the back playing a classic country song. No one knew, but old country songs were her weakness. She wanted to sit in the darkness and not think for a while. Besides, this didn't seem like the kind of place anyone from her dad's campaign would go, meaning they wouldn't catch her.

So she followed the guy in. A couple of downtrodden-looking men and women nursed beers at the bar, and two guys were halfheartedly playing darts in the back.

The bartender who'd coaxed her inside had now taken his post behind the counter. "I'm Jackson, by the way," he'd said. "What can I get you?"

Hanna didn't really want anything to drink, but she asked for a margarita anyway. As she inhaled the drink's syrupy sweetness someone called out from the other end of the bar, "Watch out. Those things are super potent."

It was a slender girl a few years older than Hanna with wide blue eyes and high cheekbones. There was something sporty about her broad shoulders, freshly scrubbed skin, and high blond ponytail. She nudged her chin toward Hanna's drink. "Seriously. Jackson should have warned you."

Hanna licked her fingers clean. "Thanks. I'll remember that."

The girl grabbed her cocktail, got up, and slid into a seat next to her. "He's kind of cute."

Hanna shrugged. "He looks like he rows crew. Not my thing."

The girl sipped her drink. "I dare you to ask him to do a shot with us."

"That's okay," Hanna said quickly. She wasn't in the partying mood.

The girl cocked her head. "Is someone scared?"

Hanna flinched. Ali used to dare Hanna, Emily, Aria, and Spencer to do all kinds of things they didn't want to do, teasing that they were scared when they refused. She always made them feel like such losers.

"Fine." Hanna flagged Jackson over and ordered three lemon drops—one for him, too. The bartender and the girl knocked theirs back, but Hanna dumped hers on the floor when they weren't looking.

The girl sloppily wiped her mouth and gave Hanna an approving grin. "What's your name, anyway?"

"Olivia." Hanna blurted out the first name that came to mind. It was the name of her father and Isabel's wedding planner, whom she'd spoken with earlier that day.

"I'm Madison." Madison raised her empty shot glass. "I'm having one last hurrah before I head back to Penn State. I'm on academic probation there, and if they catch you with even the teensiest bit of alcohol on your breath, they go ballistic. Where do you go to school?"

"Temple." It was another think-fast answer—Emily was starting a summer program at Temple next week.

Madison asked Hanna more questions about herself, and Hanna made up more details. She said she was a cross-country runner, that she wanted to be a lawyer, and that she lived in Yarmouth, which was near Rosewood but *not* Rosewood. It felt good to slip into someone else's identity for a few hours. This fictitious Olivia didn't have two murderous BFFs and various stalkers. Her life seemed so enviously simple. The only real thing she shared was that she was going on a trip to Reykjavik, Iceland, soon with Aria, Noel, and Mike. "Is that the place where you can smoke pot in the streets?" Madison asked excitedly.

Hanna shook her head. "No, that's Amsterdam." Madison looked disappointed.

Madison told Hanna that she lived in the area, though she didn't say where. At first, she put on a good face about going back to school next fall, but as she downed drink after drink, her enthusiasm seemed forced and manufactured.

Within an hour, Madison became aggressively flirtatious with every guy at the bar—especially Jackson, who she said shopped at the store where she worked. Eventually, she slurred her words, dropped things, and spilled her sixth drink across the bar. As Hanna ran for napkins, Jackson scooped up the empty glass. Hanna wanted to tell him to cut Madison off—she could barely stand up.

"We're taking a quick break, but we'll be right back!"

43

the steel drum player boomed, jarring Hanna from her thoughts. She looked around. The plate of fries was now empty. James was gone, and Mike was fiddling with his cell phone. She gritted her teeth, annoyed she'd given Madison any thought. Hadn't she just told herself *not* to think about all the crappy things in her past?

"I still have no signal," Mike grumbled, punching buttons. "What if it stays this way through the whole trip?"

"The crew told us the service is spotty," Hanna reminded him. "Besides, why do you need your phone so badly right now? Are you secretly texting with a Villa girl?"

"Never," Mike said, then stood. "I'm going to unpack. Wanna meet up later in your room?" His eyes danced playfully.

"Yes, but only if my roommate *isn't* a Villa girl," Hanna said. "I'll let you know."

Then she headed toward her cabin, which was two decks down and through a labyrinth of hallways. On her way there, she spied Zelda Millings, a cool girl from Doringbell Friends who was always at Noel Kahn's parties. "Hey, Zelda!" she called out.

Zelda looked at Hanna, then sniffed and pretended to talk on her cell phone. Hanna glanced around, horrified that someone might have seen.

As she slipped the keycard into the lock and opened the door, the room looked different than when she'd left it. The lights Hanna had turned off were on again, and the TV was blaring.

"Hello?" Hanna called tentatively, peering around. Someone had dumped their suitcase on the second bed. A pair of bright-yellow skinny jeans lay on the floor. A silky scarf, several T-shirts—in size extra-small—and a pair of espadrilles were spread across the mattress. Hanna's gaze scanned the rest of the room. There wasn't a plaid Catholic schoolgirl uniform in sight. *Yes.*

"Hello?" she called again, more happily this time.

A figure appeared in the balcony doorway. "*Hanna?*"

Hanna's eyes adjusted. Standing before her, in a cloud of her signature Kate Spade Twirl, was a girl with long, supple limbs, white-blond hair, and ice-blue eyes. It was someone Hanna hadn't prepared for at all.

"Oh," Hanna said stupidly. It wasn't a Villa girl. It was Naomi Zeigler.

She braced herself, waiting for an insult to spew from Naomi's mouth—probably something about her being a stalker. Or maybe Naomi would groan and march out of the room, disappointed that she'd gotten stuck with Hanna, the ship's biggest dork.

But the corners of Naomi's lips edged up in a grin. "Oh thank *God*," she blurted, slumping in relief. "I was so afraid they were going to stick me with someone like Chassey Bledsoe!"

She strode up to Hanna and linked her arm through her elbow, which was stiff with caution. "I am *so* glad you're here," Naomi gushed. She squeezed Hanna's arm. "I need someone to party with. What do you say?"

Hanna licked her lips. She wanted to ask Naomi where her BFF, Riley Wolfe, was, but now that she thought about it, she hadn't seen Riley anywhere. Maybe she hadn't come.

She glanced at her reflection in the mirror over the

45

bureau. Her auburn hair hung glossily down her back, the zits on her forehead seemed to have suddenly cleared up, and her arms looked toned and trim, not bloated from stress eating. Even though Naomi was probably glomming on to Hanna because her other friends weren't aboard, it had been a long time since a popular girl had begged her to hang. And with everyone still snickering about her little stalking episode, the offer felt even more tantalizing. With Naomi at her side, she'd become a queen bee again in no time. And isn't that what she'd wanted, forever?

I'm Hanna Marin, and I'm fabulous, she used to say when she was friends with Mona. And, okay, maybe she didn't feel *quite* as fabulous these days, but surely she still had a little bit of sparkle left in her.

She turned to Naomi and squeezed her arm back. "Let's party."

5
Speaking of Villa Girls ...

At 10 P.M. that same night, Emily stood on the Fiesta Deck next to Spencer, Aria, and Hanna at the Welcome to Paradise Luau. Fragrant leis hung in loops from the archways. Palms sprouted out of brightly painted pots. Pink and yellow strobe lights flashed from the ceiling. The place was so stuffed that Emily had had her toes stepped on a zillion times. The air had a sweaty, humid quality to it, and every few seconds a flash popped.

"It's great to see you all groovin', people!" Jeremy called from the stage as the DJ launched into "I'm Sexy and I Know It." A bunch of girls screamed.

Emily watched them as they barreled toward the dance floor, keeping her eyes peeled for a tall girl with dark hair and haunting eyes—Ghost Girl, she'd begun to call her. She'd thought of little else since their interaction on the balcony. Had there been something magical between them, or was it just her imagination? And why had she let the girl go without asking who she was?

Spencer, whose eyes kept wandering all over the crowd,

47

too, pointed at a table across the room. "How about some ice cream?"

She was looking at the make-your-own sundae bar in the corner. It was slightly less crowded than other parts of the party, so Emily and the others made a beeline for it.

As they chose their glasses and long silver spoons, Aria nudged Emily, her gaze on someone across the room. "Hey, is that your roommate over there?" she asked.

Emily looked through the dancing bodies. A tall girl with dip-dyed blond-to-brown hair in a tight black dress and black boots was holding court in a booth. Her chocolate-brown eyes were heavily lined and shadowed, and her lips were a vampy red, reminding Emily a little of Angelina Jolie. The silver cross around her neck made her seem both untouchable and irresistible. A few snooty-looking blond girls were sitting with her, and about eight guys flocked around them, flirting.

Emily rolled her eyes. "*Yes.*"

Hanna, who had just plopped a modest-sized scoop of vanilla into her bowl, gasped. "Your roommate is Erin Bang Bang?"

Emily gave her a crazy look. "*What?*"

"Erin Bang Bang. But just the guys call her that, not the girls. She's from Villa Louisa, that Catholic school that's obsessed with sex."

"I heard a rumor about that girl today," Spencer said as she deliberated over chocolate or rainbow sprinkles. "She's the one who dumped Justin Bieber because he was too boring, right?"

48

"Noel told me she made out with the pastry chef minutes after the boat disembarked," Aria piped up. "He created a dessert in her honor."

Hanna made a face. "She's not *that* great."

Emily stared at the labels on the tubs of ice cream. They all had politically correct names like Free-Trade Vanilla, Sensitively Harvested Chocolate, Organic Strawberry, and Cruelty-Free Rocky Road (No Marshmallows). Then she eyed Erin again. "This afternoon, she walked into our room for about one minute, took one look at me, and walked out again," she said stiffly. "I guess she thought I was a sucky choice for a roommate."

"Aw, Em." Hanna placed her hand on her shoulder. "I'm sure it wasn't because of anything *you* did."

"I'd love to be your roommate," Aria added. "I'm stuck with this girl from Tate who's obsessed with the talent show at the end of the trip. She's already working on a song—and her voice is *awful*."

Emily smiled at all of them, instantly feeling better. One good thing had come out of this A mess: She'd reunited with her friends for real.

They moved closer to Erin Bang Bang's booth. Now she was sitting on the lap of a tall guy with surfer-dude blond hair. "What do you say to a *Titanic* moment later on?" she cooed to him loudly, sounding a little drunk.

Surfer Dude widened his eyes. "Which moment would that be? 'I'm the king of the world'? The part where Leo sketches Kate in the nude?"

"Whatever moment you want," Erin Bang Bang said, trailing her finger up the boy's cheek. "Want to meet in your room in an hour?"

49

Emily turned away. So much for a heart-to-heart bonding session tonight. For some reason, she felt like Erin was rejecting *her*, not just being a slut.

Spencer grabbed a napkin from the stack. "Forget about her, Em—we'll have a great time together." She pointed at a talent show poster on the wall, which featured silhouettes of kids dancing à la the iPod ads. "Why don't we do an act together?"

Hanna rolled her eyes. "Why is everyone so into this stupid talent show? Didn't they go out in, like, fourth grade?"

"Come *on*." Aria nudged her. "We could all make up a dance routine."

"What about a hula dance?" Emily suggested, spooning up whipped cream from the top of her sundae. "We could wear bathing suits and make grass skirts."

"Perfect," Spencer said. When she noticed Hanna's sour face, she poked her arm. "You're doing it with us whether you like it or not."

"Fine," Hanna said, rolling her eyes.

Sundaes in hand, they pushed through the crowd toward a booth that had just opened up. Emily slumped into the seat and gazed around the huge room once more. Kids hung on the railings and crammed against the bar. When she saw a flash of a white dress, her heart sped up a little. *Ghost Girl?*

But then the girl stepped out from the crowd. She had a stubby blond ponytail and a big nose. Emily's shoulders drooped in disappointment.

A new song came on, and Jeremy's voice boomed through the speakers. "This is going to be the last song of the night. I hope everyone had a great time, but we gotta get our beauty sleep!"

Spencer snorted into her hand. *"Beauty sleep?* That dude is *so* weird."

"Does anyone else think he's sort of a lech?" Hanna whispered. "I swear I've felt someone watching me all day. And when I turn around, he's always there."

"Are you sure it's not *A*?" Aria asked.

"A's not on the ship," Emily insisted. "Didn't you see all that security checking IDs at the gate?"

Aria raised an eyebrow. "Who says A doesn't have an ID? I'm with Hanna. Ever since I boarded the cruise, I've felt ... *weird*. Like someone is watching, but then ducking away before I can see who it is."

"But ... " Emily trailed off. She didn't even want to *consider* the idea of A being on the boat.

She glanced around. A shadow slipped behind a large potted plant, but when Emily turned to see who it was, no one was there. James Freed was grinding against a few girls from Pritchard. Phi Templeton carried a big dish of ice cream to her seat.

As Beyoncé launched into a new verse, Jeremy cleared his throat. "One other thing, guys. Not to be a buzzkill, but some items have gone missing from people's rooms. Please know we don't tolerate this behavior. Respect the earth, respect people's stuff, you know?"

Zora-Jean Jaffrey, a bookish girl from Rosewood Day whom everyone called Z-J, banged her spoon against her sundae glass from the next table over. "That thief took my makeup bag!" she said to her group of friends. "My mom quilted it for me and everything!"

51

When the song ended, the lights came up. Kids started toward the exit. Spencer leaned forward. "So what's our game plan, guys? What should we do about A?"

"We should try to put together all the clues as to who A might be," Emily said, shrugging. "It's someone who knows everything, who was in Jamaica *and* Rosewood. I feel like the answer is right in front of us, and we just don't see it."

"Watch what you say," Aria said warily. "A *might* be right in front of us—literally. If anyone sees anything weird, send a text, okay?"

"And maybe we should just enjoy ourselves a little, too." Spencer dabbed her mouth with a napkin. "We haven't had a chance to breathe since Tabitha's body was found. This might be a good opportunity."

"That's not a bad idea," Aria murmured. "I just hope I *can* relax."

Then Hanna mumbled something about hanging out with Naomi Zeigler, her roommate. As Emily was tossing her napkin in the trash, Aria touched her arm. "Are you going to be okay alone?"

Emily shrugged. "I'll be fine." *Lonely*, she thought, *but fine*.

"If you need to talk tonight, call me. Promise?"

"I promise." Emily hugged her. "Same with you, okay?"

"Same for *all* of us," Spencer said.

They parted ways. Emily boarded a stuffed elevator to the Sunshine Deck. When the car stopped on her floor, she got off and walked down the hall, looking at the marker boards the ship had affixed to everyone's doors. Most of them had dirty drawings or scrawled messages making plans for when and where to meet. When she arrived at her own door, though, there were a bunch of hearts on the board and *eleven* notes for Erin, all signed with guys' names. A guy wearing a Lacoste polo with longish blond-brown hair and a beaky nose was penning a note as she approached. He stepped back and watched Emily pull out her keycard, then shrugged.

"Do *you* want to do something tonight?" he asked after a moment.

"Ew, *no*," Emily said, brushing past him and slamming the door.

Her room had a preppy, nautical theme, with navy-and-white-striped bedspreads, lots of wood trim, and light fixtures and drawer pulls in the shapes of anchors, swordfish, and manta rays. The bathroom light was on, the timer ticking away, and there was a sky-blue towel on the floor that Emily didn't remember putting there. A type of perfume Emily had never smelled before lingered in the air, and a discarded T-shirt lay on Erin's bed. But Erin was nowhere in sight.

She flopped back on the mattress, shut her eyes, and felt the almost imperceptible sensation of the boat cutting across the sea. She heard a slight rustling sound, but figured it was probably the water lapping against the side of the ship. But how was that possible? This room was eight flights up from ground level, nowhere close to the water.

There were more rustles. Emily looked around. The room seemed eerily still all of a sudden, as though all of the sound and air had been sucked out through a straw.

The sound came from the little closet in the corner on Erin's side of the room.

Bump.

She swung her legs off the bed and stared at the small door. Something was scraping against the walls desperately, as if clawing to get out. Suddenly, the bathroom timer dinged, and the only light in the room clicked off, drowning the room in darkness. It was so black, in fact, that Emily couldn't see an inch in front of her face. A horrible thought took shape in her mind. What if the others were right? What if A—Real Ali—*was* on the boat?

There was another bump, and then a scrape. It seemed like someone was inside, trying to break free. Emily shrieked and scuttled to the opposite wall, ducking behind one of the long curtains. And then, she smelled it: a slight whiff of vanilla, wafting out from across the room. It was the soap both Alis, Real and Theirs, had always used.

Emily's fingers trembled as she reached for her cell phone, ready to dial Aria, but then the phone slipped from her fingers, banging to the floor and tumbling under the bed. Then there was a loud, long, nerve-rattling *creak*. She peered at the closet through a gap in the curtains and could just make out the door in the darkness. The little starfish-shaped doorknob began to turn, and the door began to open, revealing whoever it was inside.

She yelped, untangled herself from the curtains, and dove for the door that led to the hall, but her foot caught on one of Erin's discarded boots and she went flying onto the carpet. She scrambled to her hands and knees, then glanced behind her and screamed. The closet door was

54

wide open now, and a figure matching Ali's height and weight was staring at her.

"Stay away!" she screamed, crawling toward the door. "I'll call security!"

"Please don't!" the figure cried.

"Then get out of my room!" Emily screamed. "Get out *now*!"

"I *can't*!"

Emily paused with her hand on the knob. It was a plaintive, desperate cry, not a threatening one. The voice didn't sound like Ali's, either.

"W-why?" she stammered.

"Because I'm a stowaway!" the figure said. "I have nowhere else *to* go!"

Emily noticed a small, quilted makeup bag on the floor of the closet, illuminated by a thin strip of moonlight. Stitched on the side was the name *Zora-Jean*.

"My name is Jordan Richards," the girl said. "I snuck on this boat because I had no money. I didn't think it would actually work, but now I'm here, and I don't have a room, and ... "

Then she stepped into the moonlight. She had large green eyes, full lips, and thick, dark hair held back by a velvet headband. She wore a white eyelet dress and ballet flats with grosgrain trim.

Emily gasped. "*You?* "

"Me," the girl answered, and then faintly smiled. Ghost Girl.

Emily sank down to her bed, trying to focus. "You snuck on the boat?" she repeated.

Ghost Girl—Jordan—nodded. "This morning. I wanted

to come on the cruise, but my parents didn't have the money." She made a wry face. "Actually, they didn't want to *spend* the money. We're not exactly close."

"Okay," Emily said slowly. "How did you get *on*?"

Jordan leaned against the wall next to the closet. "There was so much confusion when everyone was checking in that I thought, *What if I just walked on? Would anyone notice?* So I did. But then the ship pulled away from the dock, and I panicked. I didn't have my passport. I didn't have any stuff. And I didn't have a room to sleep in. I was screwed."

"Don't you know other people on the ship who could help you out?"

Jordan shook her head. "I just moved to the Philly area a few weeks ago, so I don't really know anyone yet."

"What school are you going to?" Emily asked.

"Ulster," Jordan said, staring absently out the little circular porthole.

A crack formed in Emily's brain when she looked at Z-J's bag again. "You were the person stealing stuff from people's rooms, right?"

Jordan looked sheepish. "A lot of people left their doors open while moving in," she said. "It was easy to slip in and out of the rooms. That's how I got into your room, too. I camped out here for a couple hours and took a nap." She grabbed Z-J's bag and a couple of other duffels from inside the closet. "Anyway, I'll let you get some rest now. Sorry I freaked you out."

"Wait!" Emily caught her arm before she could go. "D-do you want to stay here?"

Jordan froze, halfway standing. "For the night?"

"For . . . maybe *longer* than the night," Emily blurted. "I have a feeling my roommate isn't going to sleep here much. There's a spare bed."

Jordan squinted. "Why would you do that?"

Emily traced her finger over the threads on the comforter. She'd surprised herself by asking, but maybe it wasn't such a bad idea. She felt sorry for Jordan, definitely, but she was also lonely being in the room by herself. Besides, Emily found it almost impossible to take her eyes off Jordan's high cheekbones, her kissable lips—in a platonic way, of course.

Her cheeks flushed, and she was suddenly afraid Jordan could read her thoughts. "We can't have you sleeping on a chaise by the pool." She patted the bed next to hers. "It's yours if you want it."

Jordan nodded slowly. "I'd *love* that, if you're sure."

"I'm sure," Emily said, and then, because she thought it sounded buddy-buddy, added, "roomie."

Jordan held her gaze. "Roomie," she repeated, as if it were an antiquated word she'd never heard before. Then she stood up, walked toward Emily, and gave her a huge hug. "Thank you so much. This is wonderful."

Emily remained as stiff as she could, though she wanted to bury her face in Jordan's neck and inhale the sweet scent of her skin. "You're welcome so much," she said back.

But really, it was Jordan she should have been thanking.

6
Spencer's Last-Ditch Effort

The following morning, Spencer and her roommate, Kirsten Cullen, stepped out of their room and started toward the elevators. The air smelled of lingering shampoo from people's bathrooms; bacon, eggs, and coffee from the restaurant; and sunscreen. The turquoise sky and navy-blue sea loomed large out the huge windows at the end of the corridor, and the hallway walls were papered with flyers reminding everyone to sign up for the end-of-cruise talent show. Spencer made a mental note to sign up their hula routine later that day.

Kirsten stretched her arms over her head and let out a low moan. "I am *so* jealous of you for not getting seasick last night. I'm exhausted. I don't even know if I'll be able to dive today!"

Spencer nudged her playfully. "We're at sea. Where do you think we're going to dive?" The two of them were taking scuba, which counted as a class credit, and they were headed for the first lesson, which was taking place in one of the fitness centers. Spencer was overjoyed that she'd been randomly paired with Kirsten, especially hearing about her friends' matches. Field hockey buddies for years, she and Kirsten had already roomed together when traveling to out-of-state games.

"This is just a getting-to-know-you, everyone-try-on-the-equipment, here-are-some-water-safety-tips kind of thing," Spencer added knowingly. "I've been through plenty of these before." Spencer had gotten her scuba certification at fourteen; she could probably write the book on scuba safety.

After getting off on the top floor, they passed one of the restaurants, which teemed with guys loading their plates at the buffet line, girls whispering at the tables, and kids flirting and gossiping near the espresso bar. Then Spencer spied someone's tall, straight back in front of the giant aquarium, and she suppressed a nervous squeak.

"Reefer?" she called out, her voice cracking only a little.

Reefer turned. His whole face lit up when he caught sight of her. This was the first time they'd seen each other on the boat. They'd tried to connect yesterday, but, like Kirsten, Reefer had spent the evening in his room, seasick. "Can I walk you to scuba?" Reefer asked, a little bashfully.

"Sure," Spencer said, trying to temper her smile. She glanced at Kirsten to see if it was okay, but Kirsten had tactfully walked on.

"Oh, and surprise." Reefer proffered a smoothie from behind his back. "This is for you. It's banana-papaya."

"My favorite," Spencer breathed, thrilled he'd remembered. She'd mentioned liking those flavors together just once on the phone.

59

Their hands touched as she took it from him. Chills zinged up Spencer's spine. She snuck a peek at Reefer's face, taking in his chiseled jaw and his amber-colored eyes. This was the first time she'd laid eyes on him since Princeton—since she'd realized she liked him. How could she have not remembered his strong shoulders or how pink and kissable his lips were? Why hadn't she taken note of the cute freckles on his cheeks? Even his dreadlocks, threadbare hemp sneakers, and oversized tie-dyed shirt were suddenly endearing.

She pushed a lock of hair behind her ear, feeling the back of her neck redden. "Um, how are you feeling?" she blurted, suddenly needing to fill the silence. "You must have been bummed to miss out on the Welcome Party." She'd almost been tempted to knock on his cabin door with a glass of ginger ale and some Dramamine, but she'd worried that might seem too forward.

"Eh, it's all good," Reefer said, starting down the hall toward the scuba class. "I watched movies on pay-per-view. Did you get sick? Those waves were pretty vicious."

Spencer shook her head. "I've never been seasick. I'm used to boats."

"Lucky," Reefer sighed. "Have you been diving for a while?"

Spencer nodded. "I've been certified for a couple years. I'm hoping to go on some private dives without the rest of the group. I don't really like diving around a lot of people."

Reefer held the door to the stairwell open for her. "Would you mind some company? I mean, I only got certified last year, but I'm a quick learner, I swear. And I bet you're a pretty good tour guide."

60

Spencer put a finger to her mouth, coyly pretending to contemplate the offer. "But what if I wanted those dives to be private? What do I get in return for bringing you along?"

Reefer paused on the staircase, his eyes sparkling playfully. "How about my most cherished 1977 Grateful Dead concert T-shirt?"

Spencer gave him a skeptical look. "The one you bought off eBay that still smells like pot after all those washings? No thank you."

"It doesn't smell like pot!" Reefer urged. "It smells fine. I wear it to school all the time and no one questions me, I swear."

Spencer secretly felt thrilled at the idea of wearing a T-shirt that Reefer had worn, too. It seemed so ... *boy-friendly.*

They'd reached the door to the Seahorse Gym, the site of the first scuba class, by then. Elliptical machines, stair climbers, and treadmills lined the window wall, and about thirty folding chairs stood on the mats. Kirsten was in the front row, filing her nails. Quite a few kids grabbed coffee and bagels from a catered tray in the back. Tim, the instructor Spencer had met at the Activity Fair the day before, stood over a couple of cardboard boxes, sorting through oxygen tanks and wetsuits.

Spencer faced Reefer again, feeling a tingly, excited rush. Reefer was smiling at her, too.

Then she was suddenly gripped with a wonderful idea. She touched Reefer's arm. "Let's ditch."

Reefer widened his eyes. "*Class?*"

"We both already know how to dive. Why not?"

Reefer, clapped a hand over his mouth, feigning shock.

61

"Aren't you the girl who's gotten the Perfect Attendance award every year?"

Spencer shrugged. "I'm on vacation." She could just picture it: grabbing Reefer's hand and pulling him down to one of the lower lounges, which were probably empty at this time of morning, and sitting in a back booth. They'd gossip about people on the boat, plan outings for after their dives, and then their heads would move closer together, and then . . .

"*Raif?*"

It was coming from someone inside the classroom. Reefer turned. His eyebrows shot up, and he took a step through the door.

"It *is* you!" a girl whooped. "Oh my God!"

"Wow!" Reefer said. And then he was hugging her. *Really* hugging her. Spencer stood in the doorway, feeling like a forgotten child's toy tossed out a car window.

She cleared her throat a little more loudly than she meant to, and Reefer turned around, his dreadlocks bouncing. "Oh, Spencer. Sorry. This is—"

"Naomi," Spencer blurted, staring at the girl who had stepped into view. She gave Spencer a haughty, threatening look.

"Hi, Spencer," Naomi chirped. "You're taking scuba, too?"

"Uh, yeah," Spencer mumbled, eyeing Naomi's fingers, which were grazing Reefer's. She glanced at the door, considering ditching without him.

But suddenly, it didn't seem like a very fun idea at all.

62

7

A Partner in Crime

That morning, Aria and about thirty other kids stood in the shade of the giant pink waterslide on the top deck of the cruise ship, eagerly awaiting the start of the Eco Scavenger Hunt. The air smelled like wood-floor cleaner, spicy deodorant, and boat fuel that the captain had insisted was totally eco-friendly, though Aria had her doubts. Everyone fanned their faces, applied high-powered sunscreen to ward off the punishing Caribbean sun, and chattered excitedly about what the activity was going to entail.

Finally, the activity leader got off her cell phone and turned to the group. "Welcome!" she cried, her freckly face breaking into a smile. "My name is Gretchen Vine, and you guys are in for a treat. Think of this hunt like *The Amazing Race*—we give you clues and cash to get to your destination, and the first group to figure out all the riddles wins."

"Wins what?" a brunette girl whose string bikini straps peeked out from underneath her shirt asked.

Gretchen smiled and unveiled two white gift certificates to the Apple Store, and everyone oohed. "They're worth a thousand dollars each."

Then Gretchen passed out little red wallets that said ECO TREASURE HUNT on the front. "Carry your clues in here," she instructed. "You'll need to show me what you found at the end of each day."

"Will we get to do any camping? Extreme hikes? Role-playing?" a boy called.

Gretchen frowned, fiddling with her necklace. "Well, we need you to return to the ship every night—otherwise we'd have to send out a search party. The hikes take you over a lot of terrain, but I wouldn't call them extreme. And I'm not sure what you mean by role-playing—perhaps you can elaborate?"

The speaker, a guy with longish brown hair and thick eyebrows, waved his hand dismissively. "Forget it."

Gretchen told them they would have to scour beach-heads, traipse over dunes, bushwhack through tropical rain forests, and navigate busy city streets to extract information that would lead them, ultimately, to the prize. Aria exchanged excited glances with kids next to her. There were quite a few couples holding hands in the group, and she felt a longing pang. Maybe Noel would have chosen the scavenger hunt if he had known about the prize.

"Okay, the first thing I need you guys to do is split up into groups of two," Gretchen said after she'd called roll.

The couples paired up. Other kids turned to people they knew. Aria spun around, but everyone from Rosewood Day had already found partners. Even her roommate, a sweet, quiet girl named Sasha who'd also signed up for the scavenger hunt, had paired up with another bookish-looking girl from her school. As more and more people grouped together, she felt a self-conscious twinge. Years ago, when kids at Rosewood Day teamed up at recess, formed partnerships in art class, or picked groups for an English project, goofy, friendless Aria was often the last to be chosen. *Is it because I have a pink stripe in my hair?* she would wonder. *Or is it because of some innate, loserish quality that I don't even know I have?*

"Those of you who don't have a partner, raise your hands," Gretchen announced.

Aria sheepishly lifted her palm a few inches. Several other kids did, too.

Gretchen matched those who didn't have partners with one another. When she got to Aria, she pointed her toward the guy who'd just asked about camping and role-playing. "You two okay to work together?"

The boy looked at Aria and shrugged. "That's cool." He extended a hand to Aria. "I'm Graham Pratt."

"Aria Montgomery." She smiled at him. He had pretty hazel eyes and wore gray Toms shoes, beaten-up Army-surplus shorts, and a faded T-shirt with what looked like a shield on the front and a small hole in the shoulder.

"Do I know you from somewhere?" she asked. He seemed familiar, but she couldn't quite place him. "Do you go to a school on the Main Line?"

Graham's brow crinkled. "No, I go to school in Philly." Then he brightened. "Wait. Are you in SCA?"

"What's that?"

"Society for Creative Anachronism!" Graham grinned.

Aria hid a smile. Her cousin Stewart was in SCA, and

he talked about it nonstop. It was like a year-round Renaissance Fair, where people role-play parts in a medieval society. He'd met his wife there, in fact—she'd been a kitchen wench, and he played the guy who collected dead plague victims in a wooden cart.

"Uh, no," Aria answered after a moment. But then, in an attempt at diplomacy, she added, "But it's always sounded really cool."

"You should join!" Graham looked excited. "There's a meet-up in Camden next month."

"I'll get back to you on that," Aria said. "But I *still* think I know you from somewhere. Did you spend time overseas? I lived in Iceland for a few years, but I traveled to France, Germany, Austria, Holland ... "

Graham shook his head. "The last time I went to Europe was with my parents when I was six. Last summer I backpacked through Chile, though."

"That must have been amazing!"

"It was." Graham looked wistful. "It was for an SCA conference—we anointed a new king." Then he peered at her curiously. "What was Iceland like?"

"Magical," Aria said softly, though when she opened her mouth to wax poetic about Iceland, all she could think about was her *last* trip to the country, the one she'd taken with Noel, Mike, and Hanna—the one she never wanted to think about again.

She fixed her gaze across the boat instead. Several kids were swimming laps in the pool. Emily, who had volunteered to lifeguard, sat on the stand, twirling a whistle around her finger. Aria considered waving, but Emily seemed like her thoughts were a million miles away.

66

She turned back to Graham. "So anyway, I'm really excited about the scavenger hunt," she said, deciding to change the subject.

"Me too," Graham said. "A buddy of mine was supposed to do it with me, but he changed his mind at the last minute."

"Yeah, I tried to get my boyfriend into this, but he wanted to surf instead," Aria said. "It's cool, though. He seemed really excited for it."

Graham nodded. "I'm not sure my girlfriend would have wanted to do this, either. She was more of the tanning type."

"Is she on the cruise?"

Graham scratched his nose, looking uncomfortable. "No. And, uh, well, we're actually not together anymore, so . . . " He trailed off and sat down on one of the benches that lined the pool. "So you're from the Main Line, huh? Does that make you a snob?"

"Far from it!" Aria scoffed. "Most of the time, I feel really out of place there. Like it's not really where I'm supposed to be."

"I used to feel that way in my old town—it was a really stuffy suburb, too," Graham said. "I was thrilled when my family moved to Philly last year."

"Where did you live before that?" Aria asked.

"Maplewood, New Jersey," Graham said.

"*Maplewood?*" Aria blurted. According to the Tabitha Clark Memorial website, Tabitha had gone to high school in Maplewood.

Graham gave a resigned sigh. "Let me guess—you've been following the Tabitha Clark case."

Aria's stomach felt like it had been filled with hot, explosive fizz. "Did you know her?"

Graham stared into the middle distance, his blue eyes muddy. And then, before he said another word, Aria knew why he looked so familiar. She recalled a video she'd seen on the Tabitha Clark website of a cute boy dancing with Tabitha at prom. She saw his name next to posts about a pizza party fund-raiser in Tabitha's honor. She even recalled his voice on CNN, talking about the last time he saw Tabitha, a few months before she died.

All of this passed through her mind in a matter of seconds. And then Graham raised his teary eyes to Aria, uttering exactly what she feared. "Yeah. Tabitha was my girlfriend."

8
License to Kill

Later that night, Hanna took Mike's hand as they stepped off the elevator on the Palm Tree Deck. "Nine-oh-seven is that way," he murmured, then turned right and started down a long corridor. Hanna followed him, shooting a haughty look at Phi Templeton, who had paused eagerly at her cabin door. Hanna and Mike were on their way to a top-secret, exclusive party in Mason Byers's suite, but not everyone was invited.

They passed a long mirror, and Hanna gazed at her reflection. She was definitely party-ready. Her skin glowed with a brand-new tan; the gauzy, burnt-orange sundress she'd bought at the King James floated softly away from her hips; and the gladiator heels she'd purchased just before the trip made her legs look so superlong that she didn't mind that they pinched her feet a little.

Mike stopped at the last door at the end of the hall. "Here we are."

They listened for a moment. Bass thumped from inside.

A girl squealed, and a bunch of guys laughed. The scent of booze and cigarettes wafted under the door.

Hanna bit her lip. "What if the chaperone hears us? I don't want to get in trouble."

Mike's thick brows knitted together. "Since when do you care about getting in trouble?"

Hanna wound a piece of perfectly curled auburn hair around her finger. "I don't want to have to give up any more tanning time to sit in some cruise ship's idea of detention. It's bad enough I have to work in the dungeon." She hadn't bothered to sign up for a volunteer job before the cruise, so she'd been randomly assigned a position in the ship's administration office. The office was in the bowels of the ship, run by a woman named Vera who wore a thousand tiny barrettes in her hair and was obsessed with country music. Hanna was supposed to do mind-numbing data entry about the ship's capacity the whole morning—Vera tried to make it seem so interesting that this particular vessel could hold almost a hundred more guests than were on board. Mostly, she'd just googled how she could make a grass skirt look sexy for the end-of-trip talent show.

"Don't worry," Mike said. "Mason paid off this hallway's chaperone to keep quiet. We're cool."

Then he knocked on the door. It opened a crack. "Password?" said a gruff voice.

"*Flipper*," Mike whispered.

The door opened, and they walked into a suite packed with bodies. The patio door was open wide, letting in the warm, fragrant air, and a bunch of people leaned over the railing or sat on the deck chairs. On the kitchen's counter

70

were a bunch of airplane bottles of liquor, a half-drained jug of rum, plastic cups, and pretzels, peanuts, and M&M's from the minibar. Rihanna blared from an iPod dock, and a few people were dancing on one of the beds. The room smelled thickly of perfume, sweat, and all-natural carpet cleaner.

"Welcome to our soiree." Mason strode forward and offered Hanna and Mike cups filled with rum and Diet Coke. He was wearing his Rosewood Day blazer, a striped tie loosely knotted around his neck, and a pair of seersucker shorts that looked suspiciously like boxers.

Hanna accepted the drink, then started through the crowd. A lot of kids from Rosewood Day were here, as well as people from Doringbell Friends, Pritchard, and Tate. A couple of blond bombshells from Villa Louisa were doing shots with James Freed and a few other boys from the lacrosse team. Maybe it was something about the hot, humid air, or maybe it was the smell of the coconut sunscreen everyone was wearing, but suddenly Hanna was reminded of the parties they'd attended in Jamaica—especially that crowded dinner the night they met Tabitha. They'd all been sitting at the table, drinking and having a good time, when Emily had grabbed their arm. "It's *Ali*," she'd said, and there was Tabitha on the top step, looking eerie and familiar in that yellow dress . . .

Jesus. Why was she thinking about it *again*? She grabbed Mike's arm. "Let's dance."

"Aye, aye, captain," Mike said.

They hit the dance floor and started moving to a Wiz Khalifa song. Hanna shook her arms and legs like a dervish, trying to purge the negative thoughts from her

71

mind. A Lil Wayne song came on next, and then there was a medley of stuff from Madonna's latest album. By the time someone put on vintage Nirvana, she was slightly winded from dancing and much more relaxed.

"I'll get more drinks," Mike said. Hanna nodded woozily and wandered out to the balcony, where kids were staring at the moon. A hand touched Hanna's bare shoulder, and she turned, thinking Mike was back. Instead, it was Naomi. Hanna instantly inhaled a heady whiff of her fruity Kate Spade perfume.

Hanna brightened. "What's up?"

"Hey, girl," Naomi chirped. "Good to see you here."

Hanna smiled but didn't answer, not wanting to seem too eager. It still baffled her that Naomi was being *nice*. They'd hung out at the welcome soiree a little and had gotten breakfast this morning, which had instantly upped her cool-girl cred—a few girls had said hi to her in the corridors afterward. Naomi had even asked if Hanna wanted to tan this afternoon, but Hanna had had her jewelry-making class. Hanna kept waiting for Naomi to prank her, ditch her, or laugh in her face, but so far, so good. Naomi had finally woken up and realized Hanna was cool.

"I don't know how you dance in those shoes." Naomi pointed to the high, strappy gladiator heels on Hanna's feet. "They're incredible. Are they from Salt and Pepper?"

Hanna flinched. Actually, the shoes *were* from Salt and Pepper, but the store was in the slightly down-market section of the King James Mall—*definitely* uncool. The only reason Hanna shopped there was because their knockoffs were so good people often couldn't tell the difference.

72

"Um, my mom bought them for me," she mumbled. "I don't know where she got them."

"C'mon, Han," Naomi said in a knowing voice. "I saw those in the store window." Then she leaned closer, a conspiratorial look in her eye. "I almost bought them myself, actually. Shopping there is my little secret. It's such a great store, but everyone would make fun of me if they knew. Look—I'm wearing Salt and Pepper shoes, too."

She lifted her foot to show off a pink kitten heel that Hanna did, indeed, recognize from the store's shelves. "It *is* a pretty great store."

"Are you kidding? It's the best!" Naomi's eyes gleamed. "We can't tell anyone about it though—it has to be our little secret. Otherwise *everyone* will go, and there will be nothing good left."

"Definitely," Hanna said in a mock-haughty voice, secretly thrilled that she and Naomi were in on something together.

"Not even Riley," Naomi went on. "And definitely not your stepsister. Got it?"

"Got it." Hanna ran her fingers over the plastic ridges on her cup, feeling triumphant. Naomi and Kate had been BFFs since Kate had started at Rosewood Day. Hanna and Kate had been getting along lately, and Kate had told her she was in a fight with Naomi. The way Kate had put it, though, Naomi was the one at fault.

Naomi propped her elbows on the railing and stared back in at the party. "Zelda Millings looks pretty good in that halter dress, don't you think?"

Hanna studied the pale blond girl who'd snubbed her the day before across the room. "Eh," she said, feeling

73

triumphant that the tables had turned. "It makes her boobs look really small."

"True." Naomi nodded sagely. "But at least that color doesn't make her look like an albino."

"She's going to have a wicked sunburn at the end of the week," Hanna mused.

Naomi twisted her mouth. "You know who I *wish* would get wicked sunburns?"

"The girls from Villa Louisa?" Hanna blurted out.

"Yes!" Naomi whooped, then touched Hanna's arm. "Oh my God, don't you think they're *so* annoying?"

"Absolutely." Hanna felt a rush of satisfaction. It felt good to bash the Villa Gorillas. "Did you know Emily Fields is rooming with that Erin Bang Bang girl?"

Naomi winced. "She's the *worst*. I got stuck working in the administration offices on the boat because I was really lazy about signing up for something else, and she works the shift with me. That bitch didn't say one word to me the whole time."

Hanna frowned. "Wait, you're working in the admin office? So am I!"

"With Vera?" Naomi asked.

"Oh my God, *Vera*!" Hanna giggled. "What's with all those sappy love songs?"

"And those barrettes?" Naomi added, holding in a laugh. "She looks like a poodle!"

"Doesn't that office have the weirdest smell?" Hanna pretended to gag.

"Yeah, like a mix of feet, wet dog, and old lady," Naomi groaned.

"It could be worse, though," Hanna said. "I heard

74

some people who signed up late are on cleaning duty. They have to scrub the boys' toilets."

"Ew!" Naomi shrieked.

Hanna grinned as she sipped her drink, feeling light-headed and free. She felt like she'd just discovered a new clothing designer whose jeans and tees and dresses fit her perfectly—and her name was Naomi. That Naomi was giving Hanna the same *Where have you been all my life?* look made her feel even better.

Then Naomi shifted her weight. "I've wanted to ask you something for a while. Did you ever get help for ... you know. That eating thing?"

Hanna bristled. A million years ago, Mona-as-A had forced her to confront Naomi and Riley last year and admit she had an eating disorder. Hanna glanced through the door, considering running away.

"The only reason I ask is because I wanted to get a referral," Naomi added when Hanna didn't say anything.

Hanna frowned. "For who?"

Naomi looked down. "For myself," she murmured quietly.

Hanna almost laughed out loud. "*You* binge? Yeah, right." Naomi was a size 0. Hanna had barely ever seen her *eat*.

Naomi lowered her eyes. "With exercise. It's something I've struggled with on and off for years. I've wanted to talk to you about it, actually—you're the only person I know who's suffered with it, too. It's not like I can talk to Riley or Kate about it."

"I don't really do it anymore," Hanna said cautiously.

"I didn't, either." Naomi traced her finger around the

lip of the glass. "Until last summer. Some weird stuff happened, so I started again."

Hanna blinked hard. "I'm really sorry," she said softly, still not quite believing what she was hearing. But Naomi's expression looked earnest and guileless. Hanna had yearned to talk about bingeing with someone who'd been through it as well, but so far she hadn't come across anyone who'd admit to it.

"If you ever want to talk about it, I'm here," she offered after a moment. "I know how hard it is."

"Thanks," Naomi murmured, reaching across and squeezing Hanna's hand.

Just then, Mason Byers stumbled out onto the patio. His hair was mussed, and he was wearing a gold Rosewood Police badge on his lapel. "The name's Officer Byers, ladies," he slurred. "Are you two old enough to drink?"

"Of course we are," Naomi winked.

"Can I see some ID?" Mason demanded.

Mike stuck his head out, too. "We're making up a strip card game that uses everyone's fake IDs. Wanna play?" He waved his own fake ID in the air.

"Let me see that." Hanna stepped back into the room and grabbed for it. Mike had bragged about a new fake ID, but he'd been cagey about showing it to her. She burst out laughing. Quincy Thomas, the name on the card, had a blond crew cut and glasses. The description said he was six foot ten, almost a foot taller than Mike was.

She tossed it back to him. "No one's going to think that's you!"

Mike held it protectively to his chest, his cheeks blazing. "All right, smart ass, let's see yours."

Hanna reached into her purse and pulled out her own fake ID, which she'd bought last year online *and* which featured her own picture and stats. Mason offered up his ID, too, which he'd gotten in New York City. Other kids added their IDs to the pile. One girl had a very convincing-looking Japanese passport, even though she herself wasn't Japanese. Erin Bang Bang used her own photo for her fake. The picture was so arresting and model-gorgeous that Hanna guessed no bouncer or bartender would even bother to look at her birth date. *Bitch*.

"Hey, yours is pretty good," Mike said to Naomi as she dropped hers on the pile. "She even looks like you."

"That's because it's my cousin's," Naomi explained. A strange look came over her face. "It's not like she needs it anymore."

Hanna glanced at the photo, then did a double-take. Even though she'd seen the girl for only one night, the face was unforgettable. It was like a ghost staring back at her.

Madison.

She backed away, tripping over an upended suitcase and nearly falling on her butt. As she righted herself, her hands were suddenly shaking so badly she had to shove them into the folds of her dress. The room felt hot and close, and so many people were staring at her, Naomi included.

"Um, I have to . . . " Hanna fumbled past everyone to the door.

She ran to the end of the hall, desperate to catch her breath. Then she noticed a French door that led to a small, open-air courtyard. She slid it open and staggered to a shuffleboard court, leaning over onto her knees.

Madison was Naomi's *cousin*. And what did Naomi mean when she said she didn't need the ID anymore? Was she dead?

Beep.

It was Hanna's phone. She pulled it out of her purse, figuring it was Mike. But then she looked at the screen. *One new text message from Anonymous.*

"No," she whispered, scanning the dark courtyard. Then she looked down at the screen. With shaking fingers, she pressed READ.

Be careful who you hit and run, jailbird. See you on the Fiesta Deck! —A

9
Pretty Little Stowaway

Tuesday evening, Emily and Jordan sat on the bed in Emily's room. Empty potato chip wrappers from the vending machines were strewn around them, and Jordan had made them virgin banana daiquiris from some drinks she'd found in the mini bar. One of Emily's swimming mixes was playing through her portable iPod speakers, and Discovery, the only channel that had a signal besides CNN International—which Jordan said she hated—was airing a show about Yosemite Park in the background, though neither girl was watching it.

"Okay, I need a verb," Emily said, staring down at a book of Mad Libs she'd found at the bottom of her bag, left there from an overnight swimming trip.

"Um, *kissed*," Jordan said after a moment, popping a chip into her mouth.

Emily wrote *kissed* into the space. "Next I need a noun."

"*Boobs*," Jordan said quickly.

Emily laid down her pen and looked at the other words Jordan had chosen. *Sexily*, *tongue*, *humping*, and *sensual*

79

massage. "You realize this is a kid's game, right? Not a porno?"

"What can I say?" Jordan snickered. "I'm inspired by the spirit of Erin Bang Bang. Even *I've* heard rumors about how many guys she's been with."

Emily shuddered. "Every time I see her, she's with someone different."

Jordan glanced at the door. "Are you *sure* she's not going to mind me staying here?"

Emily shrugged. "I doubt Erin's going to be back for the rest of the trip, to be honest. And if she *does* come in, we'll just say you had a fight with your roommate. You can even sleep in my bed if it makes you feel more comfortable." Her cheeks reddened a little at the suggestion, but surely Jordan knew she meant it in a friendly way, right?

Jordan gave Emily a relieved smile. "You're a lifesaver, you know that?"

Emily rolled her eyes. "You've only told me that a zillion times." Then she stared back down at Mad Libs. "Okay, I need an adverb."

"*Lustily*," Jordan spouted quickly, and they both dissolved into laughter.

After Emily penned it in, she breathed in the sudden scent of freshly popped microwave popcorn. Someone must have made some in the kitchen at the end of the hall. "That's one of my favorite smells," she mused.

"Mine too," Jordan said, clutching a pillow. "You got any others?"

Emily thought for a moment. "Rubber balls and gasoline, I guess. And the smell of my old best friend's bedroom."

"Alison's?" Jordan asked.

Emily nodded. She'd told Jordan about Ali almost immediately. It was one of those things she just had to get out of the way when she made new friends these days—everyone had seen *Pretty Little Killer*, the docudrama about what Ali did to them, anyway. "I used to sneak into her bedroom during sleepovers," she admitted, blushing. "Her room smelled like flowers and powder and just ... *her*."

"You really loved her, huh?"

Emily cast her eyes downward. That was something else she'd admitted to Jordan right away: There was no use in hiding her attraction to girls anymore. It was easy to tell Jordan things, though—she was so accepting of everything that came out of Emily's mouth. She'd just smiled faintly and said that was fine with her.

She cleared her throat and looked up at Jordan. "I meant to ask you. Do you need to call your parents? I have a phone card you can borrow. They're probably wondering where you are, right?"

Jordan shrugged. "I said I was staying at a friend's house for a while. They won't check up on me."

"Are you *sure*? For a whole *week*?"

"They probably don't even notice I'm gone." Jordan fiddled with her velvet headband. "My parents are way more concerned with their own lives. They don't really have time for me. Add in the fact that I'm not the perfect daughter they always wanted, and they'd probably rather I was just gone for good." She said it nonchalantly, finishing with a sarcastic laugh, but the pain was obvious in her voice.

81

Emily drew a squiggle in the margin. "Sometimes I think my parents want me to disappear, too."

Jordan looked up at her, clearly waiting for Emily to say more. "I've done some stuff to make them really mad," Emily said vaguely. Even though she'd shared a lot, she wasn't ready to get into *that*.

But suddenly, Jordan's face had moved closer. The air smelled heavily of jasmine perfume. "I don't know why anyone would want *you* to disappear," she blurted. "No matter *what* you did."

Emily held her breath, noticing for the first time that Jordan's eyes were the color of tourmaline gemstones. Then her cell phone let out a few sharp bleeps. She groaned, rolled over, and looked at the screen. Hanna had sent a text.

A is on the boat. Meet me near the tiki bar now.

Emily turned the phone over so Jordan couldn't see the message. "I-I'll be back," she whispered, and was through the door before Jordan could ask what had just happened.

Ten minutes later, Emily stood at the tiki bar, a steady rain pelting the awning above her head. Naturally, the deck was empty. Somewhere down below, she could hear the strains of New Age music from a late Cirque du Soleil performance in the theater.

The elevator doors opened, and Spencer and Aria walked out. They spied her and jogged over, shielding their heads from the rain.

Hanna emerged up a staircase wearing a long sundress,

high heels, and an incongruous oversized white hoodie that stretched to her mid thighs. Her eyes were wild, her face was pale, and she held her phone tightly in her right hand. "The bitch somehow made it on board with us," she snapped when they approached.

She thrust the phone at the girls. Emily stared at the text message on the screen. *Be careful who you hit and run, jailbird. See you on the Fiesta Deck!*

Aria squinted at the note. "Hit and run? What is A talking about?"

"Isn't it obvious?" Hanna said. "The accident on Reeds Lane? That horrible night in the rain? A knows."

Emily's mouth dropped open. The night of Hanna's accident felt so far removed—it had happened at the beginning of the summer, before anything else. She'd found out she was pregnant just after spring break in Jamaica, and though she'd still been living at home when Hanna had called, she was moving in with Carolyn the following week, much to her sister's chagrin. When Hanna called Emily, she had almost declined—she had a little belly bulge at the time, and what if the other girls guessed what was going on? It was hard enough to hide it from her parents. Her mother had even commented on Emily's new billowy-shirt style.

But a split second later, she'd felt terrible. Hanna needed her. And then Aria had called, saying she'd swing by and pick her up, and Emily didn't know how to say no. In the end, if any of them noticed her belly, no one said anything. They were all too preoccupied with the car crash.

Emily leaned against the bar. "How does A know about

that?" she asked, looking at Hanna. They'd been on such a desolate stretch of road, and they'd driven away before the ambulance had arrived. But then more of the night came back to her. They'd possibly hurt the girl. And then they'd run, like it was a prank.

Hanna fiddled with a large, carved tiki-head candle on top of one of the tables. "I'm not sure. But you know that girl in the car, Madison? It turns out she's Naomi Zeigler's cousin. Naomi and I have been getting along, and at first I *thought* it seemed suspicious, but then I figured she'd turned over a new leaf. Until I saw her fake ID—it's Madison's picture."

Aria's brow furrowed. "So you think Naomi was being nice to you because she's A?"

"I'm not sure," Hanna said. "But if she's not, A is going to tell her about the crash. Naomi will turn us in for sure."

"Yeah, if A doesn't turn us in first." Spencer pointed at Hanna's phone. "A called you *jailbird*."

"Hanna, did Naomi say anything about the accident?" Aria asked.

"Sort of," Hanna admitted, looking at Spencer. "She mentioned going through some terrible stuff last summer. And she got this weird look on her face when someone asked her who it was on her fake ID. She was like, My cousin doesn't need her ID anymore."

"Like she was dead?" Spencer gasped.

Emily's eyes widened. "In the crash?"

"She couldn't have died in the crash." Hanna's eyes darted back and forth. "She was still breathing when you guys got to the scene."

84

"*Was* she?" Aria squinted. "Did anyone actually check?"

Emily looked around at the others. "I don't remember if we did or not."

"I don't, either," Aria said.

Spencer's face was green. "What if we killed her when we moved her?" She slumped against one of the metal posts that propped up the awning. "I *dropped* her."

"Don't jump to conclusions yet, Spence," Aria said quickly, though she looked just as sick.

"How do you think A knows about that?" Emily asked.

Hanna shrugged. "If A is Naomi, she could have seen the accident from her house. It is just over the hill from the crash, not that I'd ever made that connection."

"Or maybe Madison lived, and she saw the girl playing you in *Pretty Little Killer* and figured it out," Aria piped up.

"No, Madison would've had to figure it out before that," Hanna insisted. "If Naomi is A, she must have known almost immediately—and decided to stalk all of us. That could be how she found out about Gayle and Kelsey."

Emily nodded, considering this. She had spent time at Gayle's house that summer, and Gayle had offered to buy Emily's baby in a café. If Naomi had been following her, it would have been easy for her to figure out what was going on.

Aria ran her hands down the length of her face. "I'm not sure Naomi makes sense as A, though. How could she know about all the other secrets A knows? Like Jamaica—that happened *before* the thing with Madison."

"Well, it's easy to explain how she knew about what happened to us in the summer—Naomi lives in Rosewood."

85

Hanna's eyes were wide. "She's friends with Kate—she's been at my house hundreds of times. She definitely could have dug up tons of dirt on me like *that*." She snapped her fingers.

Spencer bit her lip. "Actually, Naomi was around a lot when A was threatening me about Kelsey, too. She was one of the witches in *Macbeth*."

"And she latched onto Klaudia—a lot of my A notes were about her for a while," Aria added thoughtfully. "And she was at Noel's when I got a message from A about his family."

Everyone looked at Emily, waiting for her to contribute her own Naomi story. She just shrugged. "I haven't had any interaction with her."

"She was at Gayle's funeral, remember?" Hanna pointed out. "Don't you think that's weird?"

Emily stared at the flag flapping on the pole overhead. She wasn't sure if it was weird or not. "A *lot* of people live in Rosewood, though—someone else could have been watching us. And Jamaica still doesn't make sense," she whispered. "Naomi wasn't there—we would have seen her. How could she know about that?"

"There's got to be a connection," Hanna said. "Maybe she was there and we didn't know it."

Spencer's fingers flew on her phone. "Nope, Naomi was in St. Bart's for spring break—it says so on her Facebook page."

"Okay, maybe there are *two* As—one who saw what happened in Jamaica, and then Naomi, who's carrying out all the evil deeds," Hanna suggested.

Spencer squeezed her eyes shut. "God. My head is

going to explode. Now we have to think about who a *second* A could be?"

Emily breathed in. "I think I have an idea."

Hanna looked at her sharply. "Let me guess. Real Ali?"

"Yeah, Ali," Emily said in a small voice. If Jordan had snuck aboard so easily and effortlessly, who was to say Real Ali couldn't have done the same thing?

She glanced over her shoulder, terrified that Real Ali was watching them. A bolt of lightning flickered at sea. Puddles glistened under the lights. The idea of coming face-to-face with Real Ali on a boat terrified her. There were only so many places she could hide.

"Real Ali is dead," Spencer said dismissively. "It's got to be someone else."

Aria cleared her throat. "Something weird happened to me today, too." She took a deep breath. "You know how I signed up for that scavenger hunt? I got partnered with this guy who'd recently transferred from a school in New Jersey. We talked for a while, and I found out he knew Tabitha."

"You're kidding," Hanna said worriedly.

Aria nodded. "It gets worse, though. He used to be Tabitha's *boyfriend*."

"What?" Hanna shrieked.

"Are you serious?" Spencer gasped.

"I know." Aria looked tormented. "I think the universe is out to get us."

"Or *A* is out to get us," Spencer said. "Couldn't *he* be A? He has a better motive than Naomi—*or* Real Ali. Maybe more of a connection, too—he could have been in Jamaica with Tabitha."

Aria rocked from foot to foot. "I don't know about Jamaica, but I doubt it. And Graham said he was in Chile last summer—how could he have witnessed our secrets, or stolen that money from Gayle's mailbox? I could probably get him to prove it somehow the next time I see him."

Spencer's eyes boggled. "You can't see him again! What if you slip and say something?" Then she blinked hard. "And does this mean that *more* people who knew Tabitha are on the boat, too? She could have tons of friends here—they could *all* be A, together!"

Aria shook her head. "No, no, Graham *transferred* from Tabitha's school to a school in Philly. None of her friends are here."

"Still, I agree with Spencer," Hanna said. "Stay away from that guy. It sounds like a situation you don't need right now."

Aria looked annoyed. "I can't just *drop* him. I'd feel terrible."

"Why?" Spencer demanded.

Aria stared at her fingers. "Do you guys really think we're going to get away with this in the end? This might be my last chance to make things right with someone who cared about her before I go to jail."

Spencer looked at her crazily. "Are you going to *tell* him?"

"No. But I feel I owe him something. I want to make his life better somehow."

"You don't owe him anything!" Spencer roared. "The only reason you feel that way is because A is screwing with your mind!"

"Well, that's a good reason, isn't it?" Aria shrugged helplessly. "A totally has us cornered! I don't know what else to do!"

Everyone shut their eyes. A huge rush of dread swept through Emily. A *did* have them cornered. What if A turned them in for everything? They'd done so much, especially if Madison had died. And A seemed to know absolutely everything.

Spencer cleared her throat. "Look. If we figure out who A is, we can nail Gayle's murder to him or her and protect ourselves." She looked at Hanna. "You're Naomi's roommate. Search through her stuff. See if she has a second phone, like Mona did. Or break into her e-mail and see if any of the A notes are in her sent box."

Hanna bit a fingernail. "You really want me to get that close to A's stuff? Haven't you forgotten the *other* things A has done? Like with Gayle? Or what about how she laced your brownies with LSD?"

"But—" Spencer protested, then froze. A footstep on a loose plank squeaked across the deck. Spencer grabbed Emily's arm. Emily squinted hard through the shadows, terrified of what might be there. The scent of fruity perfume wafted through the air toward her, then vanished. For a few moments, all she could hear was her heartbeat pounding in her ears.

Hanna's phone chimed, and everyone jumped. "It's just Mike," Hanna said, checking the screen. "He's sneaking me into his room for the night."

"You're staying with Mike?" Aria looked worried. "You guys could both get in trouble."

"I'd rather get in trouble than get killed," Hanna said,

then hurried away, looking back and forth into the shadows before descending the stairs.

After a moment, Spencer peered at the others, let out a despairing moan, then walked off, too. Only Aria and Emily remained. They stepped out from under the awning and exchanged a terrified glance.

"Tell me this isn't happening," Emily whispered.

Aria wiped raindrops out of her eyes. "I can't live like this much longer, Em."

"I know. Neither can I."

Another bolt of lightning snapped at sea. Emily stepped forward and wrapped her arms around Aria's shoulders. Aria squeezed back, and the two of them remained that way for a few seconds, shielding each other from the elements.

And maybe from A, too.

10
Diving Right In

On Wednesday morning, Spencer stood on the docks of St. Martin. The cruise ship, which had pulled into the island at sunrise, sat in the harbor among much smaller speedboats and ferries, looking a little like an eighteen-year-old in a classroom of first-graders. The sky was a pinkish-gray, the air smelled like sun-baked pavement, and shopkeepers lifted the metal grates of their jewelry stores and placed plaques in the windows that read DIAMOND SALE! and BEST PRICES ON THE ISLAND!

About twenty or so kids from the diving class were on the dock, too, struggling into rash guards and picking through the rented diving equipment. Kirsten slathered sunscreen on her arms, then offered the tube to Spencer. "Are you really thinking of diving away from the group?"

Spencer opened her mouth to say that she was, but then hesitated. Maybe it wasn't such a good idea to dive alone—not with A around.

She gazed up and down the docks, feeling a nervous

pull in her stomach. *A is on the boat with us.* On one hand, it seemed impossible. But on the other, it made perfect sense—A was everywhere. Of *course* A was on the boat. A could be watching her that very second.

"Morning, Spencer."

Reefer stood behind her, wearing plaid swim trunks that showed off his muscled legs and holding a pair of neon-green swim fins.

"Isn't it a lovely day?" Naomi, who was standing next to him, added with a smirk. Instead of wearing a rash guard, like a sensible scuba diver, she had on a skimpy, metallic string bikini that showed off her ample cleavage. When she noticed Spencer looking her up and down, she moved a little closer to Reefer, practically stepping on his foot.

"Hi," Spencer said woodenly, then turned her back on them. Ever since scuba class, Reefer hadn't had any time for her. She'd received a sweet text from him at dinner the night before, saying he'd look for her, but then he'd sent another a few minutes later, saying, "Sorry, Naomi needs to talk, let's catch up soon." After dinner, when she and Aria were wandering around the arcade, she'd noticed Reefer sitting with Naomi in a corner, their heads angled together intimately.

She bent down and grabbed a dive tank in her arms. When she caught a glimpse of her reflection in the chrome, she winced. Her skin looked sallow in her bright-yellow Body Glove rash guard. And she'd been so tired last night, she hadn't bothered to take a shower, so her hair hung in dirty, salty clumps. How could she compare with Naomi?

92

And what about what Hanna had said about Naomi? Was it possible that she could be A? Even if she wasn't, she had a lot of reasons to be angry at them—especially if A told her what they'd done to her cousin. Last night, after Hanna had gotten that message, Spencer had lain in bed, thinking about the car accident on Reeds Lane. She couldn't believe she'd nearly *forgotten* about it.

As they'd driven away from that horrible scene, she'd turned to Hanna nervously. "What if the girl wakes up and realizes who you are?"

"Well, I told her my name was Olivia and that I was from Yarmouth," Hanna mumbled.

"But what if she sees a picture of you in an old *People*?"

Hanna turned her head sharply and stared out the window. "Well, let's hope she doesn't."

Judging by the fact that no cops had knocked on Spencer's door, asking questions, or that the news didn't even *report* on the story, Madison *didn't* seem to remember. Spencer had hoped it was because Madison had been too drunk, but there had always been a little voice inside her, whispering that it could have been because of something else. The first rule of lifesaving class said never to move someone who'd been in an accident. And then there had been that horrible *crack* of bone when Spencer had dropped Madison, a sound that now rang in Spencer's ears as though on autorepeat. She was the worst person in the world.

She felt Naomi's eyes on her and shuddered. Then she felt Reefer staring at her, too. She rolled back her shoulders and started toward the drive truck. Reefer broke away from Naomi and followed behind. "I looked for you by the aquarium this morning," he said.

"Um-hmm," Spencer murmured, biting down hard on the inside of her lip.

"I thought that was going to be our regular meeting spot."

"I decided to get an early start," she said in a clipped voice, not making eye contact.

"Spencer." Reefer caught her arm, but Spencer wrenched it away and kept going, not bothering to stop for a swim mask that slipped from her fingers and rolled across the pavement. Reefer scooped it up and ran after her. "*Spencer*. Stop."

Spencer rolled her eyes and paused. Reefer stared at her plaintively. "Are you mad about something?"

Of course I'm mad! Spencer wanted to scream. But she plucked the dive mask from Reefer's fingers and smiled tightly. "Nope."

Reefer glanced over his shoulder at Naomi, who was now talking to Tim. "We're just buddies, you know. We met at a Princeton party. She was touring the campus."

Spencer frowned. Naomi wanted to go to Princeton? She hadn't known that.

"She sort of hijacked me last night," Reefer whispered. "I wanted to have dinner with you, but she dragged me to the arcade and talked about some family stuff she was going through."

Spencer felt a prickle. "Family stuff? Like what?" *A cousin's death? A driver fleeing the scene?* What if A had *already* told Naomi what had happened?

"Just like, a family fight or whatever, I don't know."

94

Reefer shrugged. "I didn't want to just *ditch* her. Okay, to be honest, we *did* hook up in Princeton. But it's in the past. I'm into someone else now."

He stared into Spencer's eyes meaningfully. Even though Spencer wanted to remain hard-hearted, she couldn't help but melt a little.

Tim slammed the door of the van open and gestured everyone closer. Spencer looked everywhere but at Reefer, not wanting to forgive him *too* easily. Then Naomi sidled up next to him and placed her arm on his shoulder. "I had such a great time with you last night, Raif. It's so good to reconnect."

Spencer really hated how Naomi called him *Raif*, like they had some sort of special understanding. Reefer opened his mouth, about to answer, when Tim clapped his hands. "Okay, everyone! Before we head to the first dive, I want everyone to pair off. You and your partner will look out for each other when we're in the water. You'll make sure you're always safe."

When Spencer turned to Reefer, Naomi had already touched his arm possessively. Spencer stepped away—*So much for that*. But suddenly, she felt a hand on her back. "No way. You're with me."

Reefer was grinning at her hopefully. Naomi stood behind him, looking shocked. A second later, she shrugged and huffily stalked off across the group.

"If that's *okay*, that is," Reefer added in a lower voice. "Do you want to be my partner?"

Spencer pretended to think about it. "I suppose. But you owe me for ditching out on dinner last night."

"How about I take you *out* to dinner?" Reefer asked,

looping his arm in her elbow. "Somewhere on an island. I don't know about you, but I'm already getting sick of those organic sweet-potato fries and all the garlic they put in the veggie burger."

A brief flurry of guilt washed over Spencer—it seemed crazy to want to go on a date when A was so close to telling on them. But maybe she should enjoy these last few moments of freedom. She'd probably never get to do this again. "Sounds good," she answered.

They climbed into the van together and took seats next to each other in the middle row, while Naomi was relegated to a back seat by the equipment. As they pulled out of the parking lot, the sun came out from behind a cloud. The warmth felt delicious on Spencer's skin. And for the first time in weeks, at least for a minute, she felt at peace.

11
Aria's Pygmalion

That morning, Aria stood with Graham on a street corner of the French section of the island of St. Martin. Rickety-looking buses whizzed past at alarming speeds. Old, sun-weathered men sat at an outdoor café, drinking cappuccino. The surf pounded in the distance, and there were about a hundred seagulls in a nearby parking lot, fighting over an open bag of potato chips.

Aria took a deep breath and stared at the Eco Scavenger Hunt clue again. It was written in poem form and attached to a large lump of coal.

"*Use me for jam, cabinets, and wood,*" Graham read aloud. "*And when I'm a barrier, I protect sea turtles— that's good!*" He looked at Aria. "Any ideas?"

Aria touched the coal. Black dust came off on her fingers. "How can a piece of charcoal also make jam?"

Graham fiddled with a string on his hooded sweatshirt, which smelled overpoweringly like flowery fabric softener. "Maybe it's a plant. One part of it is used for charcoal, but maybe another part—the berries—makes good jam."

"That makes sense!" Aria grinned. "How did you think of that?"

Graham shrugged. "We have to be resourceful at our SCA meet-ups in the woods. I can almost guarantee you that part of this tree we're looking for probably could provide a decent component for gunpowder, too." He smiled proudly. "I'm in charge of ammunition within my unit."

Aria wanted to comment that she was pretty sure people in medieval times didn't *have* gunpowder, but she held her tongue. She looked around. "Maybe a local would know what tree around here could be used to make jam."

Graham nodded, then headed down the uneven sidewalk in the direction of a sign that Aria was pretty sure said *juice bar* in French. She took in the drawing of a knight on the back of his T-shirt. Besides the gunpowder trivia, she'd had to listen to a long aside about the virtues of makeshift toilets and cooking over a cauldron at his Society of Creative Anachronism gatherings.

It still hadn't really sunk in that Graham had dated Tabitha. After Gretchen had dismissed them, she'd run back to her cabin and scoured the Tabitha memorial sites for Graham's posts. Most of them were vague, innocuous—just saying things like *RIP* and *Miss you, Tab*. But when Tabitha's father spoke out about the resort's negligence, Graham had chimed in, saying he thought The Cliffs shouldn't have served alcohol to minors. When the news broke that Tabitha hadn't died an alcohol-related death, Graham's posts had turned irate. *Whoever did this, the cops are going to find you and take you down.*

Just reading that post had made the vegetarian chili Aria had eaten for dinner rise up in her throat. Last night, she had a dream of finding Tabitha in the sand. As she'd turned Tabitha's limp body over, Graham had come up behind her. "Aria?" He'd seemed so surprised. "What are *you* doing here?" And then, slowly, his face had registered what she'd done. "It was an accident!" Aria had cried. "It was almost like she *pitched* herself over the side—I hardly pushed her!" Tears had welled in Graham's eyes. And then he reached out his arms to strangle her. That was when she woke up.

She felt like she needed to do something for Graham. Her friends might have been dead-set against her seeing Graham again, but she'd meant what she said the night before about how this was the only way she could think of to make the overpowering guilt lift. By being Graham's friend, by being his shoulder to cry on about Tabitha—if that was what he needed—maybe she could make small amends for everything she'd done.

Bells jingled, and Graham emerged from the juice bar, looking triumphant. "The guy running the place says that the sea grape makes good jam. He says sometimes they serve as a natural barrier for sea turtles, too."

Aria frowned. "I've never heard of a sea grape tree."

Graham pulled out his cell phone, pressed the BROWSE button, and typed *sea grape* into Google. Pictures of a large-fronded tree with green grape clusters appeared on the screen. "The largest group of sea grape trees is on the southernmost tip of the island," he read aloud.

"I guess that's where we're going," Aria said, then turned on the sidewalk toward the ocean.

Graham exited out of Google, and his phone returned to the main screen. When Aria saw that the wallpaper was a picture of Tabitha, a scream froze in her throat. Tabitha was sitting on a stone wall, dressed in a pink shirt and skinny jeans.

She turned away, but not before Graham caught her looking. "Oh. That was my girlfriend. The one who was ... you know."

Aria nodded, taking in Tabitha's familiar blond hair, big blue eyes, and the faint burn scars on her neck from a childhood fire. "She's, um, pretty."

"Yeah." Graham sighed heavily. "She was gorgeous." His voice got a little choked up.

Aria paused at a corner. "You miss her, huh?"

Graham nodded. "It's ... hard. And weird. I don't know anyone our age that's died, you know? I've sort of had a hard time with it, which is totally lame, because we weren't even together when she passed away."

A car whizzed past, kicking up the ends of Aria's hair. "You weren't?"

He shook his head. "We dated in tenth grade, but I always felt like she was just waiting for something better to come along. Even when I asked her to the tenth-grade dance, she was so blasé about it, like she would've rather gone with someone else." He kicked a loose pebble on the ground. "I said some pretty awful things when we broke up, mostly about her being crazy. But then, after she went to the hospital again, I felt like the biggest jerk in the world."

"S-she was in the hospital?" Aria asked, hoping she sounded surprised.

"Yeah. She was in and out of a hospital for years," Graham answered, stepping back from the edge of a curb to avoid getting clipped by a fast-moving scooter.

"For what?"

"Depression. She had a lot of problems with her family."

There were no more cars coming at the corner, so they crossed the street. "Did you ever visit her?" Aria asked.

"Once." He made a wry face. "The place she was in looked really beautiful on the outside and had this amazing lobby, but once you went to the patient rooms, it was pretty miserable."

"Huh," Aria said, keeping her features completely neutral. That sounded like The Preserve at Addison-Stevens, all right. "Did she have any friends there?"

Graham stared up at the sky for a moment, thinking. "There were these two blond girls who were, like, the queen bees of the place. They insisted on hanging out with Tabitha when I visited her—I think they were sizing me up, deeming if I was worth talking to or not."

Even though the sun was blaring down hard on the top of her head, Aria shivered. She wondered if one of them was Ali.

"There was a guy, too," Graham went on. "I could tell he was into her—he kept giving me these nasty looks across the room." He set his jaw. "She was probably hooking up with him. All the girls thought he was pretty hot."

Then he glanced at Aria. "I'm making her sound crazy, but she wasn't—she was pretty awesome. Everyone was after her—I don't know why she picked me." There was another sigh. "I've talked to a therapist about it. She was actually the one who told me to go on this trip. She thought it would help me get over what happened, separate from the craziness surrounding Maplewood right now."

"I hear that." Aria's skin felt so prickly she just wanted to scratch and scratch. What would Graham think if he knew he was standing next to Tabitha's murderer?

They approached a public beach with a small boardwalk. A weathered man stood under a striped umbrella, selling sodas out of a cooler. Two tanned boys sat on a lifeguard stand, gazing at a few swimmers in the water. To the left was a heavy thicket of trees. Green, globelike fruit hung in bunches from the branches, and a sweet, pleasant odor filled the air. The trees looked just like the search images on Graham's phone.

Thick leaves waved over their heads, and Aria spied an envelope pinned to one of the trunks. It had the cruise line's logo in the upper right corner. "The next clue!" she cried.

She tore it off the trunk. Inside were instructions to put the clue back in the envelope for other hunters to find it, and then a link to a website that would tell them where to go next.

She showed Graham what she'd found. "We rock! High five!"

She raised her palm in the air, and Graham slapped it. Suddenly, his eyes widened at something on the beach. Aria swiveled. Two girls stood near the lifeguard stand, slathering sunscreen on their bare legs.

"What is it?" she asked.

Graham stuffed his hands in his pockets and turned away. "Nothing."

Aria squinted at him, then back at the girls. One had long, hippie-wild hair and wore Birkenstocks, and the other had pixie-short brown hair and a nose ring. She recognized both of them from the cruise ship—they'd been behind her in the waffle line at breakfast this morning. "Do they go to your school?"

"Uh-huh," Graham mumbled.

"They're cute."

Graham looked tortured. "Yeah, but whatever."

"You wouldn't ask one of them out?"

Graham snorted. "Like they'd say yes."

"Why not?"

Graham chuckled sadly. "Honestly? I don't know how to talk to girls—especially after Tabitha dumped me. And I don't know why they'd want to go out with a dork who pretends he's a knight."

Aria stopped next to a French-language No Parking sign and stared at him. "You're not a dork! Look at you! You're cute, you're funny, you're smart—so many girls would be dying to go out with you!"

Graham blushed. "I doubt that."

Aria placed her hands on her hips. "*I* don't. And you know what? I'm going to prove it to you. With my help, you're going to be dating one of those hotties by the end of this trip."

Graham's head snapped up. "*No!*"

"I'm serious! Now which one are you into? Elf Girl, with the nose ring, or Miss Hippie?"

Graham chuckled at the nicknames. "Fine. I'm sort of

103

into Elf Girl. Her real name is Tori. But seriously—nothing's going to happen. I've liked her for two months, and it hasn't gone anywhere."

"Have you actually ever *talked* to her?"

"Well, no." Graham buried half his foot in the sand.

Aria groaned good-naturedly. "That should be your first clue that nothing's going to happen. She seems perfect for you. Go offer to get her a soda from the drinks cart."

"Now?" Graham looked panicked.

"Yes, now!" Aria really, *really* liked this idea. Here was her chance to do something nice for Graham. It was a chance to atone for Tabitha, too. Square things up with the universe. Restore her karma.

She marched over to the drinks cart and purchased four Oranginas, two for them and two for the girls. "Now you don't even have to buy her a drink. Just go and offer these to Elf and Hippie. That'll strike up a conversation."

"About what?"

"I don't know!" Aria exclaimed, laughing out loud. "French beverages, whatever! Now c'mon, do it!"

Graham licked his lips. But after a moment, the tortured look on his face fell away, and he seemed almost a little excited. "Okay," he said.

He padded across the sand, holding the squash-shaped bottles in his hands. The girls shaded their eyes when he approached. They accepted the drinks and unscrewed the tops. Graham squatted down and said something to Elf Girl, and Elf Girl giggled.

Yes, Aria thought, taking a swig of her Orangina. She felt like Cupid.

Suddenly, her phone chimed from inside her bag. She

reached for it. *One new text message.* The sender was a jumble of letters and numbers.

A shiver snaked up her spine. Two tourists wearing fanny packs stared confusedly at a map across the street from the beach. A beautiful black woman in an island-print bikini spread out her towel on the sand. A girl approached the drinks cart and asked for a limeade. When she moved out of the way, Aria locked eyes with her. It was Naomi. Her blue eyes didn't blink. There was a nasty smile on her face, and she held a cell phone tightly in one hand.

Aria spun away fast, almost walking into a moving car. Then she looked down at her own phone and pressed READ.

Good for you for helping him get back in the game, Aria.
Everyone needs a little "push," don't they? —A

12
Duets

Late that afternoon, after her Caribbean jewelry-making course finished, Hanna plopped down at a bistro table with Mike and perused the big leather menu the waitress had just delivered to them. Mike sniffed the air and made a face. "*Ugh*. Something smells like goat poop. I think it's me."

Hanna snickered. "That's what you get for working on the on-board organic farm." Naturally, the cruise ship had its own chicken coops, alpaca pens, and greenhouse, and Mike had signed up for volunteer duty. "What possessed you to work there, anyway?" she asked. "You should have asked to be on the gym staff or something."

Mike shook his head woefully. "When I saw *hydroponic* and *greenhouse* in the description, I thought it was a pot farm. I didn't know I'd have to spend two hours milking goats. Do you know how badly those things reek?"

Hanna poked him. "Well, you'd better take another shower, stinky. Otherwise you're sleeping on the floor tonight."

Mike sat up. "So does that mean you're staying in my room again?"

Hanna stared absently at the shuffleboard tape marks on the deck. "Is that okay?"

"Of course it is," Mike said emphatically. "But c'mon, Hanna. Squeezing into a twin bed isn't really your thing. Did you and Naomi have a fight?"

Hanna pretended to be fascinated with the ice cubes in her glass, not wanting to meet Mike's eye. Though it was really cozy to snuggle in bed with Mike, she was the type of sleeper who thrashed around at night, needing a lot of space. She'd woken up several times last night on the verge of falling out of the bed. Besides that, Mike's room smelled kind of like a wet dog, and his roommate, a kid from Tate, farted in his sleep.

"It seemed like you guys were getting along at Mason's party," Mike added.

Hanna winced as she relived the moment when she'd clapped eyes on Naomi's fake ID. "It doesn't matter."

Mike buttered a piece of bread. "I don't get you girls and your stupid feuds. You know what I think you and Naomi should do? Strip down, have a good old-fashioned mud-wrestle, and pretty soon you'll work out all of your problems!"

"And then we'll kiss, I suppose?" Hanna deadpanned.

Mike's eyes lit up. "Only if you want to!"

Hanna smacked him, then gave her order to the waitress. She knew Mike wanted a better explanation, but what could she say? *I'm afraid to be around Naomi because I crashed her cousin's car and left the girl for dead, and now I'm worried that Naomi either just found*

107

out or that she's always known and is torturing me as A. Sorry I never told you any of this until now!

She really, *really* didn't want Naomi to be New A, especially because of how they'd bonded at the party. Things had felt so natural between them, like they were long-lost friends. And what about all that stuff Naomi had said about exercise bingeing? Had she made that up simply to gain Hanna's trust, so she could carry out her diabolical plans?

It did make sense that Naomi was A, though—at least one of the As. She could have effortlessly eavesdropped on so many secrets, what with her fast friendship with Kate. And she could have trailed Hanna to the photo session with skeevy Patrick, who had wanted to post her slightly inappropriate pictures online. Naomi had been at the flash mob when Hanna met Liam Wilkinson, her father's rival's son—she could have spotted them making out in the alley. Gathering dirt on Hanna's little Colleen-stalking mission would have been a piece of cake, too.

And she had plenty of motive. How many dirty looks had Naomi and Riley given Hanna and the other girls after Ali invited them into her brand-new clique? How many times had Naomi tried to take Hanna down—and failed? Okay, so Jamaica didn't really make sense—but maybe she *was* working with someone else, someone who'd recruited her onto the A-Team once Madison died. If Naomi knew Hanna had been the driver, had potentially hurt Madison while moving her, and then had abandoned her—well, that would push anyone to seek revenge.

It wasn't like Hanna had *meant* to crash the car,

though. She'd actually thought she was being a good Samaritan for driving Madison home. At the end of the night, it was clear Madison was in no state to drive—she had been slurring her words and practically falling asleep on the bar. Hanna had looked at Jackson, the bartender. "Do you have numbers for cabs?"

Jackson propped his elbows on the counter and chuckled, as though this were a frat party. "Yeah, she's pretty wasted, huh?"

"No cabs!" Madison crowed. "I'm fine!" She twirled the key ring around her finger, but it flew off and skidded under a video poker machine. When she bent down on her hands and knees to retrieve it, the whole bar got a view of her pink thong.

"That's it," Hanna had said, slapping down a twenty to cover Madison's bill. She gathered Madison's purse from under the stool and yanked the girl to her feet. "I'm driving you home, okay? Where do you live?"

"I can drive, Olivia," Madison whined, using the fake name Hanna had given her. "I'm *serfectly pober*! I mean perfectly *bober*! I mean ... "

And that was when she turned green, bent at the waist, and puked on her Coach flats. Patrons backed away, looking disgusted. Jackson wrinkled his nose. "Come on," Hanna said, dragging Madison out the door before she could vomit again. She felt a tiny spiral of worry as she took Madison's keys—she'd had a drink, too. But it was hours ago, and she'd nursed it. She'd drive a few miles under the speed limit to make sure no cops would stop her.

Now a bunch of girls rushed to the side of the ship,

pulling Hanna from her thoughts. "Are those dolphins?" someone cried.

Mike rose to see, but Hanna remained in her seat, her thoughts still churning. It seemed so unlikely that Naomi could have found out she was the driver that night—not unless Madison woke up and remembered, which would have been impossible if she'd died. Had she seen the crash happen from her new house, taking in everything through the trees? But that didn't make sense, either—if she'd watched, surely she'd seen that car come out of nowhere and run Hanna off the road.

"*There* you are!"

Hanna looked up. Naomi stood above her, dressed in a green Diane von Furstenberg wrap dress and raffia sandals. She held a glass of grapefruit juice in her hand and smelled, as usual, of Kate Spade Twirl.

"I just heard the best gossip about that Erin Bang Bang girl," Naomi said conspiratorially.

Hanna blinked, unnerved by Naomi's approach. "What was it?"

Naomi plopped down in Mike's seat. "Apparently, someone heard her talking on the phone with her mom. And get this—she was pretending like she was a complete angel, saying how she was praying every morning, spending a lot of time with her classmates, and avoiding parties and boys. Can you believe it?"

Hanna eyed Naomi carefully. Her eyes were twinkling, and she had a sweet smile on her face. She seemed so harmless, not like a malicious killer. But this was probably part of her plan as A. Still, Hanna thought about the strategy Spencer had suggested to earn Naomi's trust and figure out if she was A. She could fake-friend her. All of a sudden, it seemed feasible. Maybe Hanna could even figure out if Naomi really knew about the accident with Madison, too.

She cracked a tiny smile. "If only we could post Erin's dalliances in a place where Mama Bang Bang would see."

"Seriously." Naomi chuckled, taking the bait.

Hanna laid down her napkin. "I saw a sign that it's Karaoke Night tonight. Want to go?"

Naomi raised an eyebrow. "Only if you'll sing a duet with me. I hate doing karaoke alone."

"You got it!"

"Let's go now," Naomi suggested. "I have the perfect song for us."

Hanna stood just as Mike returned from dolphin-spotting. He gave her a confused look, which she avoided with a kiss to his cheek. "I'll see you later," she said breezily, then glided away. Hopefully he didn't notice how badly her hands were shaking as she followed Naomi to the elevators.

The karaoke lounge was two levels down, and they could hear caterwauling all the way from the elevator bank. There was a small, dimly lit stage at the front of the room, and the room's small, round tables were filled with kids. Hanna noticed a cute, dark-haired guy sitting by himself near the bathrooms. It was Graham, the boy Aria was partnered with for the scavenger hunt. Aria had shown her pictures of him on the Tabitha Clark Memorial website.

As if sensing her gaze, Graham turned and looked at Hanna, too. He didn't blink. Hanna flinched and turned away. She followed Naomi to peruse the book of songs, her heart banging the whole time. *I could be standing next to A right now*, she kept thinking. *This girl could know all the horrible things I've ever done.*

She eyed "California Gurls" by Katy Perry and considered suggesting it, but then decided it was too cheesy. But suddenly, Naomi pointed at it, too. "I think we could rock this one, don't you?"

"Let's do it." Hanna wrote it down next to their names. There was no way she was quibbling with A.

They sat down at a table and waited their turn. Though Hanna had to keep jiggling her leg to assuage her nerves, she pretended to be completely calm, watching as a bunch of guys from Ulster growled out something by a metal band and three girls with the same blond haircut pretended they were Britney Spears. Naomi pulled out her cell phone, and though Hanna was dying to look at what she was writing, she kept her gaze pasted on her drink, her heart thudding hard.

Naomi dropped her phone back in her bag. "I wish they would serve us," she sighed. "I *so* need a cocktail. I'm having major guy issues, and I want to drown my sorrows."

"What's going on?" Hanna asked, shakily resting her chin in her palm. Fake-friending Rule #1: Always pretend to care about the fake friend's boy problems.

Naomi sighed. "The guy I'm into likes Spencer."

Hanna sipped the water that had been placed in front of her, surprised Spencer hadn't brought this up when they'd talked about A last night. "That sucks," she said fumblingly.

112

"It *does* suck." Naomi's eyes widened. "Hey, got any dirt on her? You know, something that would make him run screaming?"

Hanna coughed. "I don't really know anything *that* good." *Except that she's a murderer*, a voice growled in her head. *Or that she took drugs last summer and framed someone else for possession. Or that she helped me move your cousin into the driver's seat of the car I was driving.*

Then again, if Naomi was A, she already knew all of that.

"Aw, I'm just kidding." Naomi nudged her playfully after a moment, probably registering Hanna's uncomfortable expression. She squeezed Hanna's hand. "You're so lucky you have Mike, you know."

"Yeah," Hanna said, feeling herself relax, smiling as she thought of him.

"He's better than Sean Ackard," Naomi added. "You know I dated him too, right?"

Hanna nodded. "In ninth grade."

Naomi looked surprised. "How did you remember that?"

Hanna laughed. "I pined over Sean for years—I knew everyone he dated. But, you know, when I got him, he was a huge disappointment. He was just so ... *good*."

"You mean the no-sex thing, right?" Naomi rolled her eyes. "He's always been like that. I was at this party with him once, and all the couples were peeling off to make out. But Sean and I sat on the couch, watching this stupid movie on TV like we were the parents. It was so lame."

"What does Kate see in him?" Hanna giggled.

113

"Maybe she's into virgins," Naomi snickered. "I heard she's going to V Club with him now."

"Actually, I—" Hanna was about to say she'd seen Kate and Sean leave a V Club meeting a few weeks ago but stopped herself just in time. She'd been with Liam when she caught Kate and Sean at the V Club meeting.

Then again, if Naomi was A, she would know that, too.

Hanna straightened up, feeling nervous. "You know, if you really want a cocktail, we could sneak off the boat when we get to Puerto Rico and go to a bar or something. I have a fake ID. And you have your, um, cousin's, right?"

A strange expression flashed across Naomi's face. "Yeah."

"Are you guys close?" Her heart was pounding hard. She felt ridiculously transparent.

Naomi picked at her nails. "Like sisters. Her name's Madison. She went to St. Agnes. Now she goes to Penn State. Or, well, she *did* go to Penn State until the accident."

Hanna's stomach dropped. "Did she ... *die?*" She braced herself for the answer. Or for Naomi to start screaming that she knew everything and wanted Hanna dead.

Naomi glanced at Hanna for a long moment, almost as though she were sizing her up. But before she could answer, the beginning notes of "California Gurls" boomed through the space, and the lyrics appeared on the screen behind the stage.

Naomi leapt up. "God, I'm such a buzzkill! C'mon. Let's forget about this and have fun."

114

They rushed up to the front and grabbed the microphones. But when Hanna opened her mouth to sing, her voice sounded unsteady and thin. She kept picturing Madison in a hospital bed, post-crash, one of those horrible masks on her face breathing for her. She pictured Naomi, Madison's favorite cousin, sitting by her side, a blubbering mess. Finding out that someone else was to blame would drive anyone to revenge. But how was Naomi able to play it so cool right now?

She glanced over at Naomi now. Her eyes were clear, her tears gone, and she was singing gleefully into the microphone as though she'd put the pain behind her. As the peppy chorus began, a bunch of kids in the audience sang along. Naomi's voice rose. She turned around and slapped her butt. Hanna couldn't help but snicker.

Then Hanna threw her head back and sang louder, too. Her voice sounded good blended with Naomi's. When she opened her eyes, Naomi grabbed her hands and spun her around. She flipped her skirt, and Hanna grabbed two glowsticks from a nearby table, pretending firecrackers were exploding from her boobs. The crowd cheered. When Hanna looked out at their faces, even Graham was smiling.

When the song ended, a bunch of guys sitting along the wall chanted, "En-*core*! En-*core*!"

"The public loves us!" Hanna giggled as they stepped off the stage.

"That's because we're awesome!" Naomi looped her arm through Hanna's elbow. "We should perform that at the talent show, don't you think?"

"Um, sure," Hanna said, remembering her promise to

Spencer and the others to do the hula with them. But it wasn't like she could say no—not to the girl who was potentially A.

And then, as if on cue, when she got back to her seat, her cell phone light was blinking. There was a new text message.

Naomi's head had turned and she was talking to Ursula Tippington, paying no attention. Hanna cast a glance at Naomi's phone on the table beside her. All she had to do was reach over and grab it, but her limbs felt as if they were filled with sand. Swallowing hard, she opened her text.

Hanna Marin got in a crash
Moved a girl to cover her ass
Hanna Marin fled the scene
But someone saw it all—me.
—A

13
People Who Float in Glass Boats
Shouldn't Throw Stones

"Welcome to Puerto Rico!" Jeremy boomed over the loudspeaker on Thursday morning. He said it with a flamboyant Spanish accent, rolling the *r*s.

Emily watched as a lot of kids waved scarves at the people on shore. An acoustic, dreamy version of "Over the Rainbow" tinkled over the loudspeakers, and everyone groaned. That same song had played when they'd pulled out of Newark, then the following morning at sea, *then* to summon them to dinner the night before. It was getting a little old.

She sat down on a bench, inhaling the humid air. Jordan had left her a note on her bedside table earlier, saying she was grabbing coffee but that Emily should meet her. When her phone rang, she expected to see Jordan's name, but it was Hanna instead.

"I have Spencer and Aria on the phone, too," Hanna said as soon as Emily answered. "I hung out with Naomi.

She doesn't seem to know that we were involved in Madison's accident—but *someone* does. A sent me another note about it."

"Did you find out if Madison died?" Emily asked, her heart stopping in her chest. *Please say she didn't*, she thought. If someone else died because of her, she wasn't sure how she could go on. But then, finding out that Madison hadn't been just passed-out drunk, as they'd all thought, was enough of a mind game. How could she have fled the scene, leaving a hurt, innocent girl behind? Emily kept picturing the police reading her charges, the looks on her parents' faces. Her mother would probably keel over dead—and that would be yet *another* death Emily was responsible for.

"I don't know if she died yet," Hanna admitted. "We were interrupted before I could get to that, and I felt weird pushing it."

"You have to try to find out what happened, Hanna," Aria urged. "If she did die, or if she was hurt, that makes a stronger case for Naomi being A."

"I know, I know." Hanna sounded distraught. Then she sighed. "But I'm confused. Naomi seems so poised and innocent. Could she be that good of an actress?"

"I got a note from A yesterday, and when I looked up, Naomi was staring right at me," Aria said. "My note made another reference to Jamaica. We need to figure this out soon and bring A down before A ruins us."

"You know who I'm *not* so sure about?" Hanna said. "Tabitha's ex. He was all alone in the karaoke bar, Aria, and it seemed like he was watching me."

"He's not A," Aria said stubbornly.

"How can you be so sure?" Spencer asked. "*He* was there when you got the A note yesterday, too, wasn't he?"

"But how could he know about everything else we did?" Aria said. "He was in South America last summer, remember?"

"So he says."

There was a tense pause on the line. Finally, Spencer sighed and said she had to go. The other girls hung up, too, but they promised to meet up later to talk about their hula dance. After she hit END, Emily chewed hard on her gum. Though she didn't believe Naomi was A, she also remembered something from the previous summer— maybe she and Naomi *did* share a connection. After the accident, when Emily was in Philadelphia, she'd been waddling home from the fish restaurant where she worked, deep in conversation with Derrick, her friend and coworker. They'd been talking about how heartbreaking Real Ali's return to Rosewood had been for Emily, especially the kiss they'd shared.

"Are you sad she died in the fire?" Derrick had asked.

"Sort of," Emily said, looking away. It wasn't like she could tell Derrick that Ali *hadn't* died in the fire—that she'd escaped through the door Emily had left open. Ali *had* died when Aria pushed her off the roof in Jamaica, though.

Then she had stopped short, spying someone across the intersection. There, standing at the window of the BCBG store, was Naomi Zeigler.

"Oh my God," she'd gasped, pulling Derrick around the corner. She waited until Naomi had walked on, then figured she was safe. But what if Naomi had seen?

119

Emily's phone bleated again, bringing her back to the present. *Aria,* said the Caller ID. "What are you doing today, Em?" she asked. "Do you want to get breakfast?"

Just then, Emily spied Jordan rounding the corner. She was wearing a pair of khaki Bermuda shorts and a sky-blue T-shirt Emily had loaned her. The same silk headband held back her long, dark hair.

"Uh, I can't," she said.

"Why not?" Aria sounded worried. "Is everything okay?"

"Everything's great," Emily said in a lower voice. "*Better* than great, actually." She peeked at Jordan as she strode toward her, a huge smile on her face. "I've made an amazing new friend."

"Oh!" Aria sounded pleased. "That's nice. At least *something* good is happening on this trip. Do I get to meet her?"

Emily chewed on the tip of her sunglasses. Aria might not approve of the fact that she was hiding someone in her room. They were in enough trouble as it was.

"Um, I'll get back to you on that," she said abruptly, and then hung up.

She dropped her phone in her bag and smiled at Jordan. "What are we up to today?" She nudged her playfully. "It had better be good. I'm skipping bird-watching for this." Her bird-watching instructor had a beach expedition planned, though if it was anything like yesterday's watch, Emily would be so bored that she'd almost fall asleep while staring through the binoculars. There was only so much excitement she could muster up for sea terns and pelicans.

Jordan extended a hand to help Emily up. "We're going ashore."

"Are you sure it's a good idea to leave the boat?" Emily asked incredulously. "I don't want you to get in trouble."

Jordan raised one shoulder. "Live a little! Now c'mon, cutie!"

Cutie. Jordan had also called her *hot stuff, honey,* and *hot cakes.* Maya St. Germain used to call her names like that, and Emily had to admit she liked it. Since Emily had met Jordan, her fascination had morphed into a full-blown crush. They'd stay up each night, talking about their lives. Jordan didn't make fun of Emily for any of the babble that spilled from her mouth, like Ali had. She just listened with an intrigued smile on her face, as though Emily were the most interesting person in the world.

They walked down the ramp off the boat and stepped into the humid Puerto Rico air. The sun glimmered on the water. They passed a clump of kids wearing T-shirts from Ulster Prep, Jordan's school. "Do you want to say hi?" Emily asked.

Jordan looked at her blankly. "To whom?"

"To . . . " Emily trailed off. They'd already passed the Ulster kids; the moment was gone.

"So what are we going to do?" she asked instead. "Wander the streets? Sit at a café and listen to mariachi music?"

"Patience, grasshopper." Jordan bumped Emily's hip, then took a sharp left and walked to a second dock full of tethered yachts and sailboats. She marched down the dock as though she knew it, stopping at a long, square, motorboat bobbing gently on the waves. "This'll work," Emily thought she heard her mumble.

She stepped onto the boat. It rocked slightly under her weight, and she stretched out her arms for balance. She strolled to the cockpit and peered at the gauges. Then she opened a hatch next to the steering wheel. After a bit of fiddling, the motor started up.

"Well?" she called to Emily over the growling sounds. "Are you coming aboard or not?"

Emily blinked. "Is this *your* boat?"

Jordan laughed. "No, silly!"

"Then what are you *doing*?"

Jordan leaned against the steering wheel. "Whoever it belongs to hasn't tended to it for a long time." She pointed to a sticker on the side. "See? The license is out of date. And there's a ton of film on the side—it hasn't been cleaned in years." She patted one of the leather seats. "Poor old girl. You miss going out to sea, don't you?"

"But we could get in huge trouble! I thought you were trying to stay under the radar!"

Jordan grabbed a captain's hat that was hanging from a peg by the wheel and popped it on her head. "Life isn't worth living if you're scared all the time."

Emily glanced over her shoulder, half expecting to see A's shadow slipping behind a Chris-Craft parked near them. But no one was there. It was just her and Jordan and a dockful of boats. Jordan was right: She *was* scared all the time. When had she last actually had fun?

She tentatively put one foot onto the boat. "Just a *little* ride, okay?"

"Yay!" Jordan whooped, rushing over to help Emily

aboard. She gave Emily a huge hug, holding her for a few extra beats. Emily's skin tingled. The promise of more hugs like that was reason alone for breaking the rules.

Jordan untied the boat from the slip. Then, with a spin of the wheel, she backed the boat into the harbor. A salty-smelling breeze kicked up, blowing Emily's hair around her face. In seconds, they were passing the cruise ship, then a bunch of sailboats. As they rounded the old fort on the outskirts of town, Emily looked down and noticed something. The bottom of the boat was glass. Fish swam gracefully just inches below her, visible in the bright sun-light.

"Oh my God!" She placed her palms on the glass. "Jordan! Come see!"

Jordan let the boat idle and walked into the hull, too. Tropical fish glided under her feet. Ocean plants waved gently. "Wow," she said.

"I've never seen anything like it," Emily breathed. "We don't even need a dive mask!"

They watched the water in awe for a few minutes. But as Emily stared at the abyss, her happy mood began to shift. Not even a year ago, Tabitha had been washed away in this very same sea. Fish just like these had swum around her body impassively, witnessing it wasting away. Seaweed had lodged in her hair and ears. The salty water had eroded her slowly, meticulously, until only bones were left.

A strange noise gurgled from the back of her throat. Jordan turned. "Are you okay?"

"I'm fine," Emily managed.

Jordan inched closer, her green eyes wide. "No, you're not. Are you freaked that we took this boat?"

Emily wrapped her arms across her chest, suddenly cold. *I'm freaked about everything*, she wanted to say. But if she opened her mouth, she feared all her secrets would spill out in a matter of minutes. She couldn't tell Jordan about Tabitha. It was too dangerous.

"I'm glad we're out here," she finally managed. "I needed to do this. Get away from my life."

Jordan cocked her head. "Things at home are really that bad, huh?"

Emily nodded, feeling a lump in her throat.

"Your parents?" Jordan guessed. "You said they didn't want you around."

Tears pricked Emily's eyes, and she nodded again. "They hate me."

"What *happened*, exactly?"

Emily eyed her, then took a deep breath. This was one secret she *could* share. "They found out I had a baby last summer. When I told them last week, they didn't just freak—they shut down."

Jordan blinked slowly. "You had a *baby*?"

Emily winced at Jordan's shocked tone of voice. She was probably disgusted. But then she looked at Jordan's face. It was kind and accepting. *Go on*, her expression seemed to say. *I'm listening. I'll like you anyway.*

It all spilled out of her. The part about Gayle. Even reneging on the offer and leaving the baby on the Bakers' doorstep. "After Isaac found out, I just thought it was time for my parents to know," she said. "But now it's like I'm no longer part of the family. They've been pissed at me before, but this is in a totally different league. I know I should hate them, but I miss them so much."

She stared down at the fish floating by, tears in her eyes. Everything she said was painfully true. She'd been through a lot with her family, but she thought they were all beginning to understand one another. What she'd done had ruined things between them for good.

Jordan moved closer and touched Emily's hand. "You are so, so brave," she said quietly. "I couldn't do what you did. Not any of it."

Emily blinked away tears. "It was really, really hard."

"What was it like?" Jordan's eyes were wide. "To be pregnant, I mean. To give birth. To go through something so ... *earth-shattering*. I can't imagine it."

"Scary," Emily answered. "But also amazing. My favorite part was feeling her kick. I would lie down at night and put my hand on my belly and just stay that way for hours. At first, it's like this little flutter inside of you. But then, as she got bigger, the kicks were stronger. It was kind of mind-blowing."

"Wow," Jordan whispered.

Tears welled in her eyes, and she glanced at Jordan gratefully. "No one ever asked me that, you know. It was always about what I'd done wrong or what a horrible person I was."

"You're not horrible," Jordan said. "You're incredible."

Emily peeked at Jordan bashfully. "I think you're incredible, too," she whispered.

Jordan placed one finger on Emily's knee. Instead of pulling away a split second later, she let it remain there. Emily stared at Jordan's pink, moon-shaped nail, then slid closer. Her heart started to pound. Before she knew it, their lips were touching. Emily's nose filled with the heady aroma of jasmine perfume. She ran her fingers up and down Jordan's bare arms. Her skin was as soft as petals.

They pressed close together, inhaling each other, and when they broke away, they stared into each other's eyes.

"Yay," Jordan whispered giddily. "I was hoping that would happen."

"Yay for *me*," Emily insisted, curling up in Jordan's lap and staring at the clouds.

"Yay for *us*," Jordan corrected. And then she took off the captain's hat, placed it on Emily's head, and opened her arms again.

14
Spencer's Unexpected Swim

"Here you are!" A Latin waitress plopped down a large tray in front of Spencer and Reefer. "The six ceviche tasting menu! *¡Buen apetito!*"

As she strode away, shaking her ample hips, Spencer stared down at the six small bowls. "I can't believe you talked me into this. I've been to the Caribbean seventeen times, and I've managed to avoid ceviche until now."

"Aw, a ceviche virgin!" Reefer pushed a fork at her. "C'mon. You have to try some. You'll love it."

Spencer looked up, stalling. It was Thursday night, and they were at an outdoor Latin restaurant in Old San Juan. Palm trees surrounded them, and every table bore a flickering votive candle and a vase of tropical flowers. A band played upbeat, wild music, and several couples were salsa-dancing near the stage. To add to the sexy vibe, a blue infinity pool rippled off in the distance. Spencer had already seen two couples strip down to bathing suits and dive into the pool as an alternative to dessert.

Before their dive that morning, the dive class had

watched a film about Jacques Cousteau. For the rest of the afternoon, Spencer had prepared for their dinner out. Now her blond hair spilled down her back, her skin glowed from a body scrub, and her nails had been painted a shade of red called Vixen. She'd pored through her and Kirsten's cruise wear until she'd decided on a turquoise strapless linen dress that screamed *I'm gorgeous, but I don't try very hard*. As soon as Reefer had seen the dress, he'd remarked that it was his favorite color.

She'd chosen this restaurant, too, clicking through San Juan nightlife websites and picking the place that seemed the most romantic. Other kids from the boat had the same idea: In the corner were two couples from Tate. Across the way, Lanie Iler and Mason Byers snacked on fritters. And Naomi Zeigler had just sat down with a bunch of girls from Rosewood Day, shooting Spencer a nasty look when she spotted her and Reefer together. Spencer gritted her teeth at Naomi's clonelike turquoise dress. What, had Naomi spied on her while she was getting ready?

Then again, *Spencer* was the one on the date with Reefer, wasn't she?

But on the heels of that dart of triumph came a stab of dread. Perhaps Naomi had followed her here because she was A.

Swallowing her worry, she took the fork from Reefer and daintily tried a bit of ceviche. A sharp, acidic flavor hit her first. Then she tasted something cool and mild. "It's okay," she decided.

"Have the one with the chilis." Reefer pushed another bowl closer. "It's amazing when you make it with real chilis, not the dried kind. I was on a ceviche kick for a

128

while a few years ago. I'm trying to remember my favorite recipe ... " He tapped on his iPhone, tilting it toward Spencer. REEFER'S RECIPES FROM A TO Z, read the screen. Ceviche, naturally, was filed under C.

Spencer snickered. "You're so organized."

Reefer covered the screen with his hand, looking embarrassed. But Spencer wasn't surprised. He kept his pot supply in little individual, carefully labeled drawers. Earlier, when he'd opened his wallet for his fake ID, his cards were alphabetized, an AAA membership at the front, a business card for Justin Zeis, Personal Trainer, in the back.

"I like everything in its place," he admitted. "I can't stand it when things are messy." He bit into a chip. "You can say it. I'm a dork."

Spencer leaned forward on her elbows. "If you're dorky, then so am I. All of the money in my wallet has to be in order according to the serial number on the front of the bills. If it's out of order, I panic."

Reefer's eyebrows rose. "How long have you been doing that?"

"Since my first allowance. And before that, I arranged my bath toys along the side of the tub by height and color."

Reefer grinned. "I used to sort my LEGOs by size and theme. And I insisted on ironing my school clothes myself—I hated how my mom did it."

"I still iron my jeans sometimes," Spencer admitted, then felt a little self-conscious for saying so.

Reefer chuckled. "When I first got into botany, my mom gave me a spice rack to organize my seeds. I woke up several times a night to check to make sure no one had put them in a different order."

Spencer grabbed a chip and popped it in her mouth. "I begged my father to let me do his filing. He thought there was something wrong with me."

"You would have been such an asset to the Ivy Eating Club," Reefer joked. "A perfect secretary."

"Too bad that'll never happen." Spencer stared morosely at the salt on the rim of her margarita glass. She'd been so desperate to get into Ivy, but after the pot-brownie fiasco, it was clear that would never happen.

When she felt Reefer's large, warm hand cover hers, she looked up in surprise. "You'll have way more fun at Princeton without being part of an eating club, you know," he said softly. "I'll make sure of it."

"You will?" Spencer dared a smile.

"Of course. We're going to have an amazing time. I know tons of fun things to do—things that are much cooler than what those Ivy people are into."

Spencer's heart thumped. He'd said *we*. Like they were going to be a couple. Maybe even an *exclusive* couple.

A trumpet blared in her ear, and she turned. The jazz band stood next to their table for a private serenade. The guitarist strummed a slow rhythm. The drummer shook a maraca. The singer launched into song. Even though the lyrics were in Spanish, Spencer recognized the melody as "I Only Have Eyes for You."

"You've got a beautiful girlfriend, man," the singer said in a broken Spanish accent between verses.

"I know," Reefer said, glancing at Spencer cautiously, as if he'd said too much. Spencer smiled giddily.

Girlfriend? She tried it on like it was a dress, and it felt pretty damn good. She smiled at him and squeezed his hand.

"Want a picture?" A waitress materialized with a Polaroid camera. Spencer and Reefer leaned close and smiled. The flash went off, and the device spat out a photograph. Spencer took it from the waitress and laid it on the table to dry.

Reefer stood and offered his hand. "Want to dance?"

"Yes," Spencer breathed.

They chose a spot on the dance floor close to the pool, and Reefer wrapped his arms around her.

"I never took you as the dancing type," she murmured as they swayed.

Reefer made a *tsk* noise with his tongue. "You should know by now that looks can be deceiving. I like to dance—especially if it's with the right person."

Spencer's heart thudded as he leaned closer to her until his nose grazed her cheek. She swallowed nervously, then tipped toward him, too. The trumpeter let out a series of notes as their lips touched. Spencer shut her eyes and tasted lime and ceviche and salt. Tingles shot through her body.

They pulled away and grinned. A muscle twitched by Reefer's mouth. But then, a half-second later, his gaze focused on someone behind Spencer.

"Mind if I cut in?"

Naomi's angular face swam into view. She stared sweetly at Reefer, her head cocked and her lashes fluttering.

Spencer stiffened, wanting to say no. But before either

131

of them could move, Naomi nudged her body in front of Spencer's, grabbing Reefer's hands. Spencer tried to hold her ground, but then Naomi gave Spencer a little shove with her hip. Spencer staggered backward. Her heel caught on the uneven stones, and she wheeled her arms for balance. The moments in the air felt like an eternity, and suddenly her body hit cold water with a loud splash. Water gushed into her ears and drenched her dress. Her butt hit the bottom of the pool, and she quickly pushed off and swam to the surface, coming up sputtering.

She pushed her hair out of her eyes and looked around. The music was still playing just as loudly, but a lot of people on the dance floor had stopped and were staring at her. Waiters froze in place, trays in hand. Reefer's mouth hung open. Naomi's eyes were wide. After a moment, she stepped carefully toward the pool's edge.

"My goodness, Spencer, are you okay?" she said in a fake-concerned voice. "You should be more *careful*!"

Spencer wanted to grab Naomi's ankle and pull her in, too, but Naomi had already glided back to Reefer, assuming, perhaps, that they were going to continue dancing. But Reefer turned to a waiter, who rushed forward with a towel.

Spencer climbed out of the pool and let Reefer wrap the towel around her shoulders. "That was weird," he murmured, oblivious, as he ushered her back to their table. "Maybe we shouldn't have danced so close to the pool, huh?"

Not with Naomi around, Spencer thought bitterly. Her phone beeped from inside her tote, and she bent down. *One new message from Anonymous.*

She glanced behind her. Naomi stared out the window, her phone in her lap. There was a wisp of a smile on her face, as if she was keeping a delicious secret.

Spencer eyed Naomi, who was now gliding toward the exit with her head held high, as if her job here was done. Then Spencer peered down at the text.

If you know what's best for you, Spence, you'd stay away from him. There are plenty of fish in the sea. Or, after I get through with you, the prison yard. —A

15

A Picture's Worth a Thousand Words

On Friday morning, Aria and Noel stood in the ship's kitchen at separate workstations. In an attempt to do something together, they'd signed up to volunteer in the all-natural, all-organic kitchen. Little did they know they'd be assigned to the breakfast shift at 6 A.M.

Aria peeked into Noel's bowl and frowned. "I think you put too much flour in the batter," she whispered, glancing surreptitiously at Bette, the large woman who was in charge of the kitchen.

Noel's brow furrowed, and he peered at the laminated recipe next to him. "It said twelve cups for this size of a batch. I *think* that's what I did."

Aria fluffed the batter with a fork. "I think it's supposed to be thicker. It's way too flaky."

Noel snickered. "*You're* flaky."

He tickled Aria's side, and she swatted him with an oven mitt. She had to admit the early morning breakfast thing was fun: They were the only kids in the kitchen, there was a romantic classical-guitar station on the radio, and the air felt fresh and clean, not yet tropically humid. True, Aria hadn't realized most of her kitchen chores would involve handling meat: removing thousands of strips of free-range turkey bacon from the freezer, frying up lumpy grass-fed beef sausages, even dealing with something called scrapple, which she was convinced contained pig snouts—albeit *organic* pig snouts. But even that was a small price to pay for having some solid Noel time.

Noel poured more milk into the batter. "Hey, since we're up early, we should go for a walk on the beach. I could show you the rap Mike and I are going to do for the talent show on Sunday." He nudged her.

"That would be great!" Aria said, but then bit her lip, remembering. "But I can't today. I promised I'd mini-golf with Graham this morning."

"Oh." Noel stared into his bowl. "That's cool."

Aria tossed another tray of bacon onto the griddle. It sputtered loudly. "I'm really sorry. If you'd asked me earlier, I could have rearranged things." They'd had dinner with a big group of kids last night. Aria and Noel had barely talked.

"I said it's fine," Noel said stiffly. "You sure are spending a lot of time with that Graham guy, though."

Aria wrinkled her nose. *That Graham guy?* That was something her mom would say. "It's not like I'm into him. He's one of those guys who dresses up in armor and goes to jousts."

"But is he into *you*?"

She laughed. "Definitely not. I'm trying to get him to talk to his crush, in fact. His old girlfriend died, and he's too shy to talk to her on his own."

Noel looked up, surprised. "How did she die?"

Aria bit down hard on the inside of her cheek. "Um, I'm not really sure."

Really, she shouldn't have told her friends about Graham, either—they couldn't get it out of their heads that Graham might be A. Yesterday evening before dinner, when they'd met to go through their hula routine, Emily had told her she'd seen Graham lurking around one of the halls. And Hanna, who was hanging out with them even though she was now doing an act with Naomi, remarked that it seemed like Graham didn't have any friends on the cruise—he was always sitting alone at meals. "What if he came aboard for other reasons—like stalking us?"

"He's *not* A," Aria had urged. "It wasn't even like his relationship with Tabitha was recent."

"Yeah, but you said that he liked her more than she liked him," Hanna reminded her. "Maybe he thought she was his true love or something. Maybe he's one of those crazy guys who is just dying to get revenge on someone."

"You don't even *know* him," Aria had said defensively.

"Yeah, but neither do you," Hanna retorted.

Now, she cleared her throat and looked at Noel. "I just feel like I need to help the guy out. It's fun to play match-maker."

Noel took a sip from the mug of coffee sitting next to him. "Just as long as you don't play matchmaker and match him with *you*. You might be leading him on and not even know it."

The bacon sizzled loudly. "You don't trust me?" Aria asked.

"Of course I do," Noel said quickly. "It's just ... I

136

thought this cruise would be different. I didn't think this Eco Hunt of yours would take up so much time."

Aria pointed her spatula at him. "*You're* the one who didn't want to do the Eco Hunt with me. *You're* the one who insisted on surfing. You knew I couldn't do it with you. You know I can't swim very well. But you did it anyway."

"You *said* I could!"

"And I meant it," Aria said. "I think it's awesome that you're having so much fun. But don't guilt me because *I'm* having fun."

Noel's eyes widened. "Fine. I won't say anything. I won't bother you at all."

"Good," Aria answered, hardening.

She turned back to the bacon. Noel stirred his mix. His movements became so forceful and impassioned that all of the excess flour rose up in a cloud and covered his face in a fine white mist. He blinked hard, looking like a mime.

Aria couldn't help but laugh. After a moment, Noel laughed, too. He shook his head and gently knocked her shoulder. "I'm sorry. I'm being an ass."

"No, *I'm* sorry," Aria said, grabbing a paper towel and wiping the flour off his face. "I don't want to fight. I want us to have fun. But you shouldn't be jealous about Graham, okay? I love *you*."

Noel spit flour from between his lips. "You're both really arty, though. You probably have a lot in common."

Aria's mouth fell open. *Seriously?* There had been plenty of times she'd felt inferior around Noel—he was so wealthy, good-looking, and popular that sometimes she still felt like kooky sixth-grade Aria, Ali's dorky sidekick.

But this was the first time he'd ever told her *he* didn't feel good enough for her.

"Noel ... " She touched his arm. "You're being ridiculous. I promise."

"Okay," Noel said after a moment. "It's just that I really wanted to take a walk today so I could give you this."

He brushed off the flour from his hands and pulled out a gold necklace from his pocket. A pendant spun slowly on a chain. It was tarnished and a little battered, perhaps antique, with an intricate, swirled design on the front.

The locket looked vaguely familiar. "Did you get this at one of those expensive jewelry shops in Old San Juan?" she asked.

Noel shook his head. "I actually found it on the beach at our surf spot in Puerto Rico yesterday. I almost stepped on it. It's like it was meant to be mine—or yours."

"It's like a sunken treasure," Aria whispered, letting Noel hook it around her neck. She peered down at it. There was an initial on the front—an *I*? A *J*? It was impossible to tell, as the letter was almost worn away. The necklace had had a whole life before her, a whole story she'd never know about.

"I'll wear it always," she told Noel, and wrapped her arms around him, not caring that she was getting flour all over herself. And then, as easy as that, everything felt perfect again.

An hour later, Aria and Graham stood on the green of the ship's mini-golf course. Technically, they were supposed to be discussing the next clue for the Eco Scavenger Hunt—

138

it involved figuring out which part of the ship was constructed with the highest percentage of recycled materials—but their gaze was on a girl bent over a tee at Hole 5 instead. It was Tori. She was wearing a long peasant skirt, a ribbed blue top, sandals that had little jewels on each strap, and a silver ankle bracelet, which struck Aria as both bohemian and Shakespearian. Tori swung her club and gently tapped the blue golf ball toward a clown's open mouth, but it hit the rail and rolled back down the ramp.

"So I've asked around, and I found out Tori doesn't have a boyfriend," Aria whispered in Graham's ear. "You're totally in."

Graham's cheeks reddened. "You *asked* about her?"

"How else were we going to find out anything?" Aria grabbed a club from the rack. "Now c'mon. Let's go to the hole right behind them. Then I want you to compliment her on her putting skills."

"Are you serious?" Graham snickered. "She's missed getting the ball through the clown's mouth like six times."

Aria glared at him. "Don't you know *anything*? When it comes to flirting, you *lie*! You say whatever it takes to make girls feel amazing and special!" She rolled her eyes good-naturedly. "You're hopeless!"

"I bet you're wondering how I *ever* had a girlfriend, huh?" Graham teased.

Aria waved her hand, not wanting to talk about Tabitha. "You did great with her on the beach yesterday." Graham had spoken to Tori for almost ten whole minutes before freaking out and jogging back to Aria, claiming he was afraid they were going to run out of topics. "She seemed into you, too. Now you just have to seal the deal."

She walked to the hole next to the one Tori was playing. A small windmill spun creakily. The goal was to hit the ball through a tiny gap at the bottom. As she handed Graham the putter, he smiled at her gratefully. "It's really sweet that you're doing this for me."

"I'm glad to help," Aria chirped, her confidence renewed. How could her friends think Graham was A? Beyond the fact that it didn't make any sense, he was just too *nice*. This morning, she'd picked him up at his room, which was right down the hall from Noel's, and Graham and his roommate, Carson, were playing video games, laughing. Then, Graham said a polite thank-you to the chambermaid who was coming to clean their room. Psychopath stalkers didn't get along with their roommates and thank the staff, did they?

Tori finally managed to get the ball through the clown's mouth. As her friends whooped, Aria shoved Graham toward her. "Uh, nice one, Tori!" he said a little stiffly.

Tori looked over, sized Graham up, and smiled. "Hey, Graham." Then she looked at her putter. "But you're lying. I suck."

"You're better than I am," Graham offered bashfully.

Tori smiled, then walked to the next hole. Graham spun back to Aria, looking dejected. "See? I'm hopeless!"

"What are you talking about?" Aria said. "You're doing great!" She picked up her putter, which she'd leaned against the windmill. "Let's follow them. Maybe they'll ask us to play with them."

"Isn't it going to look really obvious?" Graham whispered. "We didn't even play this hole!"

"Who cares?" Aria ran her fingertips along the tip of the clown structure as they walked. "It's not like anyone is taking this seriously, anyway." She eyed Tori as she plunked down her ball at the tee and swung her club. "Now you have to figure out what she's interested in. Then pretend you're interested in it, too."

She gave him another nudge, and Graham stepped toward Tori again. He waited until she finished her swing—which, as usual, didn't go anywhere near the hole—and then cleared his throat. "Do you, um, like Renaissance Fairs?"

Aria winced and considered aborting the operation. She didn't want Graham to impose *his* interests on *her*. But Tori brightened. "I've only been to one, but it was pretty cool. Why?"

Graham smiled. "I noticed your ankle bracelet and thought you might have bought it at this Renaissance festival outside Philly. There's a guy there who makes his own silver jewelry. I worked in the booth next to his one summer."

Tori stepped over the little divider that separated the putting green from the deck and walked closer to Graham. "What do *you* do at the festival?"

"I do a bunch of things, but at that particular job I helped this old guy build lutes."

"What's a lute?"

"They're small acoustic guitars, only they sound different," Graham explained. "I brought one on board, actually. I'm going to play a Death Cab for Cutie song on it for the talent show."

Tori raised an eyebrow. "*Really?*"

Graham started to reply, but suddenly Tori's phone rang. She glanced at it and rolled her eyes. "It's my mom," she said, lifting it to her ear. "She's called me, like, *every day* since we left."

Tori walked toward the waterfall at Hole 12. Graham looked confused. "*Now* what do I do?"

"Nothing." Aria guided him back toward the clubhouse. "Now you have something to talk about the *next* time you see each other. And your next task is to ask her out on a date."

A nervous smile slowly spread across Graham's face. "Okay." He cuffed Aria's arm. "What would I have done without you?"

"Just be sure to invite me to the wedding." Aria slugged Graham's shoulder in a friendly way. Then, Aria's phone buzzed in her pocket. Still smiling, she pulled it out and looked at the screen. *Two new picture messages.*

Her fingers started to tingle, and she looked up, feeling like someone was watching. A shadow slipped behind the windmill. The door to the clubhouse banged loudly. Something moved behind a trellis. But when Aria stared harder, she didn't notice anything amiss.

She pressed READ. The first picture loaded on the screen. The Cliff Resort's famous roof deck was in sharp focus, five heads easily visible over the top. The picture was blurry, but Aria could make out her outstretched hands. Tabitha, in her yellow dress, stood next to her, about to topple over.

When Aria hit the right arrow, the next photo appeared. This shot had been taken a split second later, capturing the moment Aria had pushed Tabitha off. Her

142

body hung in midair. Aria remained on the roof deck, her hands on her hips. She looked like a cold-blooded killer.

"Aria?" Graham stood behind her. "Is everything okay?"

Aria jumped and hid the screen with her hand. "Uh, everything's fine," she lied.

She stabbed at the keypad to delete both the photos, but for some reason, they wouldn't disappear. Every time she clicked into her photo gallery again, there they were, front and center. Her heart thudded. Just having them on her phone made her feel like there was a bull's-eye on her head. She *had* to get them off.

Her phone beeped again. *One new message*, a new alert said. Aria pressed READ.

What if a little "birdie" showed these to Graham—and the police? I can—and I will. —A

143

16
Across the Great Divide

That afternoon, Emily and Jordan waited at the top of the cliff in the rain forest. A thick layer of trees waved beneath them, frogs croaked from a hidden hollow, and a zip line swayed in the breeze. Emily watched as two kids in front of her grabbed the tandem zip line's handles and pushed off. They soared through the air, whooping and laughing, and landed safely on the other side of the ravine. It didn't look like a laughing matter to Emily, though. More like a death trap.

She edged closer to Jordan, who was fidgeting excitedly. "Are you sure we should do this?"

Jordan's brow furrowed. "You're not going to chicken out on me now, are you? I've wanted to do this for years."

"What if the lines break?" Emily looked nervously at the chasm below. The instructor had said it was at least a forty-foot drop.

"The lines are superstrong." Jordan inspected Emily carefully. "You're really scared, aren't you?"

Emily swallowed hard. "I had this friend who was sort of crazy. She took me to this gulch earlier this year, and we had a fight, and for a moment I was sure she was going to push me over the edge." She shut her eyes and thought about that horrible night with Kelsey Pierce.

Jordan's eyes widened. "Whoa."

"I was fine, of course," Emily said quickly. "My friend was fine, too. It just shook me up, that's all." She didn't even want to get into how Mona Vanderwaal had fallen off the very same cliff the year before. Although she'd filled Jordan in on the basics about Ali and A, she hadn't gotten into too many of the details. And she certainly hadn't told her about New A.

"Look, I promise *I* won't push you off anything," Jordan said. "And how about this? If your line breaks, I'll dive into the abyss after you. If we both die, at least we'll get to explore the afterlife together."

"Okay," Emily whispered. She fumbled for Jordan's hand. Jordan looked nervously back and forth, then laced her fingers in hers. Though they'd kissed in private plenty of times since their boat tour yesterday, they hadn't been public about anything yet. Emily was hesitant to ask why. Maybe it was too fast. Or maybe Jordan was worried about what her new Ulster classmates would say about her having a girlfriend, which is how Emily had come to think of her.

Jordan was totally perfect. Last night, after their secret boat cruise, they'd opened up about everything, covering topics Emily hadn't dared to explore with anyone before. Jordan revealed that she'd had a few lackluster boyfriends, and then she'd fallen for a toxic girl

145

named Mackenzie. When Emily pushed for details, Jordan couldn't go on. "It was just too painful," she admitted. "You're actually the first person I've ever talked to about her. You officially know more about me than anyone else."

Another boy went on the zip line, letting out a keening wail as he drifted across the gully. Suddenly, Emily and Jordan were next in line. "You girls ready?" the instructor asked.

Emily's feet felt buried in the mud, but Jordan dragged her forward. "Yep." She grabbed Emily's hand and squeezed it hard. "I'll hold on to you the whole time. I promise."

Emily shakily let the instructor harness her up. She could barely hold the zip line handles, her palms were sweating so badly. The instructor counted down, then yelled, "Go!" and Jordan jumped off. Emily had no choice but to go with her.

She felt her body being pulled downward toward the gully and screamed. But then, suddenly, she realized she wasn't falling—she was floating. The harness held, and the mechanism speedily pulled her across the ravine. The wind whipped through her hair. Below her, she could see the forest floor, carpeted with tons of brilliantly hued flowers. Beside her, Jordan was laughing her head off. Emily shot her a euphoric grin.

In seconds, they were on the other side, breathless. Emily's whole body trembled as the instructor removed her harness and helped her take off her helmet. Then she turned to Jordan. Her lips felt wobbly as she smiled. "Can we do it again?"

"Of course," Jordan said. "I *knew* you'd love it."

They rode the line across the ravine three more times. When they boarded the Jeep that would take them back to the boat, Emily checked her phone. Aria had texted, asking if Emily could meet her and Spencer in the common room. Emily didn't ask why, but she assumed it was to rehearse their hula routine.

"I wish you could participate in the talent show," Emily sighed, resting her head on Jordan's shoulder. "Hanna dropped out, so we need one more." She hadn't told her friends about Jordan yet, but maybe she should. Would they really care that Jordan was a stowaway? Even Jordan herself didn't seem too worried about it.

"I wish I could, too," Jordan sighed. "But you know I can't. I'll watch from the audience, okay? And if you win, you'd better give me a ride on your Vespa."

"*When* I win," Emily corrected her.

At the boat, Jordan slipped past the guard in a group of kids so she wouldn't have to show ID. They parted at the elevators, Jordan saying she was going to lie down in the room while Emily went to meet Aria. Then Jordan leaned in for a kiss. When they pulled away, Emily pushed a lock of hair behind Jordan's ear. "I thought you were uncomfortable about us being affectionate in public," she said.

Jordan shrugged. "This is new to me. But with you, I don't have anything to hide."

She kissed Emily once more, then disappeared into the elevator car. Emily glided toward the common room, humming the salsa song she'd heard on the radio on the ride back to the ship. As she passed a long bank of mirrors

147

in the hallway, she laughed. Her lips were swollen and full, her skin pink from too much sun. She couldn't remember the last time she'd looked so *happy*.

She rounded the corner for the common room and scanned the couches. Neither Spencer nor Aria were there yet. She settled down on one of the couches, staring at the satellite feed of CNN on the TV that was mounted to the wall. PREPPY THIEF STILL AT LARGE read a banner across the bottom.

A reporter appeared. "We've been following the story all morning about how an eighteen-year-old New York girl known as the Preppy Thief escaped from her holding cell in Philadelphia three days ago."

There was a video of a bunch of lawyers walking into a courthouse. "Notorious for stealing private planes, expensive boats, motorcycles, and cars for extravagant joyrides, Katherine DeLong was being held until her trial was set to begin later this week," a voiceover said. "But early Sunday morning, security guards found her missing. Authorities suspect she is trying to flee the country. She's very dangerous, and if anyone has information about her whereabouts ... "

A mug shot of the Preppy Thief popped on the screen. Emily squinted at it, then did a double-take. Was that ... *Jordan*?

"Emily?"

Emily looked up. Spencer and Aria stood behind her, the grass skirts they had made a few days ago in their hands. They looked from the television to Emily's stricken face, confused.

"I ... " Emily trailed off, not knowing what to say.

148

Her gaze returned to the TV. Now the news showed a video of Jordan walking out of a courthouse in an orange jumpsuit. Next flashed a photo of Jordan in a tennis dress and shoes, a familiar silk headband in her hair. Another video appeared of Jordan in court. A lawyer whispered in her ear. There were shiny handcuffs on her wrists and shackles on her ankles.

It felt like the ceiling was crumbling in. Anger boiled inside of Emily, sudden and fierce. With shaking hands, she grabbed her phone and composed a text to Jordan. *I know who you are, you liar*, she wrote. *I don't want to ever see you again. Get out of my room now.* As she hit SEND, she let out a sob.

"Emily?" Aria looked concerned. "What's going on?"

"Do you know that girl?" Spencer asked, pointing at the TV.

Emily's mouth felt like it was filled with peanut butter. "That's my new ... she's ... I *know* her."

"Oh my God," Aria whispered. "Is this girl the new friend you met? Is she on the boat?"

Emily nodded weakly, afraid to give away any more.

Beep.

Her eyes filling with tears, she looked down at her phone, bracing herself for what Jordan might say. But when she pulled up the screen, it said *One new text message from Anonymous.*

There was a hot flash through her chest. She looked around. The common room overflowed with kids—they were on the couches, sitting at the tables, playing pinball on the *Simpsons*-themed machine in the corner. She thought she saw a flash of blond hair disappear around

149

the corner. Emily stood up halfway and peered into the hall, but the figure had vanished.

She looked down at the message.

Cute! Maybe you and Miss Preppy Thief can room together in jail! —A

17
Friendship Has Its Ups and Downs

"*California Gurls, duh duh duh DUH duh duh!*" Naomi and Hanna sang as they walked down the cobblestoned streets of Old San Juan later that night. They were on their way to a club Naomi had been invited to that afternoon and had decided to fit in a quick rehearsal for their talent show routine on the way. Passersby kept giving them strange looks.

"Hey, we should see if we can find blue and purple wigs," Naomi suggested, sidestepping a sewer grate in her high heels. "Maybe there's a costume store at the last stop. Or maybe we can borrow a wig from someone in Cirque du Soleil." She snickered.

"Wouldn't it be funny if we found a guy to play Snoop Dog?" Hanna suggested, thinking about the video.

"Oh my God, that would be *classic*," Naomi squealed. Then she sighed. "Damn. The guy I was into would've made a perfect Snoop—he's such a pothead. But now that he's with Spencer, it's like he wants nothing to do with me."

"We'll find someone else," Hanna said quickly as they passed a closed-up boutique with bikini-clad mannequins in the window. She wasn't about to mess with a Naomi-Spencer love triangle, especially if Naomi was A. Which was something she *still* wasn't quite sure of.

Naomi breezily pushed a lock of hair behind her ear. "Or maybe I'll find a way to get him back."

Before Hanna could ask what *that* meant, they'd turned the corner and arrived at the club. Pounding bass and raucous laughter filled the air. A line of well-dressed people stood outside the unmarked double doors. When Hanna and Naomi waved their VIP invites, the bouncer lifted the velvet rope to let them in.

"Thanks!" Naomi trilled, as though she'd known the guy for years. Hanna trailed behind her, feeling the envious stares of everyone in the line. She glanced at her and Naomi's reflections in the long bank of mirrors that lined the hallway. They'd planned their outfits together, both wearing jewel-toned dresses, high, strappy heels, and coordinated jewelry. They'd sat side-by-side to do their makeup, gossiping about people on the boat as they applied foundation and swept on mascara.

The tunnel opened into a large, square, dark room with a long, stainless-steel bar at one end and a bunch of banquettes at the back. A DJ spun records in the corner, and a huge dance floor took up the rest of the space. Bodies writhed on all sides of them, each guy more gorgeous than the last. The room smelled like booze, cigarettes, and the gardenia blooms that adorned every table. As the salsa beat rocked in Hanna's ears, she unconsciously began to swing her hips.

152

Hanna touched Naomi's shoulder. "This is great!" she yelled over the music.

"Right?" Naomi grinned, strutting up to the bar and batting her eyelashes at the bartender, who came over immediately.

Naomi ordered two neon-orange cocktails and handed one to Hanna. Hanna took a small sip—she didn't want to drink too much and let down her guard. People were dancing in every nook and cranny, including on top of the banquettes. There was a photographer wandering the perimeter with a huge digital camera around his neck, occasionally stopping and taking a shot of the dancers. After a moment, he stopped in front of them. "Can I take your photo?" he asked.

"That depends." Naomi placed her hands on her hips. "What's it for?"

"The Style section of the San Juan *Hola*."

Hanna exchanged an excited look with Naomi—she'd *always* wanted to be in a Style section. She set her drink on a nearby table and wrapped her arm around Naomi's shoulders. The photographer snapped and snapped. First Hanna gave him a sultry model gaze, then threw back her head. But she knew not to get *too* carried away—the experience with creepy Patrick was still fresh in her mind.

"Gorgeous," the photographer said when he was through. Then he glanced at the crowd behind them. "I think you have some fans."

It was true. Tons of guys on the dance floor were now giving them the eye, including a dark-haired college-age kid in an oversized T-shirt and baggy jeans. When he met their gaze, he raised his drink at them from across the room and crooked his finger, beckoning them over. Hanna and Naomi nudged each other and snickered.

"He's cute, but he knows it," Hanna yelled in Naomi's ear.

"Definitely. Come on, let's dance," Naomi said, grabbing Hanna's hand and pulling her onto the dance floor. The song was something Latin and fast, and they started wriggling to the music, making sexy poses for the *Hola* photographer every time he did a lap. Then, as the DJ transitioned into a new song, Naomi tapped Hanna's arm. "Who do you think is the hottest guy in this place?"

Hanna slowed her dancing and surveyed the options. "It's a toss-up between the Enrique Iglesias look-alike and James Bond in the corner."

Naomi squinted at James Bond, who was wearing a slim-cut suit, expensive-looking shiny shoes, and Ray-Bans. "Hanna!" she shrieked. "He's, like, forty years old!"

"He is *not*!" Hanna said, studying the guy's toned physique and thick brows. "He just looks older because he's sophisticated."

"He's definitely only a six or a seven," Naomi decided, sipping her cocktail. "Now *that* guy is a ten." She used her straw to point to a blond guy by the bar. He looked like he belonged on the cover of a surfing magazine.

"Are you kidding?" Hanna wrinkled her nose. "He's an eight at best."

"What about him?" Naomi glanced at a guy sitting at a nearby table. He had a shaved head and sexy cheekbones.

"Five," Hanna decreed loudly, feeling more and more confident. "I hate shaved heads."

154

"And him?" A guy with lobsterlike sunburn on his nose and arms.

"Ick! One!" Hanna cried.

They made it into a game, going around the room, tapping guys and assigning them numbers like deranged fairy godmothers. "Six!" they called to a slightly overweight guy who had thick, lustrous hair. "Nine!" they called to an Abercrombie-model look-alike who was dancing shirtless. "Seven!" "Four!" "Eight and a half!" At first, the guys at the club didn't quite understand what the girls were doing, but they caught on pretty quickly. Those deemed eights and above looked pleased. A guy who'd gotten only a six narrowed his eyes and mouthed something that looked like *Bitch.*

Someone caught Hanna's arm as she was racing past the DJ booth. "What would you rate me?"

She stopped short and looked at him. His hair was greasy, his nostrils weirdly oversized, and he was wearing a T-shirt that had the Chanel logo plastered across the front. He reminded Hanna of the guy who worked at the Motorola kiosk in the mall.

She turned to Naomi, who'd paused, too. "Ali had a phrase for this, you know," she screamed into her ear.

"What was that?" Naomi asked.

"*Not it!*"

Hanna turned and fled. Naomi burst out laughing and raced behind her. Breathless from laughing, they spilled out onto the patio, which was much cooler and quieter. Naomi wiped her eyes. "I don't think I've ever laughed that hard in my life."

"Did you see the look on that greasy guy's face when I

155

said, 'Not it'?" Hanna squealed. "I thought he was going to kill us!"

Naomi collapsed into a chair. "Did you play that game a lot when Ali was around?"

Hanna swallowed a giggle and shook her head. "Not like that."

"She didn't have that game when I was friends with her," Naomi said. Then an uncomfortable look flashed across her face. "But I guess that was because it wasn't the same Ali."

Hanna's spirits dimmed a little. "Yeah," she said, then reached for her drink, not knowing what to say next.

Naomi spun the bracelet around her wrist. "I feel terrible about what happened with you guys and Ali in the Poconos. It was all so unbelievable."

"Thanks," Hanna mumbled. Then she looked up, realizing something. "Were you surprised when you found out that there were two of them? And that the girl *you* were friends with was a murderer?"

Naomi picked at her nails. "Well, kind of, but . . ."

"But what?"

Naomi stared at the lanterns hanging from the rafters. "The whole thing is just sad, you know? I feel like such a jerk for saying this, but sometimes I still miss her."

"You're not a jerk," Hanna said quietly. It hadn't occurred to her before that Naomi had lost Ali as well. Not *their* Ali, of course, but an Ali all the same.

"You know what?" Naomi peered at her. "You're really easy to talk to. I'm surprised."

"I'm surprised about you, too," Hanna said tentatively.

156

The statement was way more loaded than Naomi might ever know.

"I've told you stuff I haven't told a lot of people," Naomi said, leaning against the railing.

"Oh? Like what?"

"Like the bingeing, for one," Naomi admitted. The light caught her gold earrings, making them glitter. "And the stuff just now, about Ali."

"You mentioned something about a favorite cousin, too," Hanna said, her heart hammering. "A girl who got in a car accident?"

Naomi pressed her lips together. "Yeah. Madison. I *never* talk about her."

"So ... did she die in the accident?" Hanna held her breath.

Naomi shook her head. "No. But she was messed up pretty bad—a lot of broken bones, and she was in a coma for a few days. She had to learn how to walk again. It was hard on all of us." Her voice broke.

Hanna let out a huge mental sigh—Madison *wasn't dead*. But hearing what *had* happened hit her unexpectedly hard, bringing tears to her eyes. Now she had a new image in her mind, one of Madison hanging on to one of those physical-therapy walker things, struggling to take a step.

Naomi set her empty cocktail glass on the table, sniffing once more. "In a weird way, though, that crash was the best thing for my cousin. It got her straight. She was a major alcoholic before that—drinking instead of going to class, drinking as soon as she woke up in the morning, drinking and getting behind the wheel and nearly killing

157

herself. I mean, yeah, it sucked that she totaled the car and had to go through so much pain, but she hasn't had a drink since. She seems much happier now."

"That's . . . good," Hanna said, trying to keep her voice steady.

"Yeah." Naomi raised her eyes to Hanna and smiled so sincerely it melted Hanna's heart. "It is."

They sat in silence for a moment, listening to the pounding bass inside the club. All of a sudden, Hanna wanted to reach across and give Naomi a big hug. Everything she'd worried about, everything she'd feared, suddenly went up in smoke. Their suspicions about Naomi were unfounded. Naomi wasn't pissed Madison had gotten in a car accident—she was relieved because it had turned her life around. Whoever A was, it was someone who'd found out about Madison another way.

It was amazingly freeing. Now she could be friends with Naomi without worrying. She could trust everything Naomi said to be the truth.

Hanna stood up and offered Naomi her hand. "Are you ready to go back in and *Not it* some more?"

Naomi looked up at her and grinned. "Definitely."

They strutted back into the club like they owned the place. They'd been wrong about A before, Hanna thought as she squeezed Naomi's hand. They were wrong again this time, too. A probably *wanted* her to suspect Naomi— and, in turn, lose a potential friend. Hanna wasn't going to let that happen, though. Not this time.

"*Shhh!*" Naomi scolded as they bumped clumsily down the hallway of the ship toward their room. It was a few

158

hours later, and they'd gotten back onboard just before curfew, acting sober enough for a few minutes to fool the guards. "You almost took out that fire extinguisher!"

"It was in my way," Hanna declared petulantly, then burst into giggles.

She hung on to Naomi's back as Naomi inserted the key card into their door. The door opened, and the two girls tumbled inside. Hanna grabbed the door to the bathroom for balance. "It smells so good in here!" she cried, inhaling the fresh scents of baby powder and Kate Spade Twirl perfume.

"Mind if I take the bathroom first?" Naomi asked, her hand on the doorknob.

"Go for it," Hanna said, flopping down on the bed.

Naomi shut the door, and water started to run. Hanna rubbed her feet on the soft, silky sheets, feeling satisfyingly exhausted.

Ping.

She opened her eyes. Her phone, which was sitting on the nightstand, wasn't blinking. Her gaze fell on the open laptop on Naomi's bed. A message in the corner of the screen said *New e-mail from Madison Strickland.*

She looked away. Who cared if Naomi had received an e-mail from Madison? Cousins contacted one another all the time.

But one little peek wouldn't hurt, would it?

Hanna cocked her ear toward the bathroom. The shower was still running. Slowly, she eased her legs off the bed and tiptoed over to the laptop. The bedsprings squeaked as she sat on Naomi's mattress. On the right-hand side of the desktop were two folders labeled *School*

Papers and *Princeton Application*. Hanna scanned them, then exited. Next she waved the mouse over a Gmail icon. Taking a deep breath, she double-clicked on it. The program opened and launched right into her inbox. The new e-mail from Madison appeared. It was part of a thread titled *That night*. Hanna drew in a breath. The first e-mail in the thread was from early July of last summer.

Hanna scrolled back to the beginning of the conversation, dated July 1. *Are you still trying to figure out the name of the driver?* Naomi had written to her cousin. *Yes,* Madison wrote back that same day. *I think I'm getting close.* And then, on July 3, Madison wrote another e-mail: *We need to talk in person. I think I know who did this to me.* Naomi replied on July 5: *They're going down. I'll make sure they get what they deserve.* There was a long stretch of no replies, but today, Madison had written: *I'm so proud of you for doing this for me.*

Hanna signed out of Naomi's e-mail and looked up, catching sight of her all-too-sober expression in the mirror over the bureau. *They.* Madison must have not only figured out that Hanna was the driver but also that Aria, Spencer, and Emily had helped her escape. If she'd shared this with Naomi in early July, Naomi would have had ample time to stalk all of the girls and dig up their secrets. And *I'm so proud of you for doing this for me*? What did Madison mean by *that*?

Her heart pounded in her chest. She had been wrong. Again. Naomi *was* A. This proved it.

"What are you doing?"

Naomi stood in the bathroom doorway in a bathrobe. Hanna stepped away from Naomi's bed. "H-hey!"

160

"Hey," Naomi said slowly. Her gaze flicked from Hanna to the laptop, then back to Hanna again. "Everything okay?"

"Uh, I was just looking for my sleep mask," Hanna said, fumbling on Naomi's bed, then on the floor. She was sure Naomi could hear her pounding heart all the way across the room.

Naomi walked to the bed and sat down. She gave Hanna a long look but didn't say anything. For a moment, her face was illuminated by the moonlight, and when she smiled, her teeth looked long and garish, almost wolflike. "The bathroom's yours if you want it," she said finally.

"I'm cool," Hanna said. "I'm just going to go to bed." If only she could text Mike and beg to stay with him another night. But then Naomi would be on to her for sure.

"Okay, then." Naomi shifted her laptop to the floor and pulled the covers over her. "Nighty-night, bestie!"

"Night," Hanna croaked, huddling under the duvet and knowing she wouldn't sleep a wink.

18
Too Hot to Handle

Saturday morning, Spencer rushed into the empty arcade where her friends were waiting. Emily paced nervously past the unoccupied video consoles for *Modern Warfare* and *Dance Dance Revolution*. Aria tapped her nails on top of a change machine. Hanna picked at a loose thread on her jean shorts, the lights from a pinball machine flashing across her face. Her hair was matted, and there were dark circles under her eyes. She'd texted them that morning saying she needed to talk, pronto.

"I don't have much time," Spencer said, checking her watch. She was due to meet Reefer in the sauna at 10—and it was 9:45.

"I found something last night." Hanna's voice was high and tweaky, like she'd drunk too many cups of coffee. "I looked on Naomi's e-mail, just like you told me to do. There was an e-mail thread with Madison Strickland about the accident. I'm pretty sure they know it was us."

"Wait." Aria looked startled. "So Madison is *alive*?"

"Naomi said she was alive, but badly injured," Hanna said. "The thing is, Naomi also said that she was, in a weird way, *happy* that Madison had gotten in the accident. There's no way *that's* true—not with what these e-mails said."

Spencer shut her eyes and let out a breath. Once again, that *crack* of bone resounded through her mind. *She* had done that. She could empathize with Aria now for how she felt about Tabitha—it seemed different, somehow, when you were the one who'd pushed or dropped someone. "Did the e-mails name us specifically?"

"Not specifically, but one said *They're going down. They.* Naomi must know we were all involved. She wrote the e-mail on July 5, too—before we gave that money back to Gayle, before the Spencer-and-Kelsey thing happened, before everything last summer. And then there was a new e-mail from Madison that said *I'm so proud of you for doing this for me.*"

Emily ran her hand across her forehead. "Okay, so now we think Naomi *is* A. Or one of the As."

"It looks like it." Hanna looked pained just saying the words. "It seemed like she didn't know a thing, but I guess she's just a really, really good actress."

"If Naomi is A—or even working with another A— then Naomi knows everything." Aria pulled out her phone and showed it to the girls. "Look what A sent *me.*"

Everyone studied the blurry image of the face of The Cliffs resort that had popped up on the screen. At the top of the frame were five girls on the roof deck. A blond girl stood precariously near the edge; a brunette of Aria's

163

height and build had her arms outstretched, ready to push. If you knew what you were looking for, it sealed their life-in-prison sentence.

"You need to erase that!" Spencer grabbed Aria's phone and hit various buttons.

"Go ahead and try." Aria crossed her arms over her chest. "There's something wrong with my software—I can't delete *anything*. If anyone sees it—Graham, the teachers on this trip, the cops—we're done."

Hanna's head whipped up. "You're still speaking to Graham?"

Aria squeezed her eyes shut. "He's not A, okay?"

"But what if Naomi tells him what we did?" Spencer whispered. "She could have been the one who sent you those photos, Aria—whoever she's working with could have taken them and shared them with her. What if she mentions the picture on your phone, and what if he, like, goes crazy with revenge and hurts you?"

Aria flicked the coin return slot on the change machine. "He really doesn't seem like that kind of person."

Then Hanna swallowed. "What are we going to do about Naomi, guys?"

"*And* whoever this second A might be?" Aria added.

"One A at a time." Spencer leaned against a *Gran Turismo* driving console. "Is there a way to prove Naomi is definitely A?"

Hanna tapped her lips. "Spence, you said you saw someone running the other direction the night Gayle was murdered. Do you think it could have been a girl?"

"I guess," Spencer answered uncertainly. "But I didn't see her face." Spencer looked at Hanna. "Can you go

164

through Naomi's computer again? There could be something on there that links her to Gayle's murder. You should see if she has the photos she sent to Aria on her computer, too—that would prove she's A. If you find them, erase them. Otherwise she might send them to the cops."

Hanna cracked her jaw. "But she caught me looking at her laptop. I don't want to go back to my room ever again!"

"Sneak in when she's not there," Aria suggested.

"What if she *already* sent those photos to the cops?" Hanna said. "Even if we do find something about Gayle, they'll think we planted it there just to destroy her credibility."

"I doubt Naomi did," Aria said. "Why else would she still be threatening us? Why else haven't the cops knocked on our doors to arrest us?"

Everyone stared at one another, not having an answer. Hanna's hands shook. Emily wound the same piece of hair around and around her finger.

"Whatcha talking about, girls?" a voice boomed behind them, and everyone jumped and turned. Jeremy stood in the doorway, his eyes concealed behind his star-shaped glasses. Spencer shivered. How long had he been standing there?

Aria flinched. "Uh, nothing," she said, shoving her phone back in her pocket.

Everyone ducked their heads and marched toward the exit, the meeting over. Jeremy watched them, a strange smile on his face. When Spencer passed, he pushed something into her hand. "You forgot this from the restaurant last night. I grabbed it for you before I left."

She stared at the object in her palm. It was the Polaroid the waitress at the restaurant in Puerto Rico had taken when they were being serenaded. There was a sour feeling in her stomach; she hadn't remembered Jeremy being there.

"You two make such a cute couple," Jeremy trilled. "It's so nice to see young love bloom."

But as he shoved his glasses up his nose and did a military-style turn, Spencer's body filled with dread. *Reefer.* She had to break it off with him—now.

There was no way she was stealing A's guy.

Five minutes later, she stood just outside the sauna. The door was made of cracked wood slats that had darkened from moisture and time. Dry heat seeped from its pores, and the sharp scent of cedar hung heavily in the air. The smell would forever remind her of her Grandpa Hastings, who had loved saunas so much he built one in his house in Florida. She'd caught him lounging in there naked once and had never set foot in that wing of the house again.

Taking a deep breath, she adjusted the straps on her bikini and pushed the creaky door open. It was so hot inside that she immediately began to sweat. The only light in the room was from the glowing coals in the corner. She could just make out someone sitting on the bottom step. His dreadlocks hung limply on his shoulders, and he had a towel wrapped around his waist.

Her stomach flipped. This was going to be so, so difficult.

"Fancy meeting you here," he said flirtatiously, standing up.

"Reefer, I—" Spencer started, but Reefer slid his hands down her back and his lips touched her neck. Spencer shut her eyes and groaned. He smelled so *good*, like lemon and salt.

"Reefer, *wait*." Spencer pulled away from him and caught her breath.

"What is it?" Reefer asked, panting. "Is it too hot in here? Want to cool off in the pool?"

Spencer swallowed hard. "I do, but ... Reefer, I don't think I can do this anymore."

Reefer stared at her. The only sound was the small creaks of the sauna's wooden beams settling. "Why?" he asked, his voice cracking.

Spencer wiped a bead of sweat from her eyes. "It's Naomi," she said.

"What about her?"

She sat down on the bench and stared into the darkness. If only she could tell him the truth. *This is a girl who already wants to kill me*, she wished she could say. *She's killed before. I have no idea what she's capable of. And we're in the middle of the ocean, with nowhere to hide, with no police ...*

But she couldn't say any of that. Instead, she cleared her throat. "She really likes you."

"But I don't like *her*." Reefer sounded puzzled.

Spencer picked at a scab on her knee, then looked up, realizing something. "You said you met Naomi at a Princeton party. When was that?"

"Months ago. Way before I met you."

"Was she visiting any other times?"

Reefer thought for a moment. "Yeah. That same

167

weekend you were in Princeton for the Eating Club thing. But it was just in passing—nothing happened between us."

Spencer blinked. "Naomi was there *that* weekend?"

"Yeah. Why?"

Her heart thudded. "Was she at the party where . . . the brownie incident happened?" She closed her eyes and thought about all the kids stuffed into that off-campus house. She hadn't seen Naomi there, but she'd been high, and her attention had been on Harper and the other Ivy girls.

"No, a different one," Reefer furrowed his brows. "Why does it matter?"

"No reason," Spencer said faintly. Her head was spinning. If Naomi had been at Princeton the same weekend she went to the Ivy Pot Luck, she could have been the one who laced Spencer's pot brownies with LSD. Hadn't Spencer heard a freaky giggle when she'd stepped outside the Ivy house? Hadn't she thought she'd seen a shock of blond hair just like Naomi's slip into the woods?

And was it possible that Hanna's accident had started all this? Spencer had begged Hanna to come clean. After Jamaica, they didn't need another secret on their hands. Hanna had shaken her head. "I can't do that to my dad's campaign," Hanna said a few days later. She and Spencer had been sitting at Wordsmith's, a bookstore near Rosewood Day.

"But it wasn't even your fault," Spencer said, jiggling her foot. "That other car swerved at you from out of nowhere, and then just disappeared."

"I *think* that's what happened." Hanna shut her eyes,

as if trying to replay the scene on the back of her eyelids. "But now I'm not sure. Maybe I *was* in the wrong lane. The rain was so heavy, and the road is so twisty, and . . ."

She trailed off, putting her head in her hands. For a while, the only sound in the store was the classical music that played over the speakers. Spencer had looked at her cell phone; she'd received a text from Phineas, a friend she'd made at the University of Pennsylvania summer program she'd enrolled in, asking her if she wanted to go to a party that night. She was about to text him back when she looked over and saw someone standing stock-still in one of the aisles, head cocked. The person slipped out of sight before Spencer could see who it was, but it looked like she had the same color blond hair as Naomi's.

Now Spencer peered cautiously at Reefer. "I just don't want anyone mad at me right now."

Reefer lifted his palms. "Would it help if I told her to back off?"

"Don't do that!" Spencer said quickly. "I-I just don't think we should start anything until we get off the ship."

Reefer looked crushed. "You really think that's best?"

"I do."

They stepped away from each other. Reefer turned his back and adjusted the towel around his waist, and Spencer made the mistake of looking at his dewy skin and taut lats. Her stomach swooped. As though pulled by an invisible string, she fell into him again. He pressed her against the wooden wall and kissed her hard.

"I knew you couldn't resist me," Reefer joked.

Spencer laughed sheepishly. "Okay, so maybe we make out in private until we get off the boat."

"If it means making out with you, I'm in." Then he opened the door. "Let's go to the pool. My skin feels like it's boiling off."

Spencer nodded reluctantly. "But if we see Naomi, we have to leave."

"Deal."

They padded down the tiled hall toward the pool area. A bunch of kids were having chicken fights in the shallow end, and girls were tanning on lounge chairs near the bar. There was a squeak under Spencer's feet, and it wasn't until she was already in the air that she realized she'd slipped. She fell hard on the tiles, banging her elbow. White-hot pain shot through her ankle.

"Ow!" she shrieked, curling into a ball.

Reefer dropped to his knees. "Are you okay?"

"I don't know." Spencer touched her foot. It was already swelling up.

"What did you slip on, anyway?" Reefer asked.

"I don't know." Spencer looked around for something that had blocked her path, but the corridor was empty. Then the familiar scent of baby oil filled her nostrils. There was a slick puddle a few inches away from where she'd landed. Spencer had taken this route on her way to the sauna, though. The baby oil hadn't been there a few minutes ago—she was sure of it.

A cold feeling swept over her bones. All at once, a high-pitched giggle swirled down the corridor. As Reefer helped Spencer stand, her phone chimed. She clumsily removed it from her beach bag and read the new text.

Careful, careful! I might just slip, too—and tell. —A

170

19
Dead Man's Float

"Aria?" Noel called from outside a small striped changing tent near the pool deck. "Are you coming?"

"I don't know," Aria said, staring down at her body in the purple string bikini Hanna had insisted she buy for the trip. She'd been so busy with the scavenger hunt that she hadn't worn it yet, but now she felt self-conscious. It was skimpier than any suit she'd ever worn, the legs cut high, the top cut low.

"How can I teach you how to swim if you don't come out of the dressing room?" Noel pointed out.

It was Saturday afternoon, and Aria and Noel had just finished their lunch shift at the café and finally had some time to spend together. When Noel suggested teaching Aria how to swim properly, Aria thought he was kidding. "I'm the best teacher ever, I promise," he'd insisted.

She emerged from the tent. The air had turned chilly in the last hour, and the pool area had cleared out. Steam rose from the hot tub. Floating lounge chairs, kickboards, and fun noodles were stacked in plastic bins on the deck.

There was something eerie about the emptiness, though—the starfish, dolphin, and octopus decorations on the railings looked angry instead of friendly.

She lowered the towel and dropped it on one of the chaises. Noel, who was dressed in flowered trunks, sucked in a breath. "Whoa."

"Oh, stop," Aria said, smiling to herself. She walked to the steps and started into the pool. The water lapped around her toes, then her calves, then her midsection. She ducked her head under and came up sputtering. "*Cold!*"

"You'll get used to it." Noel floated up to her. "Come here," he whispered, grabbing her around the waist and holding her close.

Aria wrapped her legs around him, feeling weightless and free. They kissed for a long time, the chlorine-filled water brushing against their bodies. In the bowels of the ship, the New Age Cirque du Soleil music started to play.

"Let's see your swim technique," Noel said when they broke apart.

"Don't say I didn't warn you." Aria waded into the deeper end until her feet no longer touched the bottom. Then her legs flailed wildly. Her arms slashed this way and that. After a while, she settled into a swim stroke that Mike called the Aria Paddle.

When she finally made it to the wall, she turned around. Noel looked horrified. "You really *didn't* ever take swim lessons as a kid."

Aria shook her head. "Mike did, but my parents never insisted on it. I always took sculpting. Or drama. Or hip-hop dance."

172

"We should probably teach you the basics," Noel said. "Do you know how to do the dead man's float?"

Aria winced at the name. "Uh, no."

Noel led her back to the shallow end. "This will help you in case you ever get stranded at sea."

Aria gave him a crazy look. "Thanks, but I don't plan on that happening."

"No one ever does." Noel put his hands on his hips. "Lie facedown in the water. I'll hold you up."

Aria did as she was told. She felt Noel's hands prop her up under her waist. "Stretch out your arms!" he said. "Now totally relax!" It was weird not to thrash around to stay afloat—she kept thinking she was going to sink. But after a moment, she went with it and opened her eyes underwater. The bottom of the pool had diamond-shaped tiles. She could just make out Noel's blurry feet.

She turned her head to breathe, then plunged under again. Her limbs felt heavy, but buoyant. It was Zen, like she really *was* dead.

Tabitha's body floating in the waves flashed in her mind. Then came a voice: *You did that. You're going to be punished*. Instantly, her focus shattered. She breathed in a mouthful of water and came up sputtering, staring at Noel as if he'd seen into her thoughts.

"What happened!" Noel cried, oblivious. "You were doing great!"

Aria wiped water out of her eyes. "I got scared," she muttered. It wasn't a lie.

Over the next hour, Aria learned how to tread water with the flutter and frog kicks. She struggled with sculling, but had a pretty decent first try at the elementary

173

backstroke. By the time the sun came out again and a few kids appeared on the pool deck, Aria felt exhausted but almost successful. She and Noel retreated to the hot tub and shared a pitcher of lemonade.

"You do make a pretty good teacher," she told Noel, kissing him on the cheek. "It's romantic, too. Both of us almost naked, you holding me up . . . "

"Want to make it a regular thing?" Noel sipped his drink. "If you knew how to swim, we could surf together. You'd love it. It's addictive."

"I don't think I should surf quite yet," Aria said, shutting her eyes and letting the hot tub jets massage her legs. "But sure. We can do more lessons."

"How about later? I could take a day off surfing."

Aria opened her eyes. There was such a tender look on Noel's face that she hated to let him down. "I can't," she said regretfully. "I have to meet Graham."

"Oh." Noel looked disappointed. "Okay."

"I'm sorry." Aria felt genuinely bad—Noel looked so upset. "We're just friends."

"I know, I know. He likes you, though. A dude can tell."

"No, he doesn't," Aria said quickly. "He's *this close* to making a date with Tori. They ran into each other at dinner last night, and she invited him to sit at her table, but we're not really counting *that* as a date because it wasn't planned."

Noel snickered. "You really like playing Cupid, don't you?"

"Definitely," Aria said. "It makes me feel good." She meant that in more ways than one.

Someone turned on a radio, and a Shakira song played. Caterers began to set out a buffet, and a few kids got in line. Noel lifted the locket that hung around Aria's neck. "I'm glad you're still wearing this."

"It's the nicest thing anyone has ever given me," Aria murmured.

Noel dropped the necklace back to her chest, and she stared at it again. There was something so familiar about it, something she couldn't place.

Something next to her towel caught her eye. Her cell phone screen had lit up. She climbed out of the hot tub and looked at the screen. *One new text.*

She turned her back so Noel couldn't see. After she read it through, she pressed DELETE and, luckily, the note vanished. But she wouldn't forget the message for a long time.

Clownfish are pretty,
Starfish are pale.
Will Aria's boyfriend
Visit her in jail?
—A

20
Resisting Is So Hard to Do

An hour later, Emily stood with Aria and Spencer in a secluded corner near the shuffleboard deck, grass skirts around their waists. She listened to the beginning bars of the Hawaiian hula sound they'd chosen for the talent show swell through the portable iPod speakers. After a moment, she counted off. "Five, six, seven, eight ... "

They all waved their hands gracefully and started wiggling their hips. About thirty seconds in, Aria stopped and stared at the others. "We're all making our hands go in different directions for that part," she said. "We all need to swish to the right first, *then* the left."

"I'm doing the best I can, considering the fact that my ankle is killing me." Spencer held up her left foot, which had an Ace bandage wrapped around it. She said she'd slipped in baby oil earlier.

"And we talked about adding that waddling-like-a-duck move," Aria said as she paused the song. "Does anyone remember exactly how to do it? Ali was definitely the best at it."

"I'm so *sick* of Ali," Emily mumbled angrily under her breath.

Spencer and Aria's heads snapped up. "What was that, Em?" Aria asked.

"Nothing," Emily said stiffly, smoothing down the grass skirt. One of the blades pierced her thigh, and she winced. "Does anyone else think these skirts suck?" she snapped.

Spencer leaned against the railing, looking worried. "Are you okay?"

Emily sighed. "I just don't feel in the mood to do this anymore. I mean, what's the point?" She shoved her flip-flops back on her feet, keeping her eyes averted from her friends. "We're being tortured by A. We're practically wanted by the police. Don't you think doing a talent show routine is a little ridiculous? How are we going to ride a Vespa in jail?"

"It's a nice diversion," Spencer said quietly.

"Did something happen, Em?" Aria pressed. "Something with A? Something with that girl you saw on TV yesterday? Is she really on the ship?"

Emily looked away, biting her lip. She regretted that her friends had been there to witness her CNN Preppy Thief meltdown. She didn't want to drag them into the scandal. "She got off the boat yesterday," she lied—although, for all she knew, it was true. There had been no trace of Jordan when Emily got back to her room the day before, and she hadn't heard from her since. "And let's never talk about it again, okay?"

There was a long, awkward pause. "Okay," Spencer said, concern in her voice.

"Good," Emily said perfunctorily. But when she shut her eyes, all she could think about was that news broadcast. *The Preppy Thief*. Jordan being led to jail in an orange jumpsuit.

Google had provided a hundred links with all the awful details. Jordan—or Katherine DeLong, or whatever her name was—didn't come from a poor family, as she'd told Emily, but a very wealthy one from outside New York City. There were pictures of her at society events in Manhattan and debutante parties in the Hamptons. She'd been stealing boats, cars, planes—basically, anything she could get her hands on—for two years now, jet-setting across the world to attempt bigger and more daring heists. She had finally been arrested and thrown in jail near Philly a few months earlier, when she was caught driving her father's law partner's Ferrari. Now the FBI was after her.

The articles described her as a "con woman," capable of convincing people of anything and everything just to get her way. Other reporters called her a "sociopath," a "girl Houdini," and "a miscreant with no respect for private property." Apparently, Jordan didn't steal the vehicles because she had any use for them—it was all for the thrill.

It was crushing. Emily had felt reborn with Jordan. For a few blissful hours, there had been something good in her world again. But how could she have fallen for another liar? Did Jordan even like her at all, or was she exploiting Emily's kindness and generosity to keep a low profile? What if Emily got in trouble just for associating with her? A knew about it, too—what if A told?

Sighing, she grabbed her bag from the ledge where she'd left it. "I'm going back to my room for a while. I'll be ready for the performance tomorrow, though. I promise."

She padded toward the elevator, glancing over her shoulder just once. Aria and Spencer were whispering, probably trying to decide whether or not to follow her. She was glad when they didn't.

There was no one in the elevator for her ride to her floor, and the hallway to her room was empty. But when she saw a figure sitting at her door, she froze, her heart suddenly beating fast. It was Jordan.

Jordan glanced up at the same time. Her lips parted, and she started to stand. "Emily!"

Emily turned around and walked the other way, the grass skirt scratching against her legs.

"Emily!" Jordan called again, running after her. "Wait!"

Emily kept going, saying nothing. "I know you're mad," Jordan blurted. "I'm sorry I didn't tell you sooner. I tried, a few times, but . . . I just didn't know how."

"Well, now it's all out in the open, isn't it?" Emily said brusquely, pulling open the heavy door to the stairs. She had no idea where she was going. She just knew she had to go *somewhere*.

"So that's it?" Jordan's voice cracked. "You're just going to walk away from us?"

Emily pulled her bottom lip into her mouth and climbed the first set of stairs, the grass skirt swishing loudly against her legs.

"Emily, please," Jordan said. "You're the best thing that's happened to me in a long time."

Emily paused mid-step. When she turned, Jordan's face was stained with tears. Her pert nose was red-rimmed from crying, and her hands were worrying the hem of her T-shirt. A T-shirt, incidentally, she had borrowed from Emily's closet—because Emily was so frickin' nice and naive. The image of Jordan on TV flared in her mind. *Walk away*, a wounded voice inside her said.

But she also knew what Jordan meant. Something amazing had happened between them.

She swallowed hard. "You lied to me. I don't know anything about you. I didn't even know your real name!"

"I know. And I feel terrible about it. But it wasn't because I wanted to hurt you. I wanted to *protect* you."

Emily ran her fingers over a crack on the wall. "Did you really escape from jail?"

"Yes," Jordan said in a quiet voice.

"Why weren't you wearing that orange jumpsuit when I first saw you?"

"I was in my regular clothes in the holding cell."

"And why did you pick the name Jordan?"

"It's my middle name." Jordan stared at her feet. "And Richards is my mom's maiden name. I've always liked them both better."

"Why did you steal planes? Cars?"

Jordan lowered her eyes. "It was something my best friend dared me to do. We were in it together."

Emily scoffed. "Your best friend made you steal a *plane*?"

"It was that girl Mackenzie I started talking about. She dared me to steal bigger things, do more dangerous stuff, basically because she loved the power over me. She

180

promised she'd love me back if I did, but it didn't work that way."

Emily curled her toes. The story was awfully familiar—Ali had treated her like that, too.

"Mackenzie was the one who turned me in, actually," Jordan went on. "I told her I didn't want to steal things anymore, that it was getting too crazy. So she called the cops on me."

Emily gasped. "Did she get in trouble?"

Jordan shook her head. "Nope."

"Why not? Didn't she steal stuff, too?"

Jordan's lips twitched. "I didn't tell the cops that." She peeked at Emily sheepishly. "Really lame, right?"

Emily stared at the big number 6 painted on the wall next to the stairs. She'd covered for Ali, too. Hell, she'd even let her out of the Poconos house. "It's not lame. But your relationship with your friend isn't love. It's not even *friendship*."

"I know," Jordan said quietly. "But once I realized it, it was too late. Only now do I *really* know what love is."

Emily looked up; the air felt electrically charged. Jordan was looking so deeply into Emily's eyes that Emily felt a magnetic pull toward her. She thought about how Jordan had held her close on the glass-bottomed boat, accepting everything about her. And how she'd kissed Emily out in the open at the elevators. And how they could talk about anything, and how much they laughed, and how *right* kissing her felt.

She walked slowly back down the stairs until she was by Jordan's side. When she slipped her hand into Jordan's, it felt as though she'd come home. But then terror struck her. "What if someone else knows where you are?" She thought of A's note. *Cute! You can room together in jail!*

Jordan's mouth made a line. "What do you mean?"

Emily swallowed hard. "What if someone recognizes you from the news ... and tells?"

"I've kept a really low profile," Jordan insisted. "I don't think anyone on this ship is on the lookout for me, anyway. You shouldn't worry."

"But ..." Emily trailed off, thinking of all the things A could do with the information. "What are you going to do when this cruise ends and we're back on land? They're going to catch you—you can't run forever. What will happen to us? Will I ever see you again?"

Jordan pulled her close and rocked her back and forth. "Hey," she said soothingly, rubbing a figure-eight pattern on Emily's back. "Don't worry."

"But I *have* to worry!" Emily cried. "You need a plan! You need to figure out a way to stay safe!"

Jordan smiled placidly. "Em, I *do* have a plan."

Emily blinked. "What is it?"

Slowly, Jordan led her out of the stairwell, past the busy arcade, and into one of the lounges, which had big velvet booths and long aquariums lining the walls. Other than Jeremy, who was leaning against the bar, talking to one of the bartenders, they were the only people in the room.

They sat down in a back booth near a glowing ATM machine. The second hand of the art deco clock on the wall made a full rotation before Jordan spoke again. "I'm never going back to the States," she began. "You're right—I'll be arrested as soon as I set foot there. As long

182

as I stay in another country, though, I'll be safe. So when we dock in Bermuda, I'm getting on a plane. I was going to do it at our first stop in St. Martin, but then I met you, and I just . . . couldn't."

Emily's eyes widened. "Where are you going?"

"Thailand. I have it all worked out. There's a fake passport waiting for me in Bermuda, along with a plane ticket."

Emily pictured a mental map of the world, trying to gauge the distance between Rosewood and Thailand. It felt like Jordan was going to the moon. "What are you going to do there?"

"Live an amazing life." Jordan said wistfully, twisting a cloth napkin that had been set on the table in her hands. "It's incredible there, Em—beautiful beaches, an amazing culture, and you can live like a king on nothing. I was thinking of teaching English to make money. And I want you to come with me."

Emily sat back in the plushy booth. "*What?*"

"Think about it!" Jordan grabbed Emily's hands across the table, almost knocking over a glass of water. "We'd *live* on the beach. You'd get to swim in the ocean every day. We could travel, have amazing adventures, and you'd get to escape everything here that you hate."

A kid Emily didn't recognize passed by them to use the ATM, and Emily pressed her lips together until he finished. Then she looked at Jordan plaintively. "But what if I wanted to see my family? Wouldn't a plane ticket be really expensive?"

"You *couldn't* see your family ever again. The authorities might figure out we escaped together—you'd be

183

considered an accessory for hiding me. If you came back to the States, you could be arrested, too."

The words hit Emily like a punch to the stomach. Never see her family again? Never live in America again?

Then again, what did she have in the States that she really treasured? A family who hated her? A college future she wasn't even excited about? Good friends, yes, but they'd probably jump at the chance to get out of town, too. And there was Violet, of course, but the Bakers were the best parents she could ask for.

If Emily left, she'd never have to worry about getting arrested for Tabitha's murder. She'd never have to worry about A coming after her, and she'd never be haunted by Ali's ghost—or any other ghosts of Rosewood past again. Her family would probably celebrate her disappearance. It wouldn't even register on Isaac's radar. UNC would find a new swimmer.

She looked at Jordan's huge, hopeful eyes, her parted lips, and the adorable dimple next to her eyebrow. She had found so much in one person, and letting her go seemed like a terrible mistake.

And could she really afford to make another one of those?

21
Hanna's Slumber Party

"C'mon, people, two more reps!" the Jillian Michaels impersonator yelled as she stood in front of the small workout room, raising two pale-blue dumbbells over her head. "Do it even though it hurts! Feel the burn!"

Hanna's arms felt like rubber, but she lifted the dumbbells as high as she could anyway, letting out a grunt. When she looked at herself in the mirror, she was making a constipated, old-woman grimace.

Then she dropped the weights to the floor and sighed. "Give yourself a round of applause!" the instructor whooped. A few people burst into tepid clapping.

Hanna collapsed onto her mat. It was Saturday afternoon, and she'd been in the gym for two hours now—before taking the 7-Day Shred class, she'd pounded on the treadmill for thirty minutes, then tried to lose herself for another twenty on the StairMaster. But none of it had helped her forget about Naomi, or A, or Naomi *as* A.

Everyone in the class headed for the door, and Hanna draped a towel over her shoulders and followed. But when she saw Naomi's shining face in the window, she backtracked.

"Hey there, superstar!" Naomi said brightly, pushing into the room. She was dressed in gray terry-cloth shorts, a white tank top, and New Balance sneakers. "You vanished so early this morning! Have you been here this whole time? You should've told me you were coming to the gym—I would've joined you!"

"Uh, it was a last-minute thing," Hanna said, avoiding Naomi's gaze, which felt far too intrusive.

Naomi linked her arm through Hanna's. "I was just talking to the Pilates instructor—she sounds really awesome. Maybe we could sign up for a joint session tomorrow?"

"Uh, sure." Hanna fiddled with her towel, unnerved by how close Naomi was standing to her. A vision of Gayle's dead body on the driveway flashed through her mind. *Naomi did that.*

Naomi placed her hands on her hips. "Are you pissed at me?"

"Of course not," Hanna bleated, trying to sound innocent.

"Well, you're acting weird," Naomi said, hurt evident in her voice. "You're treating me like I have barf in my hair."

Hanna mustered a carefree shrug. "I'm just tired." Then she gestured toward the fountain, mumbled how she was dying for a drink, and made a beeline for the faucet. She knows everything, a voice inside her head roared. Everything she told you was a lie. She's not happy her cousin was in the crash—she's furious, and she's out for blood.

186

When she was finished drinking, Naomi was waiting. "Can we at least rehearse for the talent show this afternoon?"

Hanna felt trapped. Thankfully, at that very moment, her cell phone chimed. It was only an e-mail from Shopbop.com about summer must-haves, but Naomi didn't know that. "Mike wants to meet me—he says it's an emergency. Bummer."

Naomi looked suspicious. "Do you still *want* to be my partner for the talent show?"

"Of course!" Hanna lied, afraid of what Naomi might do if she said no. She shot her an I'm-sorry-I'm-so-busy smile. "We'll catch up soon, okay?" And then, ducking her head, she darted for the stairwell door and scrambled to the floor her room was on—she was desperate for a change of clothes. She feared Naomi would follow her, but she didn't appear on the landing.

Hanna unlocked her door and rushed inside. Even though it had only been a few hours since she'd been there, the room didn't seem like hers any longer. Naomi's suitcase was in a completely different place now. Different clothes were on her bed, and the chair had been moved to the window. Hanna peeked around for Naomi's laptop, but it was nowhere to be seen. She'd probably never leave it unattended again.

She collapsed onto her bed for a moment, all at once feeling as tired as she'd pretended to be at the gym. Her head sank into the cool, soft pillow. Her aching limbs relaxed into the cushy mattress. It felt so good to stretch out after so many hours of exercise. The white noise of the fan was lulling and soothing. *I'll just close my eyes for a minute*, she thought to herself, her breathing slowing. And then, darkness surrounded her like a heavy blanket, cloaking everything.

When she opened her eyes again, she was sitting in an unfamiliar BMW. A pine tree air freshener spun from the rearview mirror. The radio was set to a hip-hop station.

She blinked and looked out the window. It was pouring outside. Tall buildings surrounded her, and a neon sign for South Street Steaks flashed in the distance.

The passenger door opened, and a figure flopped into the passenger seat. "You really don't have to do this, Olivia," a familiar voice slurred. "I'm totally fine to drive."

Hanna blinked hard. It was Madison. Her blond hair was mussed, her face was flushed, and she was wearing the same striped T-shirt she'd worn that night at the bar. Hanna looked around again. This *was* that night at the bar. The air felt like summer. Madison's breath smelled thickly of booze. Hanna had a salty margarita taste in her mouth.

Then she had an epiphany. Was she getting a do-over of that night? Could she change fate? Could she get out of the car, hail Madison a cab, and send her home another way, staying out of this mess completely? Then Naomi would never have anything against them. She would never become A. This nightmare wouldn't be happening.

But when she tried to pull the door handle to leave, her fingers wouldn't respond. And then, unwittingly, she felt her hand twist the key in the ignition and rev the car's engine. Before she knew it, she was pulling into traffic.

188

Stop! she told herself, but her foot continued to press the gas.

"Get on 76 West," Madison mumbled, pointing to the sign above them. Hanna tried to steer the car in another direction, but it was useless. She found herself merging onto the highway, just as she had the first time.

She focused on the road, which was barely visible through the rain. "Stay on 76 until 202," Madison instructed.

Those were the directions to get to Rosewood. "Where do you live, exactly?" Hanna asked, even though she now knew.

Madison giggled. "You're going to hate me, but I don't exactly remember. My parents just bought a new house, like, last week, and I keep forgetting the address. But I think I can get us there."

An oncoming car sent up a plume of water against the windshield. *Pull over!* she told herself. *Wait at least until this rain stops!* But, frustratingly, she kept driving.

Madison directed Hanna to Reeds Lane. Hanna's heart thudded as she navigated the curves, dreading the moment that was about to come. And then, there it was: A car appeared out of nowhere, veering straight into her lane. She screamed and cut the wheel. Madison let out a strange *urp* sound, and her head banged against the seat. The tires skidded on the wet road, and before Hanna knew it, the car had slid down the embankment. She hit the brakes hard, and the wheels locked and the back end fishtailed.

"Help!" she screamed. A huge oak approached in the windshield. She tried to turn away from it, but it was too late.

There was a deafening *crunch*, and then a symphony of shattering glass. Hanna shielded her face and felt the airbag deploy. The seatbelt cut hard against her shoulder and waist, and then everything stopped. When she opened her eyes, the radio was still playing. The engine still hummed. A tree branch poked through the windshield. Glass had shattered everywhere.

Hanna looked to her right. Madison's head was tilted at a strange angle. A thin ribbon of blood flowed out of her nose. When Hanna looked down into the foot-well, she screamed. Madison had no legs. She was only a torso.

"Madison?" Hanna whispered shakily. She shook Madison's shoulder. "*Madison?*"

Suddenly, Madison's eyes popped open. Hanna recoiled. The girl's eyes were clear and lucid, and she stared unflinchingly at Hanna.

"Your name isn't Olivia," she said in a haunted voice. "It's Hanna Marin. I know everything about you."

Hanna's eyes boggled. She pushed the airbag out of the way and tried to scramble out of the car, but Madison caught her arm before she could. When she turned back, it wasn't Madison's face staring back at her. It was *Ali's*.

"Hey, Hanna!" The corners of Ali's lips stretched wide into a smile. "Miss me?"

Hanna shot up in bed, breathing hard. She was in the calm, quiet stateroom on the boat. The covers had been thrown back, and she was clutching a pillow with her trembling fingers. She pinched the bridge of her nose and tried to erase Ali's face from her thoughts, but her smile was burned in her brain.

190

"Are you okay?"

Naomi was sitting on her own bed, looking curiously at Hanna.

Hanna jumped. "H-how long have you been sitting there?"

Naomi smiled, her wide blue eyes seemingly innocent. "Not too long. You were really passed out, though. Saying some crazy stuff, too."

"L-like what?" Hanna gasped. The dream spun in her head. What if she'd called out Madison's name?

Naomi shrugged but didn't answer. She grabbed Hanna's hands to pull her up. "I have a surprise for you."

"A surprise?" Hanna echoed weakly.

Naomi pulled a plastic bag from behind her back and took out two candy-colored wigs. "Look what I found in one of the shops on the concourse level! Won't they be perfect for our routine tomorrow?" She plopped the blue one on Hanna's head, then arranged the purple one on her own. "I think I know why you're acting so weird, Hanna. You have stage fright, don't you? You're freaked about singing in front of all of those people. But it's going to be great. *I'll* be right next to you. Nothing can go wrong—I promise. So are you still in?"

The fruity Kate Spade perfume Naomi always wore was suddenly so overpowering that Hanna thought she might throw up. She looked down at her arm. Naomi was still gripping her wrist, and her eyes flashed, looking so much like Madison's.

She pulled her arm away fast. "I-I have to go."

Naomi frowned. "*Why?*"

Hanna stood up, her mind a blank. Her only goal was

191

to get to the front door as quickly as possible. "S-something came up," she stammered.

"But what about the talent show?"

Hanna glanced back just once. There was such a hurt look on Naomi's face, but Hanna knew now it was all just a facade. "I'm sorry," she practically whispered. Then she flung the door open, slipped into the hall, and slammed it shut before Naomi could follow her.

She was almost to the elevators when she caught sight of herself in the hall mirror. The blue wig Naomi had bought sat crookedly on her head, half of the hair sticking straight in the air, the other half sweeping across her forehead. As she reached to pull it off, something fluttered out and skidded to the floor. It looked like a receipt. On the back, something was scrawled in blue felt-tip pen. When Hanna leaned down to look closer, her heart stood still.

You can't hide from the truth, little liar. You're going to get what you deserve. —A

22
She's Made Her Bed ...

The next morning, there was a loud knock on Spencer's door. "Spencer?" Reefer called. "Are you in there?"

"Go away," she answered in a muffled voice. "I'm sick."

"What's wrong?" Reefer sounded worried. "Can I come in? *Please?*"

Spencer hid her face with a pillow and groaned. She'd remained in her room for as long as she possibly could. Texts had come in from Aria, Hanna, and Emily, bright and early, reporting that Hanna hadn't yet been able to sneak on Naomi's computer and find out anything else. Then Emily and Aria had called, asking Spencer if she wanted to run through the talent show routine one more time—the performance was that night, and they still hadn't nailed all the dance steps. They'd stopped bugging her after she said she wasn't feeling well, but Reefer hadn't given up. "*Pleeeease?*" Reefer drawled again.

Spencer sighed, stood up, and hobbled toward the door, wincing as she put weight on her twisted ankle. The light was bright in the hall, and she squinted. Reefer's jaw dropped when he saw her. "What *happened* to you?"

"What part?" Spencer turned away. "The fact that I smell like vomit, or the fact that there's gum all through my hair?"

"*All* of it!" Reefer cried.

Spencer glanced at her reflection in the sunburst mirror in the hall and shuddered. It was bad enough that she'd spent the whole night vomiting because of some bad shrimp scampi she'd eaten at dinner—or, well, she *assumed* it was the shrimp, even though other people had eaten the same thing and hadn't even gotten a stomach-ache. That morning, she'd also awakened to a huge glob of chewing gum as a brand-new hair accessory. It was going to take a miracle to get it out without chopping off all her hair.

"Someone put it in my hair in the crush to get out of the café after dinner," Spencer said. "I turned around, and suddenly it was there."

Reefer sat down on the desk chair, looking puzzled. "Did you see who did it?"

"No."

"Maybe you were chewing gum before you went to sleep and forgot to take it out."

She shook her head vehemently. "I never chew gum before bed."

Reefer walked over to her and hugged her waist. "Maybe this is the universe's way of telling you that we shouldn't sneak around anymore."

Spencer wriggled out of his grip. "We *have* to sneak around."

"Still?" Reefer put his hands on his hips.

194

"I told you," Spencer said. "I don't think it's fair for Naomi. And you said you were fine with it."

Reefer sniffed. "I didn't know you were going to be so serious about it."

Then Reefer ran his hands through her hair, seemingly not grossed out by the gum. She tried to resist, but Reefer smelled like sunscreen and chlorine, and in a second, his lips were on hers and they fell onto Spencer's bed. His skin was warm from the sun. Spencer shifted positions so she could help Reefer pull his shirt over his head.

Crack.

Suddenly, the bed was on the ground. The floor shook. The picture of the ship hanging above Spencer's bed wobbled on its nail, then fell. Spencer covered her head just before it crashed to the mattress.

Reefer blinked. "I knew I was wild, but I didn't know I was *that* wild."

Spencer crawled to the carpet and stared at the bed frame. All four legs splayed horizontally, as though no longer able to bear the weight of the mattress. The wood wasn't splintered, as she might have expected, but had broken off clean, as if it had been sawed through.

Then she stood up and examined the nail on which the picture over the bed had hung. It dangled precariously from the wall, in danger of falling out itself. It had clearly been messed with. The first evening of the trip, the seas had been rocky, and though Spencer and Kirsten's tubes of toothpaste had tumbled off the shelf in the bathroom, not a single piece of furniture or decoration had budged. They'd both joked that everything in the room was probably bolted down, not hanging by a faulty nail.

Spencer's skin prickled. The thought that had been quietly, insidiously swirling around her head for the last twenty-four hours pushed to the forefront of her mind. "That's it," she announced. "I can't take it anymore. This has gone far enough."

"What are you talking about?" Reefer asked.

"Don't you see?" Spencer cried, her voice cracking. "The slip on the floor, the food poisoning, the gum thing, and now the bed? Someone is *doing* this to me!"

The smile faded from Reefer's face. "You're *serious*?"

"Of course I'm serious."

"Who would be doing this to you? And why?"

She took a deep breath. "Isn't it obvious? Naomi!"

Reefer's eyes widened. "Come on. She's not *that* crazy."

"Yes, she is!"

Spencer peered around the cabin nervously. "Does that TV look like it's sitting too close to the edge to you?" she asked. Then she looked at the untouched breakfast tray she'd ordered from room service and gave the pastries an experimental sniff. "Will you taste that muffin to make sure Naomi didn't lace it with acid?"

Reefer stared at her. "Um, Spencer, if it's laced with acid, then *I'd* be on acid. But you've lost all perspective. Naomi isn't gaslighting you."

"Yes, she is!" Spencer cried. She rushed over to the closet and peeked inside, worried her bags were booby-trapped to fall on her head. Then she held her bottle of allergy pills to the light. Were they the same blue shape as before? What if Naomi had replaced them with something else—something dangerous?

Reefer placed his hands on her shoulders. "You've got

to calm down. You can't go around blaming bad luck on someone else. Everything that has happened to you is because you *made* it happen, okay?"

A lump formed in Spencer's throat. Reefer was right—but not for the reasons he thought. Maybe she *had* made her bad luck happen—maybe this was a karmic revenge for all the terrible things she'd done. Framing Kelsey. Helping Hanna with Madison. *Tabitha*. This was the universe's way of punishing her.

Then she blinked hard, reality snapping back into focus. This wasn't karma—this was A! And A wouldn't stop until she got what she wanted.

And just like that, Spencer knew what she had to do. She looked up at Reefer, a lump in her throat. "We have to break up," she said.

Reefer's jaw dropped. "*What?*"

"I'm sorry," she said in monotone. She knew she'd crumble if she looked Reefer in the eye, so she stared at her hands. "This just doesn't feel right."

"You really think she's torturing you, huh?"

"Yes."

"Why don't you let me talk to her?"

Spencer looked away. "Can you just do what I ask?"

Reefer stepped back as if she'd shoved him. His eyes glistened with tears for a moment, but then he steeled his jaw, breathed in, and turned around. "Fine," he said in a defeated voice.

"I'm sorry," Spencer called weakly. But he had already slammed the door.

23
The Wrong Idea

That afternoon, Aria and Graham stood outside the theater on the bottom level of the boat. The bright-blue walls featured photos of the Cirque du Soleil performers, who all looked freakish and possessed with their buggy eyes, weirdly tight leotards, and absurdly long limbs. Another wall was devoted to signs for that night's talent show—it started at seven, and there was a pre- and post-party.

The rest of the wall space, though, was covered with strange hieroglyphs relating to Cirque du Soleil. Aria and Graham were here because the final Eco Scavenger Hunt clue, which they'd found in a compost pail in the ship's kitchen, required them to decipher the hieroglyphs. But to Aria, the characters just looked like nonsensical squiggles.

"Any ideas?" Aria stepped aside as one of the acrobats, who had a single ostrich plume sprouting from her head, strutted through the theater door. That morning, when he and Aria had reported to Gretchen, she'd told them they were in the lead. "If we figure out this clue, those Apple Store gift cards are ours." Even though Aria hadn't been into the idea in the beginning, she'd mentally browsed through the Apple Store, contemplating whether to buy a white iPad with tons of memory or a MacBook Air.

"That's probably why they made it so impossible." Graham's forehead wrinkled as he studied the wall. "That one looks like a cloud." He pointed to a puffy-looking image. "And that one looks like a falling girl."

Aria flinched. If she turned her head a certain way, it *did* look like a body descending through space. The photo of Tabitha's tumbling form appeared in Aria's mind, followed by A's latest note. *Will Aria's boyfriend visit her in jail?*

The door to the theater swung open, and another acrobat strutted out. She glanced at them and smiled. "Want a clue?"

Aria and Graham nodded eagerly.

The acrobat edged closer. "See that picture there, the one that sort of looks like a dinner fork? It stands for an *E*. And the image that looks like a carrot stands for the letter *S*." Aria looked at the wall again. "So it's like a cryptogram?"

"Precisely," the acrobat said, then pirouetted away.

Aria peered at the symbols. She and her father, Byron, used to do the cryptogram puzzle in the *Philadelphia Sentinel* every morning. The puzzle always featured a scrambled quote. The trick was to figure out the cipher so it made sense.

When she reached into her purse for a pencil, her fingers brushed against a golf tee from the mini golf course she and Graham had visited the other day. She smacked her forehead. "Graham, I'm so rude! How did it go with Tori last night?" Graham had sent her a text the afternoon

199

before saying that he and Tori had made dinner plans. She'd written him back with a list of things to talk about, adding that he should pull out Tori's chair when she sat down and never, ever order for her. She couldn't believe she'd forgotten to ask.

Graham pushed a lock of hair off his forehead. "It was fine." Then he pointed at a three-letter word with a dinner fork icon in it. "If that stands for *E*, then that word is *the*. And so are those two."

"Oh. Right." Aria wrote it in, then filled in the *T*s and *H*s elsewhere in the puzzle, too. She cleared her throat. "So it was just fine? Not amazing?"

"And maybe that's *to*." Graham pointed to a two-letter word starting with *T*. It was like he didn't hear her.

"Yep," Aria said, writing it in. Her stomach sank. Had the date been a disaster? Maybe Graham had talked non-stop about SCA or his dead ex-girlfriend. Maybe Tori had left after the appetizers.

She was dying to ask, but all of a sudden the hall felt too quiet and exposed. They stared at the puzzle for a few minutes longer, writing in more words. Within a few minutes, they had the whole message: *Protect the seas. Save the planet. Live life to the fullest.*

"Okaaaay." Graham twisted his mouth. "What are we supposed to do with that?"

"I've seen that phrase somewhere," Aria murmured, shutting her eyes. Then the answer popped into her mind: the banner in the casino, from that first day. She'd noticed it because she'd sworn she'd seen something—or some-one—moving in the shadows beneath it.

"Come on," she said, grabbing Graham's hand.

200

The casino was dark and empty, the slot machines buzzing atonally. The banner still hung over the tables. Aria walked beneath it and placed her palms on the table's surface. When she ran her hand along the underside, her fingers touched cardboard. She squatted down; two cards had been taped right where the tabletop met the legs. She pulled off the tape and held the cards to the light. *Congratulations!* they both read.

Aria opened one. It was, indeed, a $1,000 gift card to the Apple Store. She waved it at Graham. "We did it!"

Graham threw his fist in the air. Then he scooped Aria up and swung her around. She giggled, but didn't squeeze him too hard, not wanting to give him the wrong idea. When Graham pulled back, his cheeks were a delighted pink.

"We should celebrate, don't you think?" he asked. "How about lunch at that restaurant on the upper deck?"

"Well ... " Aria's mouth wobbled. She wanted to tell him that he should do something with Tori instead. She also wanted to see Noel. But Graham seemed so happy. And they *had* just won.

"I'm in," she decided, grabbing one of the gift cards from his hand. "Just let me freshen up."

An hour later, Aria climbed up a spiral staircase to Galileo's, a little restaurant on a small landing atop the main deck. Twinkling fairy lights were strung around the railing and threaded through potted ficus trees. Kids were sitting at tables, a jazz band was tuning up in the corner, and the walls were plastered with posters advertising the talent show. FIRST PRIZE: VESPA! they all proclaimed.

201

"Aria?"

Graham appeared behind her, dressed in a blue button-down and a clean pair of jeans. His hair was neatly combed, he'd shaved, and she could smell his woodsy cologne from here. When he saw her, his face twitched nervously. "You look nice."

"Oh, I wear this old thing all the time," Aria said, waving her hand at her blue maxi-dress and espadrilles.

Graham walked to the bar and ordered them two ginger ales, then led her to a high table by the railing. Once they sat down, a sly look came over his face, and he produced a flask from his back pocket and shook it. Liquid sloshed inside.

"What is that?" Aria whispered.

"Something to help us celebrate," Graham said, then paused. "Is that okay?"

Aria must have had a strange look on her face; she was surprised Graham drank. He'd been so adamant about The Cliffs serving alcohol to minors on the Tabitha Clark Memorial website, after all.

"I guess I could have a little," she said after a moment, and allowed Graham to pour the pungent liquid into her glass. When she took a sip, she nearly coughed. "Yikes." It had to be about 150 proof.

Graham downed his drink quickly. "I need this right now."

"Why?" Aria pushed her glass away. "I thought you'd feel pretty relaxed now that we've won." Then she raised an eyebrow. "Is it because you're nervous about your talent show performance? Playing a Death Cab song on the lute sounds awesome to me."

202

"It's not that," Graham mumbled.

"Tori's going to be so into it," Aria gushed. "Speaking of which, spill it. How did the date *really* go?"

Graham shrugged one shoulder. "I told you. It was fine. We hit the restaurant on the main deck. She got sushi, I had a turkey burger."

Aria blinked. Listing the food one had eaten on a date wasn't a particularly good sign. "Did you have a lot to talk about?"

"I guess." Graham tore the napkin that had come with his ginger ale to shreds. "To be honest, I'm not really sure I'm into Tori, after all."

"Why not?" Aria cried. "She seemed perfect for you! And I'm positive she was interested." She sat back in her chair. "Are you scared to let yourself like someone else because of Tabitha?"

"I'm definitely not scared. She just wasn't for me." Graham picked up his glass and drained the rest of the drink. Ice cubes rattled at the bottom of the empty glass. When he set it back down, he gave her a long, piercing look that Aria didn't understand. "There's something I need to tell you. Something I've been trying to muster up the courage to say all day."

Aria cocked her head. "What do you mean?"

Graham continued to stare. And then, suddenly, puzzle pieces snapped together in Aria's head. *He likes you*, Noel had said. *A dude can tell. You might be leading him on and not even know it.*

She swung her hands to the right, almost knocking over her glass. "Um, you don't need to tell me anything," she said, trying to keep her tone light.

203

"No, I really need to—"

"We should just have fun tonight," Aria interrupted, reaching for her drink—all of a sudden, alcohol sounded like a great idea. "Celebrate our win."

"But . . ." Graham trailed off abruptly, his eyes widening as he stared at something on Aria's chest.

She looked down, wishing she'd chosen a dress that didn't show so much cleavage. "Isn't the sea rocky tonight?" she asked loudly, gesturing over the rail.

But Graham didn't take the bait. He pointed at the locket around her neck. "Where did you get that?"

Aria touched it self-consciously. "My boyfriend gave it to me."

Graham's hand shot forward. He grabbed the necklace and yanked it closer. The chain pressed against the back of Aria's neck, forcing her forward. His lips were inches from hers. Aria cried out, turned her head so that he couldn't kiss her, then wrenched away from him so forcefully that she nearly toppled her barstool.

When she righted herself, Graham was just staring at her again, not apologizing for what he'd done. Aria grabbed her purse, avoiding eye contact. "I have to go."

Graham stood too. "Aria, wait."

"Don't." Her head started to pound. Suddenly, everything felt so sour and sullied. "I'll talk to you later, okay?"

She tried to wheel around, but Graham caught her arm. She cried out again. When she looked at his face, it was grave, almost angry. "But I have something to tell you," he demanded.

"You're hurting me," Aria said shakily, staring down at his nails in her arm. Her heart thundered in her chest.

Graham released his grip, suddenly looking horrified. She shot away fast, diving for the spiral staircase and clomping down as fast as her high shoes could carry her.

"Aria!" Graham called after her, but she didn't stop. Only when she got to the bottom did she peer up the stairwell. Graham stood at the top, looking flummoxed. His eyes were wide and sad, the corners of his mouth turned down in a frown.

She skittered away and felt guilt wash over her. Had she led Graham on? Was he crushed now? How had this gone so horribly wrong?

The elevator couldn't come fast enough. She hit the button again and again, afraid Graham might decide to come and talk to her. Then a tinkling sound of piano keys sounded behind her. There was a baby grand piano in the waiting area, and someone was pressing a high note over and over again. It sounded like the soundtrack to *Psycho*.

She turned around, ready to tell whoever it was to stop it, but there was no one at the bench. She blinked hard around the empty room—had she heard the sound at all? But no, the sound of a just-plucked piano string echoed in the air. Someone *had* been playing the piano. And she knew, immediately, who it had been.

24
Something's Missing

"Welcome to Bermuda!" Jeremy's voice chirped over the speakers that afternoon. The opening bars of "Over the Rainbow" played. Instead of rushing to the railing and waving at everyone on the dock, as Hanna had done every other time they arrived at an island, she remained parked behind a stack of books in the lending library, her gaze trained on her stateroom door down the hall.

"How long are you going to sit like that?" Mike asked, propping his feet up on the oak desk next to her and rifling through an old *Sports Illustrated* Swimsuit Issue.

"I already told you," Hanna said under her breath. "I'm waiting until Naomi leaves."

Mike peeked over the centerfold. "You seriously can't deal with seeing Naomi for even one *second*? Are you *scared* of her?"

Hanna glared at him. "You can leave at any time, you know." When Mike had asked her what she was up to that morning, Hanna said she wanted to check out the library on her floor. Mike had offered to come with her,

206

but after a half hour of watching Hanna stake out her room and not leaf through a single book, he'd caught on to what she was really doing.

"I still think mud-wrestling is the way to go," Mike said, turning back a page to look again at a supermodel in a high-cut string bikini.

"Thanks for the suggestion," Hanna said. "I just don't really want a confrontation. She caught me looking at her computer, and she's pissed. I want to go back into the room when she's not around, that's all."

It was *almost* the truth. Hanna didn't feel it necessary to add that she wanted to go back into the room so that she could look at Naomi's computer *again*. Or that Naomi was probably extra-pissed at Hanna because she'd ditched her without an explanation.

"You were going through her stuff?" Mike said. "What's gotten into you? First you stalk Colleen, now it's Naomi . . ."

"Would you stop asking questions?" Hanna hissed, feeling more and more exasperated.

Mike laid down the magazine. "God, fine." He stood up and stretched. "I'm going to find Noel so we can run through our talent show song one more time. Call me when you're done playing Stake-Out."

As he stormed off, the door to her stateroom opened, and Naomi sauntered out, dressed in a white eyelet dress and blue sandals. Several chunky bangles lined her wrists, and she carried a small red leather bag under her arm.

Hanna held her breath as Naomi walked by the library, praying she wouldn't stop inside. She didn't. As soon as Naomi stepped into the elevator, Hanna crept down the

207

hall toward their room. When she was almost there, a figure passed through the intersecting hallway, and she froze. It was Jeremy. His fingers were entwined behind his back, and he was whistling "Yankee Doodle Dandy."

She leaned against the wall, her confidence shaken. As the elevator dinged, a horrible thought struck her. What if Naomi forgot something and came back?

She scuttled back to the library and dialed Spencer. "It's Hanna," she whispered when she answered. "I'm right outside my room, and I want to look at Naomi's computer, but I don't want to get caught. Can you be a lookout?"

Spencer groaned warily. "I don't want to piss her off even more."

Hanna glanced at the elevator again. Hopefully Naomi hadn't just taken a quick jaunt down to the gift shop. "Please, Spence? It'll take five minutes. We need to nail her."

Spencer let out a long sigh, then hung up the phone with a *clunk*. In less than a minute, the elevator chimed, and she limped out. Her face was pale, and one side of her hair was matted. Spencer caught Hanna looking and said, "There was gum in my hair. It was a bitch to get out." Then she gestured down the hall. "Let's make this quick."

Hanna let herself into her room. Inside, Naomi's bed was neatly made, her clothes folded on the bureau. Hanna looked right and left, and finally spied the laptop underneath Naomi's desk. Her heart did a flip as she lifted the cover. She found Naomi's photo folder quickly and opened it. Her gaze went immediately to a folder titled *Vacay*. She opened it up, then clicked on the first icon. The

208

same photo that had been on Aria's phone appeared. It had almost been too easy.

"Oh my God," Hanna whispered. "Here they are."

"Really?" Spencer ran from the doorway and peered at the screen. "Jesus. Delete them!"

"I will." Hanna highlighted the images and dragged them into the trash. "Go back to the door and make sure she isn't coming!" she instructed.

Spencer did as she was told, though after a few seconds she'd wandered away again. She poked her head into Hanna's bathroom. "Hey, your shower's nicer than mine."

"How do you think Naomi got those pictures, anyway?" Hanna murmured, answering *yes* to a prompt that asked if she was *sure* she wanted to delete the photos.

"I thought we covered this. The second A must have sent them to her."

"Do you understand the implications of a second A?" Hanna wished the photos would delete a little quicker. "It means someone *else* hates us, too. It also means someone else has these photos. *That's* the person who saw what happened in Jamaica."

"I know," Spencer said gravely.

"Who do you think it could be?"

"Hanna, if I *knew,* maybe we wouldn't be in this mess!" Spencer sounded exasperated.

Hanna didn't know either, but the possibility of a second A was really starting to sink in, and it was terrifying. Even if they took Naomi down and found proof that she was Gayle's murderer, they wouldn't be safe. This alleged second A could still nail them for everything.

Finally, a message popped up saying that the photos had been removed. *Phew.*

"Holy shit," Spencer cried. She emerged from the bathroom carrying a bottle of baby oil, Ex-Lax tablets, and a large package of bubble gum. "Look at what I found in Naomi's bag!"

"Don't mess with her stuff!" Hanna hissed, jumping up.

"Don't you see?" Spencer waved the bottles around. "This proves without a doubt that she's the one who's torturing me! She used the Ex-Lax to make me think I had food poisoning. She spilled the baby oil so I'd slip. And she put this"—she held up the gum—"in my hair!"

"Spence, I need you at the door!" Hanna guided her down the little hall. Then she shoved Naomi's stuff back into the bathroom and turned back to the computer. Now that she'd deleted those photos, she needed to find something incriminating about Naomi that would connect her to Gayle. An e-mail, maybe. She opened her Gmail account again, hoping to find a note signed *A.* Maybe they'd get lucky and even find something that gave away whoever it was Naomi was working with.

But when the screen loaded, there weren't any messages in the Gmail inbox at all. Frowning, Hanna clicked on some of the other folders within the server, but they were all empty. The conversation Naomi had had with Madison was gone, almost like it had never existed.

25
Forget Your Troubles

Stroke, stroke, stroke, stroke, stroke, breathe.

Stroke, stroke, stroke, stroke, stroke, breathe.

Emily reached the wall, did a flip turn, and pushed off toward the other side of the pool. Her arms cut rhythmically through the water. Her legs kicked with full power. Halfway down the lane, she had to swim around a fun noodle, then a floating toy that looked suspiciously like a giant penis. The pool technically wasn't for lap swimming at that time of day—plenty of kids were milling around in the water, soaking up the Bermuda sun. But swimming laps was the only thing that helped Emily think, and she needed to think as hard as she possibly could. She hadn't yet given Jordan an answer about running away with her, but Jeremy had just announced that they were pulling into Bermuda. She had to make a decision soon.

Stroke, stroke, stroke, stroke, stroke, breathe.

Could she really leave Rosewood forever? Never see her family again? And was it really safe, going off with a criminal? What if someone hunted Jordan down and

211

hauled her back to the States? *Then* what would Emily do?

But then she thought about Thailand. She'd looked up the beaches online last night and almost swooned. There were tons of posts about the country that said it was easy-going, clean, affordable, and accepting. *No one cares what you do here*, someone had written. *You are free to be yourself.* Wasn't that what Emily wanted? Wasn't that *not* what Rosewood—or a swimming future at UNC—could ever provide?

She could wake up every morning next to Jordan. They could go shopping in the Thai markets, travel to remote and amazing villages, make pilgrimages to other countries. Maybe she could teach English, like Jordan was thinking of doing.

Her mother's scowling face floated into her mind, then her father's. Carolyn's appeared next followed by Beth's and Jake's. Going to Thailand meant leaving her family behind. All she wanted was for them to love her, and they couldn't. Maybe it was a good thing to flee from the pain. Maybe Jordan could be her family instead.

She swam to the end of the lane and grabbed the edge of the pool. Hanna was sitting in one of the lounge chairs, and Emily flagged her over.

Hanna looked pale beneath her tan. Emily could tell she was still upset about what she'd found—and what she *hadn't* found—on Naomi's computer.

"What's up?" Hanna asked.

Emily ran her fingers across the pool's surface, unable to meet Hanna's eye. "What do you know about Thailand?"

Hanna frowned. "I've heard it's pretty cool, I guess. Why?"

Emily bit her lip. "If you had the opportunity to go there, to leave all this behind, would you?"

"Sure," Hanna said emphatically.

All of a sudden, Emily's mind felt as clear and cloudless as the sky. She pushed out of the pool, hurried across the deck, and grabbed her towel. Hanna followed her. "Wait. What's this all about? Are *you* going to Thailand?"

"Of course not," Emily said quickly. But her voice caught.

Hanna frowned. "Emily. What are you planning?"

Emily gazed at her friend for a beat. All at once, Emily thought of the sleepovers at Ali's house when she and Hanna would be the last two girls to fall asleep. "Let's look through Ali's photo albums," Hanna had whispered once, and they had turned the pages of the old book by nightlight. "She doesn't look so great in that photo," Hanna would say, pointing at one of Ali from fourth grade or one of Ali without any makeup on Christmas morning. Even though Hanna desperately sought Ali's worst shots, she seemed to understand that Emily was looking through the albums to see Ali at her very best, and she'd occasionally point out one of Ali looking beautiful. "She has the prettiest eyes, doesn't she?" she'd say wistfully. Or, "She looks like a model." All for Emily's benefit.

Her eyes brimmed with tears from the memory. She'd miss all her best friends terribly.

"I'm not planning anything," she said, running away before Hanna could stop her.

Off the starboard side of the ship, she could see the

Bermuda docks. Kids were already jamming the elevator area to be the first to disembark. Was Jordan among them? Would Emily get to her in time?

The elevators were too crowded, so Emily ran down the three flights to her room in bare feet. She flung open the door and looked around hopefully, but Jordan was already gone. Frantic, she pulled a terry-cloth cover-up over her head, then grabbed her suitcase from under the bed and stuffed her things into it. She slung the bag over her shoulder and scuttled out the door, joining the convoy of kids making their way off the ship.

She clambered down the stairs and burst through the door that led to the ramp. The gangplank had been lowered, and a crowd of kids waited to disembark. Emily stood on her tiptoes and searched for Jordan's dark hair. When she didn't see her, her heart jumped into her throat. "Jordan?" she called out. "*Jordan?*" What if she'd missed her? Would Jordan leave without her?

"Jordan?" she cried again.

"Emily?"

Emily swung around. There, under the boat's exit sign, was Jordan, dressed in a T-shirt Emily had loaned her, a pair of jeans, a baseball cap, and dark sunglasses. Emily's knees went weak. Jordan's mouth crumpled into a relieved, ecstatic smile. Emily ran into her arms.

"So does this mean you're coming?" Jordan said in Emily's ear.

"I guess it does," Emily said shakily.

Jordan stepped back and pulled her cell phone from her bag. "This is going to be amazing," she said excitedly, her eyes shining. "I promise."

Then she dialed a number and put her phone to her ear. "Hello, Jasmine? I'd like to book an extra ticket to Thailand. Her name is Emily Fields." She spelled it slowly. "I'll pay in cash at the airport, okay?"

Emily opened her mouth, ready to say she'd help pay, but then she realized—she didn't have that kind of money. She didn't know how Jordan had access to that kind of money, either, but she wasn't sure she wanted to know.

The line for the door slowly moved up. Emily grabbed Jordan's hand so she wouldn't lose her in the crush. As they got closer, Emily could see the docks out the door. The light was so bright, she had to shade her eyes. When it was their turn, Jordan started off the ramp first. Emily followed, her heart pounding. Jordan was halfway down the ramp when she stopped short. Emily bumped into her back.

"What's wrong?" Emily asked. Kids flowed around them like water moved around rocks in a stream.

Jordan's face had gone ghostly pale. Her gaze was on something out in the water. Emily craned her neck to see what she was looking at. A speedboat was docked next to the ship. A few men in serious-looking uniforms were climbing off. One was speaking into a walkie-talkie. The other looked like he had a gun in his holster. The boat had an official-looking logo on the side. FEDERAL BUREAU OF INVESTIGATION.

Emily clapped her hand over her mouth. She watched, paralyzed, as the Feds charged up the dock, straight to the ship. And then she heard one of them say "Katherine DeLong" clearly into his walkie-talkie.

Jordan whipped around to face her. "Did *you* call them?"

215

"Of course not!" Emily cried, her eyes widening. "You know I wouldn't do that to you!"

Jordan's gaze flicked from Emily to the Feds and then Emily once more. "I know you wouldn't," she admitted. "But . . . I don't understand. You're the only one here who knows who I am."

A cold, hard knot formed in the pit of Emily's stomach. She *wasn't* the only one. Someone else had known for a while now. Emily should have warned Jordan as soon as A taunted her with that first note, but she'd been too selfish.

The first FBI agent barreled quickly down the dock, his face bright red. Jordan grabbed Emily's hand hard. "Come on," she said through her teeth. "We have to get away from them."

She pulled Emily back into the ship and through a stairwell door. They raced up the stairs, taking them two at a time. At first, Emily dragged her heavy bag behind her, but then she ditched it in the stairs because it was slowing her down. They finally stopped at Deck 5, where the theater and a bunch of the restaurants were. Kids were at the buffet line and putting in their orders at the sandwich station.

Jordan raced past them and skidded around the corner toward the state rooms. Something banged behind them. "Stop right there!" a voice boomed.

On instinct, Emily froze. Both Feds had burst through the stairwell doors and were starting for Jordan. The kids at the buffet paused, agape. Someone dropped a plate. One girl even screamed.

Emily's legs felt glued to the floor. In seconds, Jordan

was going to be caught. *She* was going to be caught, too.

She jerked her head to the side, hating herself for even thinking it. As she glanced at Jordan, Jordan gave her a mournful smile. "It's okay," she said softly. "Run. Pretend you've never seen me before."

"No!" Emily cried, ashamed that Jordan sensed the thought that had crossed her mind. "I'm not going to abandon you like that!"

But Jordan just darted toward the ship railing. "Stop right there, Miss DeLong," the tall agent commanded.

Jordan groped for the railing, her eyes hard. There was something feral about her expression, like she was a cornered, wild animal looking for an escape. Everyone in the cafeteria stared. And then, Jordan hurdled herself to the top of the railing. She balanced there for a moment, gazing at the lapping waves below. It was then that Emily realized what she was about to do.

"No!" she screamed, lunging forward.

But she was too late. Jordan's body disappeared over the side of the ship. Seconds later, there was a splash. Everyone ran to look over the side. The turquoise sea rolled against the boat. Huge rafts of seaweed floated on the surface.

Please come up, please come up, Emily willed, searching for Jordan's head. But it didn't appear.

"Where'd she go?" someone asked beside her.

"That's a really long jump," another person said. "Maybe she didn't make it."

The Feds had already thundered back down the stairs, heading for their boat. Emily gripped the railing tightly,

217

scanning the waves for Jordan. There was an ugly brown froth on the surface of the sea. A fish jumped out of the waves. But there was no sign of Jordan.

At least a hundred kids were peering over the side to see if Jordan would surface. Emily wanted to scream at them, make them turn away. How could this have happened? Who could have tipped off the police? Instantly, the answer came to her. She'd be stupid to think it was anyone else.

As if on cue, her phone pinged. Emily yanked it from her purse and glared at it angrily, hating the message she knew she was going to see.

Oops! Did I go "overboard" by calling the authorities, Em? Sorry! —A

26
The Bends

That afternoon, despite the fact that she still had a teensy bit of gum in her hair and her ankle hurt like hell, Spencer sat in a fishing boat with the other members of the dive class. They had motored to a small set of naturally formed coves in an uninhabited part of the island. The rocks looked slick and wet, and the empty turquoise sea spread out behind them. The spot was beautiful, but it was also eerily remote.

Tim cut the boat's engine. "I've saved the most picturesque dive for last. The coral in this cove is amazingly preserved and in perfect health. See if you can spot all the angelfish—this is where they like to hang out. Is everyone ready?"

Everyone murmured yes, and Tim led them through the meticulous checks of their gauges and tanks. After he finished, Tim gazed at Spencer. "Do you and Reefer want to go down first?"

Reefer. Spencer peeked at him across the boat. Reefer was sitting next to Naomi, pointedly avoiding her gaze.

They hadn't said a word to each other since Spencer broke up with him. She would have skipped the last dive altogether, but ditching out would mean she wouldn't pass the course. And even though her future at Princeton *seemed* secure, she wasn't putting it past A to try and screw it up once again.

A—meaning *Naomi*. Spencer glowered at Naomi, who was possessively holding Reefer's arm. *Happy now?* she wanted to snap. *You got exactly what you wanted, like you always do.*

Instead, she shot Tim a tight smile. "Can Kirsten be my partner instead?"

Tim glanced at Kirsten, who was sitting with her partner, a girl named Jessica. "It's cool," Jessica said, and Kirsten stood up and grabbed her swim fins.

"The only thing I ask is that no one strays from the group, okay?" Tim said as he moved out of the way for the girls to climb into the water. "These currents can be very dangerous. I don't want anyone getting swept away."

A hand went up in the back. "But I heard there's even more amazing coral a few coves over," a short-haired guy with a pierced eyebrow said. "Can we check it out together?"

"Definitely not." Tim's eyebrows furrowed. "The coral in those coves is really sharp—someone could hurt themselves. It's also really deep over there—not safe for novice divers. Stay where I can see you at all times, okay?"

Spencer sighed. That meant she'd have to stay in sight of Reefer and Naomi, too.

She grabbed a dive mask from the milk crate and pulled the strap over her head. Then she and Kirsten sat on the side of the boat, counted to three, and flipped backward into the water.

The water was cool on Spencer's skin, and she felt herself sinking down, down, down. She opened her eyes, sucked in a breath, and looked around. Tropical fish darted to and fro. Fingerlike seaweed waved in an elegant ballet. She located Kirsten a few yards away and waved. Kirsten gestured to Spencer's tank and raised her eyebrows—as partners, they were supposed to keep an eye on each other's gauges. But Spencer just shook her head—they'd been in the water for only a few minutes. There was no need to check the controls yet. What she really needed was a few moments of being truly and purely alone. She turned toward the cove the boy in the boat had been talking about, eager to check out the vast depths. Screw the rules.

She watched everyone else on the boat descend into the water, including Naomi and Reefer. Once Tim's back was turned, she swam gracefully away from the group, and for a few minutes, all she could hear was the sounds of her mechanized breathing. Bubbles floated across her field of view. A school of small, neon-pink fish darted past, followed by a sinuous manta ray. Spencer swam even deeper until she was face-to-face with the coral.

Unbidden, a memory popped into her head. At the beginning of sixth grade, when they'd first become friends, the Hastingses and the DiLaurentises both took a trip to their vacation homes in Longboat Key, Florida, for a long weekend, and Ali and Spencer had taken a scuba class. As they'd walked down the dock, Ali had nudged her side and pointed to an icy blonde leading the group.

"For a second, I was afraid that was Naomi Zeigler," she'd whispered. "Her family has a condo here, you know."

Spencer had looked at Ali. "Why aren't you friends with her anymore?"

"We had a fight," Ali answered simply, adjusting her bikini strap.

"About what?" Spencer asked.

Ali shrugged. "Naomi knows what she did."

She never elaborated further. Now Spencer understood that it had been *Courtney* talking, a girl who'd never known Naomi. There had never been a fight—Naomi had never done anything.

Or ... had she? There had been something so chilling about Courtney's voice when she spoke about Naomi, a rawness not even the best actress could fake. Had she identified something dangerous about Naomi when she'd arrived in Rosewood? Was there more to the story than Spencer knew?

As she ran her fingers across a piece of coral, a sharp pain prodded at her skull. She wheeled around, thinking something had struck her, but there wasn't a person or even a fish anywhere close. She blinked hard, suddenly feeling light-headed. When she took a breath, her lungs didn't fill. Had she gone too deep? Did she have the bends?

She tried to breathe in again, but she couldn't inhale. Suddenly desperate, she fiddled with her dive mask—perhaps it wasn't lined up properly with her mouth. But it was, and yet she still couldn't draw a breath. Her heart began to pound. She tried to swim to the surface, but her arms and legs felt like dead weights. She checked her pressure gauge again, but the tank was still full. That was impossible, though—she definitely wasn't getting oxygen.

She gasped for air, an idea forming in her mind. She'd heard about this kind of thing happening. People could mess with the gauges, make them appear at the right levels when in fact the tank was empty. She knew that was what had happened. And she knew who had done it, too. *A.*

Spencer woozily glanced through the water, finding Naomi within the clump of divers in the distance. The baby oil and bed-breaking tricks were child's play compared to cutting off her oxygen supply. Of course Naomi still hated her! And to think, Spencer thought she was safe just because she'd broken up with Reefer!

"Mmm!" she cried, the sound getting swallowed up in the water. Spots were starting to form in front of her eyes. She flailed her arms and legs and weakly called out for help, but the divers were too far away to notice. She kicked closer. By now her lungs were burning, greedy for air.

"Mmm!" she called out, waving her arms some more. But all the divers' backs were to her. Spencer's eyes started to close. Her neck lolled back, and her body suddenly felt heavy. Darkness crept in, obscuring her vision. Her leg bumped a piece of rock, but she couldn't move. She had no *energy* to move. This was the end, and she couldn't even fight.

A warm feeling washed over her body, and she allowed herself to sink. She couldn't hear breathing in her ears any longer. Her eyes fluttered closed. The last thing she saw was a light coming toward her, filling her field of vision . . .

Then, air pushed into Spencer's lungs, and she opened her eyes with a jolt. She coughed violently, and salt water spewed from her mouth and exploded from her nose, burning her nostrils. She was lying on the deck of the boat again. Reefer crouched over her, his lips wet, a relieved look on his face.

"Oh my God," he breathed. "Are you okay?"

Spencer tried to speak, but another cough came out instead. She rolled over to her side and waited for the water to drain from her ears. For a split second, she thought Reefer had just been kissing her, that their breakup had been a dream. But then everything rushed back.

"What ... happened?" she croaked.

"You just started sinking," Reefer said. "I found you and pulled you to the surface, then gave you mouth-to-mouth. Tim checked your gauges—you had no oxygen left in your tank."

A chill snaked up her spine. She searched the crowd of kids that had gathered on the boat and found Naomi lurking at the back, her gaze bouncing from Spencer to Reefer. Her lips were pressed together so tightly they were almost transparent, and her eyes were round and wide. She looked shaken—maybe because Reefer was comforting Spencer.

Or maybe because her plan to hurt Spencer had failed.

27
Surprise Inside

A few hours later, Aria glanced at herself in the full-length mirror near the auditorium. She was wearing the skimpy bikini she'd had on for her first swim lesson with Noel, the grass skirt, a bunch of beaded necklaces, and her lace-up sandals. As a final touch, she'd popped a flower behind her ear.

She looked across the auditorium lobby. A girl passed carrying a portable easel under her arm. Several kids held instrument cases. Jeremy, still in his star-shaped sunglasses, ran past them with a clipboard in hand, looking frazzled. Two men in suits and a woman in a ball gown, presumably the other judges, followed behind him. Everyone was talking excitedly, and the room had a festive, free-for-all attitude about it. Hundreds of balloons floated along the ceiling and Hollywood Walk-of-Fame stars lined the ground.

She spied Noel near one of the auditorium entrances and almost burst out laughing. He was wearing a baggy, shiny tracksuit and a bunch of gold chains around his neck. She ran over to him. "You look more like a gym teacher than a rapper!"

Noel twisted the baseball cap he had on his head sideways and crossed his arms over his chest, gangsta-style. "You just wait until you hear my rhymes. Mike and I are so ready for this."

"When are you on?" Aria asked.

"Seven-thirty. You?"

Aria checked her phone; she and everyone else participating in the talent show had been sent a schedule of events. "Seven," she said. "I think we're one of the first acts." It was six-thirty.

Noel looped his arm in her elbow. "Let's check out the food."

They walked into the auditorium and down the aisles to the stage area, where a bar and food tables had been set up. Several rows of chairs had been removed to make room for a makeshift dance floor. As they maneuvered past a group of girls practicing a series of cheerleading tumbling passes, Aria punched Emily's number into her phone once more. Voicemail again. This was the third time she'd tried Emily in the last few hours. She thought about the news alert on the TV screen when she'd left her room. PREPPY THIEF JUMPS OFF CRUISE SHIP IN BERMUDA, it had said. FBI AGENTS COMBING HARBOR. It certainly explained all the FBI ships in the harbor the last time Aria had looked out the porthole. Apparently, the girl hadn't gotten off the boat at the last port, as Emily had said.

There was a beep, and then Aria said, "Em, I'm at the talent show. I hope everything's okay and you're still up to performing. Call me when you get this." She dropped her phone back into her clutch, then scanned the masses of kids running in every direction. Spencer was missing, too, as was Hanna.

Noel grabbed an empty plate and waited in line at a table filled with silver tureens full of food. "So where's Graham?"

Aria looked away, feeling a sharp pull in her stomach. "I don't know."

Noel raised his eyebrows. "I thought you guys were best buds."

Aria fingered her grass skirt. "The hunt is over. I guess we didn't have as much in common as we thought."

"Did you get him that girlfriend like you promised?"

She kept her eyes fixed on the tray of shiny forks and spoons on the table. "Turns out she wasn't his type."

She could feel Noel's gaze on her, trying to figure out what she wasn't telling him. She probably *should* tell him the truth—it was part of their pact, after all—but if he found out the guy had practically grabbed her boobs, he'd probably bust his door down and try to beat him up. It was better that he thought Graham had just lost interest. If only that really *was* what happened. The muscles in her neck ached from when Graham had yanked her forward. His furious expression flashed in her mind again and again, and her stomach clenched when she thought about how he'd chased her to the stairs.

"Hey, party people!" Jeremy called from the stage. Shabby-looking guys in roadie T-shirts and ripped jeans scuttled behind him, setting up equipment. "I realize we're still setting up, but to get you in the mood, I have a huge surprise for you. A special guest has joined us to perform

227

a few songs as a pre-show event. Without further ado, put your hands together for ... Vegan Sunrise!"

Aria looked at Noel questioningly; she'd never heard of them. Kids clapped halfheartedly, looking just as confused. But when four band members took the stage and started playing a guitar-heavy cover of "When I Come Around," everyone shrugged and started dancing.

The food line moved, and Aria and Noel filled their plates. She checked her phone a few more times, but still no Emily or Spencer. The crowd got more raucous and excited, and a girl's elbow flew out of nowhere, knocking Aria's plate from her hands. She twisted to grab it, but her ankle turned awkwardly, and down she went, too. She felt herself falling but couldn't do anything about it; in seconds, she was on the floor, vegetarian noodles in her hair. A *ping* sounded in her ear. At first, she thought it was the fork bouncing off the ground, but when she picked herself up, she realized that it was her locket. Its two halves had sprung open from the fall.

"Are you okay?" Noel asked, extending his arm to help Aria up.

"Sure," Aria said, picking up her spilled food as best she could and tossing it into a nearby trash can. Then she turned back to the locket. Inside was a picture of two blond, smiling girls, their cheeks pressed together. As she squinted, she slowly realized that she *knew* the girls. The one on the right had a round face, big blue eyes, and faint burn scars on her neck. *Tabitha.*

Then she looked at the girl on the left. Her eyes slowly scanned her familiar heart-shaped face, her big blue eyes. She drew back, startled. *No.* It couldn't be.

228

She held the locket away from her face, but the girl's eyes seemed to follow her. She had a manipulative, winning smile that had entranced Aria for years. A scream froze in Aria's throat. All of a sudden, she couldn't breathe.

Ali.

"Aria?"

Aria looked up and blinked. Noel was staring at her from a few feet away. She gave him a tight, nervous smile and shut the locket fast. The catch had broken, though, and the locket sprung right back open. She stared at the picture once more. It couldn't be. Surely her brain was playing tricks on her. She tried to close it again, then peered carefully at the front of the pendant. In the strong overhead stage lights, the initial inscribed into the silver wasn't an *I* or a *J*. It was a *T*.

For Tabitha?

Something suddenly clicked in her brain. Heart thudding, she grabbed her phone, pulled up the Tabitha Clark Memorial website, and stared hard at the picture of the girl on the home page. *That* was where she had seen this necklace before. On Tabitha, before she died.

She held up the necklace. "W-where did you really find this?"

Noel looked confused. "I told you. It was in the sand in St. Martin. Why?"

Aria's thoughts scattered in a million different directions. "That's impossible," she whispered. It couldn't be a coincidence. Had A planted it for Noel to find? And then there was the picture—Tabitha and Ali *had* been friends.

229

She took a step, but her legs felt wobbly. "Aria?" Noel touched her arm. "What is it?"

"I just have to . . ." she said faintly. She staggered toward the exit. Her phone beeped. It was Graham. Panicked, Aria hit IGNORE, then dialed Spencer's number. But the call went to voicemail.

"Where are you?" Aria demanded after the beep. "We need to talk."

But she was afraid to say anything over the phone, so she hung up and kept running. She called Emily next, but she didn't answer either. Same with Hanna. She ran up the aisle and sprinted to the elevator, pressing the UP button repeatedly.

"Aria?"

Aria turned. Graham was standing by the window, staring at her. "You walked right past me," he said, looking annoyed. "Why didn't you answer my call? I need to talk to you."

"I . . ." Aria trailed off, her gaze dropping to the locket in her hands. Graham was looking at it, too. His eyebrows met. His mouth grew very small, and all of a sudden, he reached out and touched her wrist. She gasped and closed her fist around it, but it was too late. Of course Graham recognized his girlfriend's old necklace. He'd probably recognized it from earlier.

"I-I can explain," Aria stammered.

Graham blinked hard. "You *can*?"

His cheeks were red. His eyes blazed. All at once, another barrel clicked in her brain, and a horrible thought bulldozed all others. *He knows what I did.*

It made perfect sense. Graham hadn't wanted to talk to

230

her about his burgeoning crush: He wanted to confront Aria about being a murderer.

She spun around, searching frantically for somewhere to go. The red EXIT sign for the stairs glowed in the distance.

"Aria!" Graham yelled, lurching after her. He grabbed her arm and clamped down hard. His fingers felt like hot irons on Aria's skin. She screamed and wrenched away from him, pushing through the heavy door and heading down. She'd never gone below the auditorium level and didn't know what was there. Up ahead was a door marked DO NOT ENTER.

Graham's footsteps echoed on the landing below. "Aria, come back here!" he roared.

She burst through the door anyway and spilled into a large, empty room full of ship machinery. Boilers chugged. Air-conditioning units hummed. Other utility devices rattled and churned. The space was lit by a few spare overhead lights and split into several long, mazelike corridors. There wasn't a soul around.

Behind her, the door opened. "Aria!" Graham called out, his voice reverberating.

Aria skidded behind a boiler, but Graham spied her and started running, his face red, his nostrils flaring, his teeth bared.

She wheeled around, desperately searching for someone to help her, but she was alone. Then she scrambled for somewhere to go, somewhere to hide. There was another door past the boilers marked STAFF ONLY. She ran for it and pushed it open. This room was filled with pipes and monitors and more boilers. The grumbling sound was

231

almost deafening, reminding her of a revved motorcycle engine. The doorknob rattled, and Aria rushed to turn the lock, then threw her weight against it. Frightened tears ran down her cheeks.

"Damn it, Aria, you can't hide forever!" Graham pounded on the door.

"Please," Aria whimpered. "Just go away. *Please*."

"I'm not leaving until—"

An engine sputtered. He tried to scream over the machinery sounds. "I need to—I need . . . "

"Just leave me alone!" Aria sobbed. "I'm sorry, okay? I'm so sorry! I didn't mean to do it to her! I was just so scared! We all were!"

"You can't . . . I . . . he . . . and . . . " Graham's angry voice rose and fell. Aria could only make out every other word. " . . . watching you!"

"Please go away!" Aria screamed. "I said I was sorry! Please let me go!"

" . . . there's a picture!" Graham continued. " . . . *watching* you!"

Aria blood sizzled. He had to be referencing the awful photo of Aria pushing Tabitha off the roof. Maybe *he* had taken that photo. Maybe that's what he meant by *watching you*.

Thoughts cascaded in her mind like a falling line of dominoes. What if Graham was crazy about Tabitha and hadn't let her go after they broke up? Maybe he'd followed her to Jamaica to rekindle things. Maybe he'd taken pictures of her without her knowing, and had posed on the shore to take pictures of Tabitha on the crow's-nest deck. Only, instead of documenting Tabitha with some

232

new friends, he had witnessed a murder. Maybe he'd snapped a picture of her lying on the beach, too, after she'd fallen and died. Maybe he'd even torn this necklace from her throat and planted it for Noel to find. It didn't make sense why Graham didn't tell someone at the resort right away, but maybe he'd wanted to get revenge *his* way. And so . . . he'd become A.

Aria began to tremble. Was it possible? All the warnings her friends had given her, all the times they'd said he had motive, and there she was, by his side, making *excuses* for him. He *did* have motive. He could have gotten in touch with Naomi, somehow, after the crash, and recruited her onto his team.

He could be a murderer. A torturer. And now she was trapped in this room with him on the other side.

The door thumped and thudded with Graham's pounding fists and kicking feet. When Aria shut her eyes, she saw Tabitha's terrified face as she fell. She pictured her broken body on the sand, kissed by the incoming tide. Aria *was* a terrible person. She deserved Graham to be mad at her. But she didn't deserve what he'd done as A.

Boom.

Aria screamed and covered her head. The sound was so close, and the room vibrated. The lights flickered overhead, and the sound of metal hitting the ground clanged all around her. She let out a breath and peeked through her fingers. Had something exploded? There was as horrible smell in the air of gunpowder and charred electronics. It sort of reminded her of a firework. Or, perhaps, a homemade bomb.

A fire alarm started to blare. "Everyone!" Jeremy's

233

voice crackled over the loudspeaker after about a minute. "We need you to evacuate right now! Please go to your lifeboat stations in an orderly fashion!"

Evacuate? Aria's heart started to pound. She wasn't even opening the *door*.

She cocked her ear, waiting for Graham to start pounding again. A few seconds passed, and then a minute. Finally, Aria opened the door a crack. Emergency lights flashed overhead. The room was thick with smoke. A boiler had tipped over. Pieces of metal were strewn all over the floor. Black smoke was pouring out from seemingly everywhere, and flames leapt to the ceiling. The explosion had definitely occurred right there in that room.

She let out a scream, then wrenched open the door. She had to get out of there. She looked around for Graham, expecting him to grab her. But even through the haze, the realization dawned on her fast.

Graham was gone.

28
Women and Children First

Emily followed the stream of kids toward the stairs, her nostrils burning with smoke. Above her, emergency lights flashed. Kids were screaming about the strange explosion, laughing hysterically, or making nervous comparisons to *Titanic*. And even though they'd attended a safety meeting the very first day on the boat, no one seemed to remember where their lifeboat stations were.

"Everyone!" Jeremy yelled over the loudspeaker. "If we get separated, please remember to meet us at the Royal Arms Hotel in Hamilton, Bermuda."

Jeremy repeated the message three times more. As Emily waited to go down the stairs, she glanced at the sky. A plane zoomed overhead, coming from the Bermuda airport, which was now a ten-minute boat trip away. Was it the plane she and Jordan were supposed to be on? She pictured the people sitting in their seats, the stewardesses cruising up the aisles, the smell of fresh-brewed coffee wafting through the cabin—and the two unoccupied seats meant for her and Jordan.

The line moved up a little, and a few more kids made it through the stairwell door. A girl in front of Emily with cornrows in her hair nudged her friend. "I heard terrorists blew up the cafeteria."

"No, these two guys who were in the talent show did it," her friend replied knowingly. "They knew their act sucked, so they decided to bomb the place and steal the Vespa."

"You're making that up." Cornrows rolled her eyes.

"Maybe it was that girl who jumped overboard earlier," another voice said. "Maybe this was revenge for whoever ratted her out to the Feds."

"That's crazy." Someone sounded annoyed. "That girl never came up for air. She's dead."

"Can you believe she was on this ship the whole time? Who do you think turned her in?"

Stop talking about her! Emily wanted to scream. It was like Jordan was an infamous celebrity, someone weird and unknowable. *She likes a lot of milk in her coffee*, she thought. *She's fearless. She's the most amazing girl I've ever met.*

She shut her eyes and considered Jordan's body sinking down, down, down, to the depths of the bay, just like Tabitha's had. She wanted to strangle A with her bare hands. Why couldn't A have just let them go? Why did A have to ruin Every. Single. Thing?

She felt a hand on her shoulder. Aria was on the stairs behind her, dressed in a bikini and her grass hula skirt and drenched in sweat. Hanna and Spencer were there, too, dressed normally but looking hysterical.

"What's going on?" Emily asked.

236

Aria glanced back and forth at all the kids on the stairs, then dragged Emily onto the landing, which was cool, dark, and empty. Kids swarmed past, but no one seemed to notice they were there.

"*Look*." Aria fished the round gold locket she'd been wearing all week out of her pocket and dangled it under Emily's nose. The two halves of the pendant splayed open. Emily squinted at the two girls in the picture inside. One of the girls was Ali. When she realized who the other one was, she stepped away, confused.

"Is that *Tabitha*?" she whispered.

"This was her necklace," Aria said. "Noel found it on the beach, but I checked the pictures of Tabitha online, and it was definitely hers."

Spencer shook her head, stunned. "I bet Naomi planted it for Noel to find and give to Aria."

"Or maybe Graham did," Aria said, still breathing hard. She looked like she was about to burst into tears. "I was wrong about him, guys. He stared right at the necklace like he knew what it was, and then gave me this look like he knew everything I'd done. I ran from him and shut myself in the boiler room, but he screamed at me through the door. I screamed out an apology for what we did to Tabitha, but it didn't make him stop. He said he was watching me, and he mentioned a picture. I think he was the one who set off the bomb, too. He mentioned gunpowder once when we were talking—he would have known how to make an explosion."

Spencer clapped a hand over her mouth. "You could have been killed!"

"I know." Aria swallowed hard.

Emily trembled. "What picture do you think he was talking about?"

"I don't know," Aria said. "Maybe the one of Tabitha on the beach. I think *he's* the one working with Naomi."

"Oh my God." Spencer sank onto a stair, looking woozy.

"But why would Naomi—or Graham, or whoever—plant that necklace for Noel to give to Aria?" Hanna asked.

"It proves we killed Tabitha," Spencer said, leaning closer so that a bunch of boys clamoring down the stairs wouldn't hear. "It connects us to her and that night. A is trying to build an airtight case."

Emily wilted against the wall. "I don't get it. Why would A need to build even more of a case on us? A— both of them—have the pictures. One of the As saw us. And we *did* do it. Why does A need to gather extra evidence?"

Spencer shrugged, the emergency light flashing red across her face. "I don't know. But the FBI is nearby, looking for that girl who jumped overboard." She glanced at Emily when she said this, then looked away. "This would be a perfect time to tell. We could be arrested within hours, especially if we have this necklace on us."

Hanna looked at Aria. "Where is Graham now?"

Aria tapped her nails against the railing. "I'm not sure. He disappeared after the explosion."

Spencer frowned. "That's strange, don't you think?"

Aria shrugged. "I'm *glad* he's gone. I was afraid he was going to jump out and hurt me."

"That would make the most sense, don't you think?"

Spencer hugged her knees. "I mean, I'm glad you're safe, but why wasn't he waiting for you after the bomb went off? Why did he leave?"

Emily thought for a moment, absently watching as more kids streamed down the stairs. "Maybe he miscalculated where he set off the bomb, and he had to run from it so he didn't get hurt himself."

"Or what if Graham wasn't sure it was us on the roof that night?" Hanna asked, pausing to cough. "Even those pictures of us are pretty blurry. But maybe when you ran from him, Aria, he got his proof. Maybe he and Naomi are going to tell the cops."

Spencer used the railing to hoist herself to standing. "The necklace will definitely connect us to the crime. The cops will think we tore it off Tabitha that night."

Hanna nodded. "We have to ditch this necklace *now*. We don't need anything connecting us to Tabitha—especially with the FBI here."

"You should have gotten rid of it as soon as you realized what it was," Emily said to Aria. "Why didn't you throw it overboard?"

Aria looked dazed. The fluorescent light in the stairwell made her already-pale skin look even ghostlier. "I wasn't exactly thinking clearly."

"It's *good* you didn't throw it overboard," Hanna said forcefully. "There are a zillion cops dredging the harbor. One of them could have found it. All sorts of people saw you wearing it, Aria—they'd connect it to you in a heartbeat, and then A would make sure that they linked it to Tabitha, too. We need to throw this thing away for good so that it doesn't come back to haunt us. We should weigh it down with something so that no one ever finds it."

There was a screech of feedback through the speakers, and the girls looked up. Jeremy breathed into the microphone. "Once again, that's the Royal Arms Hotel. We're sending an e-mail out to everyone in case you forget."

"I have an idea," Spencer said after the announcement clicked off. "There's a diving cove not far from here—my diving group went out near it this afternoon. Apparently it's really deep. What if we took one of the life rafts and headed for it? We could swim to the bottom and bury the necklace under the coral."

Emily's eyes widened. "But we're not all assigned to the same life raft. And usually there are more than just four people to a raft, right? What if we jeopardize someone's safety?"

Spencer shrugged. "Have you seen how many life rafts there are on this ship? There are enough to go around."

"Actually, it's true," Hanna said thoughtfully. "Some of the data-entry I dealt with in the admin office mentioned this ship's capacity and how many kids were on it now. It might seem like there are a million of us on board, but they usually cram about a hundred more people on this boat for normal cruises."

Aria swallowed hard. "Spencer, I don't know how to swim."

"I do," Spencer reminded her. "I'm scuba-certified. I'll bury it. You don't even have to get off the raft."

"What about when we're done?" Aria asked. "We'll be out in the middle of the ocean. How will we find the others?"

Spencer didn't look worried. "You heard the announcements—we're meeting up at the Royal Arms Hotel in Hamilton. We'll be able to get there."

Hanna picked at the flaky paint on the wall. "It might be dangerous to take a boat out alone, especially to somewhere so secluded."

Spencer waved the thought away. "I've been to Bermuda six times with my family. I know these waters."

"I'm in," Emily decided. "Let's go."

"I'll do it," Aria agreed finally. Everyone looked at Hanna, and she reluctantly shrugged.

They rejoined the masses of kids heading to the bottom deck, stopping at the scuba storage closet to grab a mask, a tank, and swim fins. The doors to the lifeboats had been thrown open, and the blue-black ocean and a brilliant sunset splayed out before them. Everyone was haphazardly climbing aboard the lifeboats, seemingly not paying much attention to their assignments. Friends sat with friends. Couples huddled together. Kids were still holding drinks from the talent show pre-party. Most were still dressed in their performance outfits, including Aria.

"Come on," Spencer said, pointing to an empty lifeboat at the end of the corridor. Everyone ran for it, and they climbed aboard while the ship safety staff members were busy loading up the other boats. Emily held onto the boat's rubber sides and stared at the choppy harbor in front of her. The shore looked miles away. An FBI boat bobbed in the waves to her left, sending a fizz through her stomach. Everyone strapped on life vests, which smelled faintly of mildew. When they'd safely nestled into the seats, Spencer pulled the chain to start the outboard motor.

Then, a hand grabbed Emily's arm. "Room for one more?"

Emily turned and swallowed a gasp. On the ship's deck, staring at her, was Naomi. "Um ... " she squeaked, not moving over.

Naomi's gaze darted from Emily to Spencer to Aria to Hanna. All of them looked just as shocked. The corners of her mouth turned down in a disgruntled frown. "Can I join you or not?" she asked sharply.

"Sorry, Naomi. There's no room." Hanna gripped Spencer's arm. "Go!"

Spencer hit the gas and pulled away from the deck, nearly yanking Naomi into the water. Emily rubbed the spot on her arm that Naomi had touched. Her skin prickled.

"Hey!" Naomi called after them. "What the hell?"

"Don't answer her," Hanna said under her breath.

"Hey!" Naomi called again, watching as Spencer turned the boat away from the shore. "Where are you going? That's the wrong way!"

Aria whimpered. Hanna looked like she was going to throw up. Emily's heart thrummed jackrabbit-fast. Spencer's jaw was set and hard as she steered toward the cove. In a minute, they had pulled so far away that they had a panoramic view of the entire ship. Tiny lifeboats peeled away from the hull. An alarm light blared on the top deck. Black smoke poured from the windows.

And then, Emily's gaze returned to deck where the staff was organizing the remaining lifeboats. Naomi was still standing there, hands on hips, glaring. Emily watched her rigid figure until she got smaller and smaller, fainter and fainter, until she finally vanished into the growing darkness.

29
S.O.S.

It took about twenty minutes to get to the dive spot that Spencer's group had been to that afternoon. The sun had almost set; the last remaining light danced across the sky in purple streaks. Spencer turned the boat toward a section of coast that was marred by huge rock formations, natural cliffs, and small caves. Jagged coral jutted everywhere. Water lapped against slick, high, algae-covered rocks. The cave they were closest to was deep and black, looking like a scary, angry mouth.

Spencer cut the engine, then strapped on the oxygen tank and flippers, feeling a little uneasy about using the scuba equipment after almost drowning. But she'd checked the gauges three times, and there was no way Naomi could have fiddled with them before they left. "The deepest part is in that cave. I'll go alone, okay? You guys stay here."

"Are you crazy?" Emily said. "You can't swim there alone. I'm going with you. I'll tread water on the surface while you dive down."

"So will I," Hanna said.

Aria's eyes widened. "Don't leave me here! I'm coming, too."

Spencer glanced at her worriedly. "Can you manage?"

Aria pulled a strap of her life vest. "I'll be fine. We're all in this together, right?"

"I'll stay close to you," Emily volunteered.

The girls tied the lifeboat to a natural outcropping of rocks and slipped into the cool, algae-filled water. They swam toward the narrow passage and into a dark, swirling pool. After a few more strokes, the passage opened into a wider cavern, where the water was much calmer and warmer. But it was pitch-black in there, too—Spencer could hardly see a few feet in front of her. It was barely better when she turned on the scuba flashlight she'd grabbed from the equipment room. The filmy, slimy seaweed kept slithering over her legs like leeches. She peeked worriedly at Aria, but she was bobbing comfortably in the life jacket.

She grabbed the necklace from Aria's hand. "Wish me luck," she declared, then disappeared under the water.

She sank down just like she had earlier that day. This time, her equipment worked, and oxygen filled her lungs. Once she was down far enough, she found an outcropping of rocks and pushed the necklace deep into the cove, dislodging a cloud of sand. When it cleared, the necklace was gone. It was hidden—hopefully for good.

When she popped back up, the girls were still treading water. There was a tense silence—Spencer could tell none of them had spoken the whole time she'd been down. Hanna's teeth chattered. Aria was breathing heavily. Emily's eyes darted back and forth toward the shore, which seemed a million miles away.

"It's done," Spencer said when she pulled the dive mask from her face. "Let's go."

They paddled back through the passage. The sea had grown even colder with the setting sun, and Spencer couldn't wait to climb back on the lifeboat and head for land. She squinted at the tiny sliver of sun on the horizon. There was barely any distinction between the navy-blue water and the darkening sky. The only sound she heard was the peaceful lapping of waves. She looked right and left, disoriented. Something seemed different.

Emily surfaced behind her. Aria swam through next, then Hanna. They all treaded water with Spencer, looking around in confusion.

"Where's the boat?" Emily finally said.

Spencer blinked. Just like that, her bearings came back to her. She saw the cruise ship far in the distance. And there was the finger-shaped rock she'd remembered from the dive earlier that day. But when she looked for the natural hook they'd tied the boat to, all she saw was a slack piece of rope. She pulled at it, feeling a weight rise up from the deep. An outboard motor appeared on the surface. After that, a limp shell of a raft, all of its air gone.

Aria gasped. Emily and Hanna exchanged a silent, horrified look. The waves lapped violently against the rocks. A thin, high-pitched giggle spiraled through the air.

Hanna let out a tiny squeak and stared at all of them with wide, terrified eyes. "I-I don't understand."

"Something must have punctured it," Spencer suggested, her voice trembling.

Emily whimpered. "Is this actually happening? How are we going to get back to shore?"

They stared at one another, then at the vast distance between themselves and the ship. Spencer swung around and tried to judge the swim to the land, but that was much too far, too. Emily could swim it, perhaps, but next to her, Aria was thrashing around and breathing heavily, even wearing a life jacket.

"I should have stayed on the raft," Aria blurted between gulps of sea water. "Maybe this wouldn't have happened. I could have kept it safe."

"Stop it," Spencer said sternly. "What if you'd stayed on the raft, and it started sinking, and you couldn't get out?"

Aria stared at the smooth walls of the cliffs. "How could something have punctured the raft anyway? It doesn't seem possible."

And then, as if in answer, they heard it again: that high-pitched giggle, seemingly wafting out from the ocean depths. It was a vengeful laugh, a satisfied laugh, a laugh that said, *Now what are you bitches going to do?* And suddenly, a tiny seedling of an idea formed in Spencer's mind.

"Naomi did this," she whispered.

Aria's throat bobbed as she swallowed. Hanna's chin trembled. Emily's fingers shook as she pushed her hair behind her ear. As soon as the words spilled from Spencer's mouth, she knew they were true. Naomi had seen them leave. Surely she had known what they were going to do, and surely, as A, she saw a foolproof opportunity. Spencer could just see the news tomorrow: *Four pretty girls go for a joyride on a lifeboat when a cruise ship is evacuated. Boat springs a leak, the girls drown.*

It had probably happened before. When the rescue

teams finally found them, it would be deemed a horrible accident, but certainly not foul play. No one would go to jail. It was the perfect crime.

Everyone exchanged a haunted glance. "Naomi left us here to die," Spencer whispered. "For all we know, she and Graham were in cahoots the whole time. Once his bomb didn't finish off Aria, they moved on to plan B."

Emily burst into tears. "What are we going to *do*? I don't want to die like this!"

"Help!" Hanna screamed out. But the waves drowned out her voice.

"We should have never come out here," Emily blubbered.

"This is all my fault," Aria blubbered. "If I hadn't gotten that necklace, we wouldn't be here. We wouldn't be in *any* of this mess if I hadn't pushed Tabitha."

"Don't talk like that," Spencer said.

"But it's true!" Aria wailed. "I'm the only one who deserves this from A. You guys don't!"

Spencer watched as a wave passed over Aria's head. She bobbed back to the surface, coughing, when another wave took her under again. Her arms thrashed uselessly. There was terror in her eyes.

Emily grabbed Aria around the waist and pulled her to the surface. "You have to stay calm," she shouted in her ear. "Panicking wastes energy."

"How can I *not* panic?" Aria cried. "Don't you see? A figured out a poetic end for us, tossing us out to sea just like the waves washed away Tabitha. Even if we survive, what's the use? A is going to find us again and do something even *worse*."

247

"Don't say that," Spencer soothed. "We're going to beat A. We're going to find a way." But as she stared into the dimming light, she realized that everything Aria was saying was true. Being marooned at sea seemed like the worst possible death, but if they survived, who was to say A wouldn't come up with something even scarier? How could she live, knowing A had something in store for her just around the corner?

Aria wiped water out of her eyes. "If we get out of this alive, I'm telling the cops what I did in Jamaica."

Everyone whipped their heads around and stared at her. "No, you're *not*," Spencer hissed.

"I can't take it anymore!" Aria thrashed her arms. "Don't you see what's happening? A is using our guilt and fear to manipulate us—and it could go on forever if we don't stop it! The only way we free ourselves of A is to confess. Then A has nothing on us."

The sea was calmer for a moment. Hanna wiped water out of her eyes. Spencer sniffed back tears. Finally, Emily cleared her throat.

"Maybe we should *all* tell," she said.

"We can't let you do that alone, Aria," Hanna added.

"And it's true." A wave splashed Spencer's left cheek. "A is powerless if we confess. In a weird way, it'll probably free us. Yeah, we'll go on trial, and yeah, who knows what our futures will be? But at least A will be gone from our lives."

Aria swallowed hard. "You guys don't have to ruin your lives for something I did."

Spencer rolled her eyes. "For the last time, Aria, we're in this together. We're *all* confessing. We'd never let you take the blame alone."

Then, through an unspoken understanding, they swam together and formed a protective ring. It felt, suddenly, like they were real and true best friends. Even sisters.

Spencer squinted at something in the distance. "What's *that*?" Every so often, once a wave passed, something white cut through the water.

Aria's mouth dropped open. "A boat!"

Hanna waved her arms over her head. "Hey!"

"Over here!" Emily screamed.

The low growl of an engine sounded over the raging tide. The boat headed straight for them. Hanna let out a quasi-hysterical laugh. "They *see* us!"

The boat crested atop a wave and then bounced down its face. It looked like a fishing vessel, with nets strung over the sides and poles jutting up from the hull. The driver had on a khaki fishing hat that was pulled far over his eyes. Spencer wondered if it was someone from the cruise ship.

"Grab on!" a voice cried. A rope appeared in the water. Spencer struggled for it, but just as she was about to reach out, Aria pulled her foot.

"*Don't*," she said in a low voice.

Spencer was about to protest, but then she followed Aria's wide-eyed gaze. A girl was standing on the deck. Spencer's head started to spin.

Naomi.

"Grab on!" Naomi said again. She reeled in the rope and threw it out again like a fishing line. When none of them took the bait, she narrowed her eyes. "What's *wrong* with you people? Do you *want* to drown?"

"Swim away!" Spencer screamed, wheeling around in the water. "We have to get away from her!"

249

But then another voice called out from the boat. "Hurry, girls, please! We need to get you to safety!"

Spencer stopped paddling, recognizing the voice. Emily's mouth dropped open, too. As a wave moved out of the way, a second figure appeared at the railing. He wore a tight pink polo, seersucker shorts, and star-shaped sunglasses. The look on his face was of pure worry and fear.

"Jeremy?" Spencer blurted, blinking hard.

A few other people appeared at the side. That slutty girl Emily was rooming with, Erin. Kirsten Cullen and Mike. Noel.

They were saved.

30
The Long Ride Home

"Grab on." Jeremy hung over the side of the boat with his arm outstretched. "I'll pull you in."

Hanna's gaze flicked from Jeremy to Naomi, then to the boat's captain, a guy with the brim of his hat pulled low. Then she stared at the rest of the rescue party. Familiar and unfamiliar faces gazed concernedly over the side. Mike looked like he was going to start sobbing any minute. Noel Kahn held out his hand for Aria to grab on to, the blood drained from his cheeks.

A wave hit the side of Hanna's head, and she went under for a moment. As much as she didn't want to set foot on a vessel with Naomi, the situation felt safe. She was freezing. Her arms and legs had lost all feeling, and, by the woozy way her head was spinning, she was pretty sure she was exhausted.

She grabbed on to the rope and let Jeremy, Noel, and the other kids on the rescue team haul her aboard. Someone threw a big towel over Hanna's shoulders, and she sat there for a moment, breathing hard. There was a flurry of activity at the rail of the boat as the rescue team hauled Aria, Emily, and Spencer onto the deck. Then Jeremy stood over them, his hands on his hips.

"What the hell were you four thinking, stealing a lifeboat and heading *away* from shore?" Jeremy shouted. His star-shaped sunglasses fell off, but he made no move to pick them up. "Do you realize how much trouble you're in? What do you have to say for yourselves?"

Everyone exchanged a glance. Then Spencer stepped forward. "I-I lost something during my dive earlier this afternoon. A family heirloom. I just thought since we were evacuating *anyway*, we could take a quick trip out to the cove and see if it was there."

Hanna stared at her, impressed with Spencer's quick thinking. "When we got to the cove, we all got out and swam around, looking for it," she added. "And then our life raft deflated."

Jeremy shook his head. "Don't think your parents aren't going to hear about this. *And* your school."

Hanna swallowed hard and felt Aria tense next to her. But then, something inside her released. Who cared who Jeremy told? They were about to confess to murder, after all.

A motor grumbled, and Jeremy instructed everyone to sit down. Spencer, Aria, and Emily sat on one end. Noel quickly occupied the last seat next to Aria, leaving Hanna no choice but to take a seat at the other end of the boat. A seat, unfortunately, right next to Naomi.

She sat down, avoiding eye contact. But Naomi was staring at her anyway. "Are you okay?" she asked gruffly.

Hanna turned away, shrugging one shoulder.

"God, Hanna," Naomi said sharply. "You could at least say thank you."

Hanna spun back around. "F-for what?" she blurted.

Naomi looked stunned. "Uh, for worrying about you when I saw you idiots go the opposite direction from land? For organizing a rescue team when I didn't see you on shore? You're making it really frickin' hard to be friends."

Hanna crossed her arms over her chest. "You never wanted to be my friend, Naomi. I know everything. You sank our boat. You *wanted* us to be stranded. You and Graham."

"Who?"

Hanna scoffed. "The guy you're working with."

Naomi stared at Hanna as though an extra eyeball had sprouted on her forehead. "Gee, Hanna, you're totally right. Me and Graham, whoever that is, followed you in my secret, super-fast spy boat and then sank *your* boat so you could die. We're both complete monsters."

Yes, you are, Hanna thought weakly, still shivering under the towel. *You're monsters called A.*

But something was strange. There was no knowing smile on Naomi's lips. No bemused expression. No wide-eyed, you-caught-me gasp. Instead, she was shaking her head at Hanna like she was crazy.

Hanna's mouth tasted salty, and when she breathed in, her lungs felt raspy and raw. Maybe it was the fact that she was exhausted, or maybe it was the fact that they'd decided to confess about Tabitha, but nothing seemed to matter much anymore. As Hanna stared at Naomi, she felt brave. "I know you know," she said.

253

Naomi frowned. "What?"

"You *know*." Hanna spoke more forcefully. "I know that you know I drove Madison home the night of the accident. I wasn't drunk, but a car came out of nowhere, pushing me off the road, and I crashed into a tree. I know that you know I moved Madison to the driver's seat and left so I wouldn't get in trouble. You and Madison figured it out, didn't you?"

Naomi's hands went limp in her lap, and her face grew pale. "*What?*"

Hanna took a breath and then glanced at Jeremy, who was talking to the captain. Why did Naomi seem so surprised? Her e-mails with Madison indicated they knew the truth. And her A notes made it clear she knew everything. And yet there she was, her face pale, her eyes darting back and forth, her hands trembling.

It felt like someone had reached into Hanna's mind and tilted everything ninety degrees. Was it possible she was wrong about Naomi?

"You . . . *didn't* know?" Hanna asked.

Naomi slowly shook her head. Hanna turned away and stared at the moon overhead, then at a fishing sticker on the side of the boat, then at Jeremy's stupid sunglasses, trying to hold onto something stable and knowable. If Naomi didn't know Hanna had been with Madison, then she had no reason to be after Hanna. And if she had no reason to be after Hanna, why was she A?

Was she A?

It felt like someone had just told her the sky was green, the water orange. Hanna looked at Naomi. She seemed as vulnerable and disarmed as she had during karaoke, or at

254

the club, or at the gym when she'd begged Hanna to hang out. A single tear rolled down her cheek. She bit on her bottom lip over and over again until it was red and raw.

Hanna clapped a hand over her mouth. All at once, she felt sick with remorse. "Oh my God," she whispered. "I thought you knew everything."

Naomi's eyes blazed. Her lips twitched, and she clenched and unclenched her fists, as though she were considering throwing a punch. But after a moment, she shut her eyes and sighed. "No, Hanna. I didn't know."

"I'm really sorry," Hanna whispered.

Naomi stared at her. "You think *sorry* cuts it?"

"But I *am*," Hanna protested. "It's not like I meant for any of it to happen. Madison was barely able to stand up when she left the bar. That's why I drove her home—I was afraid something awful might happen if I didn't. And you said yourself that the crash was, in a weird way, a *good* thing—it got her straight."

Naomi looked at Hanna in horror. "My God, Hanna. I would have preferred the crash had never happened at *all*."

Hanna shut her eyes, suddenly realizing how idiotic she sounded. "Of course," she whispered.

Naomi pressed her fingers to her temples. "I have half a mind to call the cops right when we get home and tell them everything. My cousin used to like to play field hockey on the weekends, did you know that? Now she'll never be able to again. She'll probably always walk with a limp. She went to grueling physical therapy for *months,* which racked up a ton of bills for my aunt and uncle. I should make *you* pay them. Or maybe your rich father."

Hanna opened her mouth and shut it again. She had no defense. Naomi was totally right.

"That accident caused a lot of anguish for *all* of us," Naomi hissed, her cheeks flushed. "It was torture when we weren't sure if Madison was going to pull through. And you think you can just say you're sorry and be done with it?"

"I shouldn't have said that." Hanna hung her head. "You can tell the police about me if you want. And your parents. And Madison. They deserve to know the truth."

Naomi set her jaw and stared at the horizon. "I just don't understand how someone could *do* something like that. And then, after you knew, you pretended you were my friend, like nothing was wrong!"

"I didn't know Madison was your cousin until I saw the fake ID," Hanna said. Tears rolled down her cheeks. "When I made the connection, I freaked. I thought you knew about me and Madison from the very beginning—I figured that's why you were being so nice to me. You knew, and you wanted to get revenge."

Naomi scoffed. "I was being nice to you because I wanted us to be friends. I was sick of our stupid fights." She stared at her in disbelief. "Is that why you were on my computer when we got back from the club? To see if I knew for sure?"

Hanna nodded, overwhelmed with guilt. "I was convinced you knew about Madison. I read an e-mail exchange between you and her, and you said you'd narrowed down who the suspect was. I figured you knew it was me."

"Have you ever thought about just talking things out? Coming clean?" Naomi asked.

"It's complicated," Hanna mumbled. It wasn't like she could tell Naomi about A.

"Did you put those photos on my computer, too?"

Hanna frowned. "What photos?"

Naomi balled up her fists. "A whole folder of new photos was mysteriously added to my desktop. I thought they were a virus, actually, so I didn't look at them, but when I went to delete them, they were gone. Were you trying to crash my computer?"

Hanna's mouth opened, but no words came out. Were the photos Naomi was talking about the ones of the girls in Jamaica? Had someone planted them there?

"I'm sorry," she said one more time, not knowing how to explain.

Naomi pinched the bridge of her nose. She watched the waves for a few moments, then turned back to Hanna sharply. "Just to be clear, I had no idea Madison had someone with her in the car. She was so wasted that night she didn't remember, either. What she *did* remember, though, was flashing headlights coming head-on just before the crash. That's who we were investigating, you idiot. *Not* you."

Hanna winced, but then nodded sheepishly. "I remember that car. It was like, one second, there was no one on the road, and the next, there it was, heading right for us."

"We managed to find a witness," Naomi said begrudgingly. "A lady lives in the house on the hill where the car crashed. She wasn't home at the time, but she has a security camera in the driveway, and it caught some of the accident. There was this shadowy image of Madison's car—I couldn't tell there were two people in it. There was an image of a second car, too, forcing the BMW off the road. It was like they meant to do it."

Hanna's heart started to pound. "Do you have any idea who it was?"

"We have part of a license plate number, but that's it. The cops asked Madison if she knew anyone who hated her so much they would want to hurt her, but she didn't know anyone. I guess I should ask you the same thing."

A shiver danced down Hanna's spine. If *only* she knew who wanted to hurt her. But maybe that was how A knew what had happened that night: A had been the driver of the other car, forcing the accident. Of course A had had a front-row seat to what happened next. All A had to do was pull over around the bend, turn off the lights, and watch Hanna freak.

The boat slowed, and the port of Hamilton rose into view. Hanna's friends, who were all the way across the boat, out of earshot, leaned over in their seats, and then turned back to Hanna. They were probably watching the conversation, trying to figure out what Hanna was saying. Hanna wondered if just by her body language they could deduce that Naomi wasn't A.

Hanna glanced at Naomi again. There were a lot of things she wanted to say to Naomi. A thank-you *was* in order—they would have died without the rescue boat. She wanted to try and make it up to her, too, although she had no idea how. But saying either of those things seemed completely inappropriate. It was one thing when what she'd done was a contained secret, something she was tortured by but internalized. It was another when she saw how many lives it touched, altered. It added a whole new layer of guilt and shame.

"I'm really sorry about everything," she mumbled once more.

"Yeah, well, you should be," Naomi growled. When she glanced at Hanna, there was disgust in her eyes, but then she shrugged. "I'm not going to tell, if that's what you're worried about. But you owe me—got it? And let's just hope they nail whoever that other driver was."

"Oh. Thanks." Hanna was surprised by Naomi's sudden generosity. But Naomi just rolled her eyes and turned away.

A wave splashed up, misting Hanna's face. She settled back in her seat, feeling a mix of shame and regret. All at once, she knew that the seed of friendship that had started to grow between them was probably lost forever. Too much had been said. Too much was damaged—and it was all Hanna's fault. They might not taunt each other in the Rosewood halls anymore, but they wouldn't sit together at Steam, either. It was just another thing A had wrecked.

The boat pulled up to the dock, and everyone lined up to get off. "You know, there's something else I should probably tell you," she said gruffly as they stepped on the docks.

"What's that?" Hanna asked.

Naomi tucked a windswept piece of hair behind her ear. "Ali called me up once, after she came back to Rosewood as Courtney. She told me everything. That she was the *real* Ali, but she'd been imprisoned in the hospital at

259

the beginning of sixth grade because of this fluke switch, and that it was sort of *your* fault it happened."

Hanna's eyes widened. "Did you tell anyone?"

Naomi shook her head. "I thought she was drunk—the story was so crazy. And she kept saying, 'I hate them, Naomi. They ruined my life. They ruined yours, too, don't you think? Don't they owe you something?'"

"*Do* you think that?" Hanna asked.

Naomi shrugged. "It was cool to be Ali's friend, and I *was* really pissed when she dropped Riley and me for you guys. But as time went on, I started to think it was a good thing. Ali was really bossy. And she kept a lot of secrets."

"Like what?"

Naomi gave Hanna a crazy look. "Maybe that she had a twin sister no one knew about?" Then she cleared her throat. "She said something else on the phone to me last year, though. She said, 'I'm going to get those bitches, Naomi. We're going to make them pay for what they did.'"

"God," Hanna whispered. Ali *had* made them pay.

Then she looked at Naomi. "I wish you would have said something earlier. I wish you would have told *some-one*." If Naomi had taken Ali more seriously, the girls might not have gone through that horrible ordeal in the Poconos. If Real Ali had gotten sent back to The Preserve—because surely she would have, if someone had known to believe her—Jamaica wouldn't have happened, either. Tabitha would've just been a weird friend of Ali's from The Preserve who acted strangely on Ali's behalf, nothing more.

Hanna pictured time rewinding, every horrible thing

260

they'd done turning to dust. What sort of life would she be living now? How happy would she be, how carefree? How amazing would it be if A wasn't in her life?

A clever, vindictive look crossed Naomi's face, reminding Hanna more of the girl she'd known for years, the girl who'd always been her enemy. "I guess that makes us even."

31
A Bittersweet Reunion

The lobby of the Royal Arms Hotel was done up in beige
and brown tones and filled with generic furniture and ugly
brass light fixtures, making Spencer feel like she was at a
hotel near the Philadelphia Airport instead of on the
shores of Hamilton, Bermuda. The only thing special
about the lobby was that it was jam-packed with kids
evacuated from the cruise ship. Boys from Pritchard sat on
couches. A bunch of kids from Rosewood Day swarmed
the little restaurant, where three televisions were all tuned
to cricket matches. Girls from Villa Louisa leaned against
the front desk, talking to their parents on their cell
phones. Everyone had gotten calls from their parents, who
were furious that their children had had to flee for their
lives on lifeboats. Rumors swirled about lawsuits against
the cruise company. Mason Byers announced that his dad
was taking a private plane to Bermuda that night and getting him the hell out of there. The story had even hit the
news already—THE BERMUDA TRIANGLE, a headline had
read earlier on a news program before cricket, followed

by footage of dozens of tiny lifeboats sailing away from the burning ship. Unfortunately, the story about the girls' brush with death got some airplay, too—reporters practically salivated once they realized they were the Pretty Little Liars. Spencer had found out through the news that the authorities were still trying to figure out what had caused the explosion in the boiler room.

"Okay, everyone!" Jeremy shouted into a megaphone, still doing his best to remain chipper. "We've got the fire out on the boat, but it isn't safe for travel, so we're booking you plane tickets. You'll leave either tomorrow or the next day. We're trying to get you all rooms here, so no one go anywhere. Otherwise you'll be stranded in Bermuda until your parents can come and get you."

"As if that's a *bad* thing?" Spencer murmured, rolling her eyes. She stood with her friends in a back hallway near a couple of computer terminals and vending machines, watching the chaos from afar. None of them had quite recovered from their time in the cold water—they all still had towels slung over their shoulders and goose bumps on their arms. Their hair had partially dried, but Aria had seaweed twisted in her bangs. Emily cupped a mug of hot chocolate in her hands, and Hanna was still shivering. But maybe that was because she'd just announced that Naomi *wasn't* A.

"She didn't know what I did to Madison," Hanna went on after Jeremy finished his announcement. "And, I mean, she organized a rescue team for us. It's pretty obvious the real A sent us down the wrong path again."

Spencer nodded, not really surprised. As soon as Naomi had arrived with a rescue team in tow, she'd begun to doubt their suspicions. But it was incredible how expertly A had made it look like Naomi was the one after them. Sending them notes when Naomi was around, for one. Organizing Hanna and Naomi to room together, for another.

She shut her eyes. "But A *was* on the boat. And A *did* deflate our life raft—right?"

Aria nodded. "It's too much of a coincidence. A definitely did it. So that leaves Graham. Maybe he's the one and only A."

"But I don't understand how Graham could have followed us to the cove without us seeing him," Emily said, looking puzzled. "We were on open water. And he must have acted quickly—we weren't in that cove for very long."

"Maybe he overheard us talking about going to the cove and headed out there first," Hanna suggested. "Or he could have already *been* there when we arrived, hiding in one of the caves."

Aria squinted. "I don't know if he could have gotten out there that fast after the explosion. But I guess anything is possible."

Spencer twisted her silver ring around her finger. "Graham probably spied on all of our conversations in the common room. And just because Naomi wasn't around, we thought we were safe."

"Has anyone *seen* Graham?" Hanna whispered. "He could be listening right now."

Everyone looked up. Spencer scanned the crowd in the lobby. Jennifer Feldman was tapping on her iPad by the check-in desk. Lucas Beattie was roving around the lobby,

taking pictures for yearbook. She didn't see Graham anywhere.

"I wonder what his next move is," she said uneasily.
"Do you think he's going to tell as soon as we get to back
to the States?"

Aria squared her shoulders. "I think *we* should confess
instead of letting Graham turn us in."

Confess. Spencer took a deep breath. Hanna and Emily
shifted uncomfortably. It was obvious they were all contemplating the promise they'd made in the water.

Emily picked at her cuticles. "I'm so afraid of what's
going to happen when we tell."

"We have to end this," Aria said. "Out there in the
water, I had this epiphany. I'd rather clear my conscience
than live a lie. Even if that means suffering for it, I don't
think I can live another day with this hanging over me."

Spencer nodded. "I feel that way, too. But you're under-
estimating it when you say *suffer,* Aria. We could spend
years in court. We could go to jail for the rest of our lives."

"A could torment us for the rest of our lives, too," Aria
said.

"But we'll never get to see our families again," Hanna
said. "Everyone we love will hate us."

Tears filled Aria's eyes. "I know. But like I said, I can
confess for everyone, and—"

"*No,*" Spencer, Emily, and Hanna all said at once.

Spencer touched Aria's hand and swallowed hard.
"You're right. We have to end this, and confessing is the
only way. I'm in."

"Me too," Hanna said after a moment. Emily nodded
as well.

They were silent for a while, listening to the din of the kids in the lobby. Jeremy once more announced that they were booking everyone on flights back to Philadelphia that would leave in the next few days. Spencer's stomach sank just thinking about it. Once they got home, their lives would be over. If only she *could* stay in Bermuda forever.

Suddenly, a figure appeared in the doorway. Reefer stood with his hands in his pockets. "Can we talk?" he asked, eyeing Spencer.

Spencer glanced at her friends, who shrugged and nodded. She walked toward Reefer tentatively, her heart suddenly thrumming. As soon as he got close, he grabbed her and pulled her into a hug. "I just found out what happened," he said into her ear. "Are you okay? What were you doing taking a lifeboat back to those coves?"

Spencer's body remained stiff and cautious, and she glanced around the room to see who might be watching. Even though A wasn't Naomi, A had still sent texts that she should stay away from Reefer.

But then she remembered that they were going to confess soon. Life was too short to stay away from him. "It's a long story," she admitted. "But I'm fine. Naomi rescued me, actually. So I guess she's not such a psycho after all."

Reefer shook his head rapidly. "No, Spencer, she *is*. She told me everything."

Spencer frowned. "Told you what?"

"She *was* the one gaslighting you." His voice dropped to a whisper. "She poured baby oil on the floor, rigged the bed so it would break, all of it. Everything you thought was happening was true."

266

Spencer blinked hard. "She actually *admitted* that?"

Reefer nodded. "I just talked to her. First she told me about the rescue, but then she admitted what she'd been up to. She seemed to feel really bad about it. *I* feel bad about it, too. I didn't believe you. Can you ever forgive me?"

Spencer stared at him crazily. "*I* should be the one begging for forgiveness. *I'm* the one who's been acting crazy. And *I'm* the one who broke up with you. I never should have done that."

Reefer squeezed her tight. "Of course I forgive you," he murmured. "It's been a weird trip, hasn't it? Naomi tormenting you, that fugitive girl jumping overboard, and did you hear about the explosion? It might have been intentional."

Spencer swallowed hard. "I didn't hear that." She hoped it sounded like the truth.

Reefer nodded. "It started in the boiler room. They think a passenger did it."

Spencer looked down, knowing eye contact with Reefer would give everything away. "Do they know who did it?" she asked.

Reefer shrugged. "No clue. They're trying to bring up security cameras from the boiler room, but two of them were knocked out. I heard that they made out two people on the third camera, though—they're just trying to figure out who they were."

Spencer glanced at Aria, who was still talking to Hanna and Emily. She was sure the two figures on the security tape were Aria ... and Graham. She shut her eyes for a moment, considering Graham as A. They didn't even *know* him. It all seemed so ... *impersonal*. What kind of lunatic stalks and torments his girlfriend's killers instead of simply turning them in to the police?

A lunatic called A, of course.

She turned back to Reefer, wanting to think about something else. "I missed you so much," she admitted.

"I missed you, too," Reefer said, and leaned forward to kiss her neck.

Spencer tilted her head back, savoring the sensation. But suddenly, as a group of tourists wearing American flag T-shirts waded through the kids, reality snapped into focus once more. They were going to call the FBI *tomorrow*. How would it go down? First a call, then a meeting with the investigator, then a tearful confession? She pictured her parents being summoned to jail, the press clamoring at the door with questions, their names in the news again, everyone staring at them. What would Reefer think when he found out?

She let out a small, quiet moan and hugged Reefer even tighter. When she was a little girl, she and Melissa used to play a game they'd made up called "Prince Charming," in which they listed all of the characteristics they wanted in a future boyfriend. At first, Spencer always copied what Melissa said—tall, dark, handsome, drives a nice car, and has a good job—until she realized they were, more or less, describing their dad. But even when she imagined a unique future prince, things like *smells like hemp* or *can quote obscure Grateful Dead songs* were never on her list. But as she gazed at Reefer's kind, gentle face, the same wistful, someday-my-prince-will-come feelings she used to have when playing the game welled up inside of

268

her. Even though Reefer wasn't the sort of guy she had anticipated ending up with, he was exactly what she wanted.

But would he want *her*, after he found out what she'd done?

32
The Boyfriend Problem

Even though the Eco Cruise company had chartered flights for the kids to take back to Philadelphia, there was still the matter of everyone collecting their stuff from their rooms on the ship. The boat pulled into the Hamilton harbor at 7 A.M. on Monday, and everyone was allowed one hour to pack up. Aria and Noel climbed up the ramp, then glanced at the auditorium, which was still decorated for the talent show. It was kind of sad to see the festive balloons, streamers, and search lights. Even the food was still set up, though flies were buzzing around it hungrily.

Noel pointed at the first-prize Vespa, which was parked near the stage. "I wonder who's going to get that?"

"No one, I guess," Aria murmured.

He shook his head somberly. "Yesterday *sucked*." He took Aria's hand. "I just can't believe you thought it was a good idea to go and get some stupid family heirloom that Spencer lost on a dive. You could have died."

Aria lowered her eyes. "I didn't think it was a big

270

deal. We didn't plan on the raft deflating. It was a freak thing."

"You just should have thought it through." Noel cupped the sides of Aria's face in his hands. "When Naomi told me that you guys sailed off into the sunset and hadn't come back yet, my heart just about stopped. I don't know what I'd do without you."

"Don't be so dramatic," Aria murmured, but tears sprung to her eyes. Those horrible moments in the water were so fresh and raw in her mind. She still couldn't wrap her mind around the fact that Naomi wasn't A, either— and that A might be Graham and Graham alone. He'd watched all of them, slipping in and out of the shadows so effortlessly. He'd been the one to kill Gayle and almost kill them.

As they walked further onto the ship, the smell of smoke grew stronger. Noel wrinkled his nose. "Nasty." As they passed the casino, Noel glanced at the table up front, which still bore a sign for the Eco Scavenger Hunt. "Did you talk to Graham after we evacuated?" he said, making a face. "I'm surprised *he* didn't want to rescue you."

Aria swallowed hard, revisiting those horrible moments in the boiler room. Spencer had told her that the ship was able to salvage one of the security cameras, but she was of two minds about what the tape would reveal: On one hand, it might be good for Graham to be identified and caught. On the other, *she* was certainly the second figure on the tape. Noel would probably lose his mind if he found out she'd almost been blown to smithereens.

She wiped her eyes and looked around the crowd of kids heading to their rooms. Graham's room was on that floor, but he wasn't among them. In fact, Aria hadn't seen him anywhere. She'd searched the crowds in the hotel lobby, restaurants, and outdoor spaces nonstop, but he'd been nowhere. Then again, if he *was* A, hiding in plain sight was what he did best.

But soon it wouldn't matter anymore. Once they told about Tabitha, Graham wouldn't be able to torment them any longer. They'd be free.

"Earth to Aria?"

She jumped. Noel was staring at her. "Are you okay?" he asked.

Aria tried to smile, but her mouth wouldn't cooperate. Reality hit her like a bucket of cold water over her head. *They were going to tell.* Didn't she owe it to Noel to tell him, too? She didn't want him to find out by watching the six o'clock news.

"I . . . " she began, her voice cracking.

Noel looked worried. "What is it?" he asked softly.

"I-I've done something horrible," Aria whispered.

"What?" Noel edged closer. It was unclear if he just hadn't heard her or was asking her to elaborate.

Someone slammed a door. Another boat on the harbor blew a loud, ugly-sounding horn. The story throbbed on Aria's tongue, begging to be set free. "I've . . . "

Suddenly, Jeremy's voice screeched over the loudspeaker. "Forty-five minutes left, everyone! Please pack quickly!"

Noel turned back to Aria. He looked at her for a few beats, waiting. Aria turned away. "Never mind," she said. There was no way she could blurt it all out now.

He gave her a big hug, then pulled away and touched her collarbone. "Where's your necklace?"

272

Aria's mind scrambled for an excuse. "I must have lost it in the water." She hoped she sounded convincing. "I guess it wanted to be returned to the sea."

Noel nodded slowly, not seeming that distressed. "I guess it's better you lost *it* than I lost *you*."

He gave her a final hug, then headed toward his room. Aria stepped back on the elevator—her room was two flights below Noel's. Every muscle in her body felt twitchy and charged. That very well might be the last hug she and Noel would ever share. Would he even speak to her after he found out she was a murderer?

Suddenly, just as the doors were closing, a man in a police uniform walked by, his posture stiff, his gaze straight ahead. Aria stabbed the DOOR OPEN button and slipped into Noel's hall once more. The cop walked to the end of the hall, then entered an open door on the left. Aria was almost positive that was Graham's room. She remembered where it was from when she'd picked him up to go mini-golfing. It seemed like so long ago now.

She watched as Noel strode to his room, inserted his key into the door, and walked inside. Then, taking a deep breath, she started down the hall, too. She passed Noel's door, heading to the end of the corridor to the door the cop had entered. It was definitely Graham's—Aria recognized the knight sticker on the marker board.

She peered inside, bracing to see Graham, but instead only the cop and Jeremy were there. Their heads were close, and they spoke in heated tones.

"How long has he been unconscious?" the cop asked, hands on his hips.

"Since the evacuation," Jeremy murmured. "I'm not

273

sure how bad his injuries are—the doctors aren't telling me much. His family is flying in soon."

Aria blinked. Was Graham in the *hospital*?

The cop made a wry face. "Unconsciousness is an easy way not to talk, huh? The security footage reveals two people, one of whom is him." He gazed at a cell phone. "He has a lot to be afraid of right now."

"Have you identified the second person?" Jeremy asked.

Aria held her breath. But then the cop shifted his weight and said, "We still can't get enough facial characteristics on the second person. We think it's a male, though."

Aria frowned, confused. She ran her fingers through her long hair, then stared at her sinewy, feminine fingers, each one painted a glittery coral color. She'd been mistaken for a lot of things over the years, but never, ever, a guy.

Suddenly, the two looked up and saw her. Jeremy's eyes widened. The cop looked angry. "Yes?" he barked.

"Um, I'm looking for Graham?" she said, surprised at how weak and timid her voice sounded. "Do you know where he is?"

Something flickered across Jeremy's face for a split second, then submerged. "You need to pack up now, okay?"

An alarm bell went off in her head. "Is Graham ... *okay*?" she asked, her voice squeaking.

Jeremy frowned and stepped toward her. "Seriously. If you don't get everything out of your room in the next half hour, we're not letting you back on for it."

The contours of his face had sharpened, making him

look older and menacing. Aria turned and walked quickly back to the elevator, feeling that she'd just seen and heard something she shouldn't. An uncomfortable feeling came over her, but before she could think too clearly about it, she sped up, wanting to be away from the room that had possibly been A's once and for all.

33
Emily Gets Her Wishes

The next day, the shuttle van pulled into Emily's driveway, and the kind driver, who'd talked Emily's ear off the whole drive about his sixteen-year-old son who would be just *perfect* for her, trotted to the back and grabbed Emily's bags.

"Looks like no one's home." He squinted at the Fieldses' blue colonial. The windows were dark, the shutters were drawn, and there were windswept weeds and branches all over the porch.

Emily shrugged. Her dad had sent her a terse text shortly before she landed at Newark Airport saying he couldn't pick her up after all and had arranged for the shuttle. He didn't offer an excuse, and Emily wondered if it was just because he didn't want to be stuck in the car with her for two torturous hours. Apparently, he didn't sympathize with the fact that she'd had to escape the ship on a lifeboat.

She gave the driver the last twenty-dollar bill in her wallet as a tip, then punched in the garage code and watched as the door slowly rose. Sure enough, both her parents' cars sat quietly in the garage. She walked around them and opened the side door.

The familiar smell of her house, a mix of slightly stale potpourri, bleach, and the musky cologne her dad always wore, made her throat tighten. For a few hours, she had thought she'd never have to come back here. And after everything that had happened, she hadn't had time to prepare to return to this life.

All of a sudden, her legs wouldn't move. She couldn't endure another sidelong glance from her parents, another heavy sigh. She couldn't tolerate the heavy, disappointed silence, her mother's closed bedroom door, those horrible dinners with her father where neither of them spoke. And it would only get worse once she and her friends confessed.

She stood in the laundry room, one hand on the top of the washer. Maybe she'd turn around, walk out the door, and stay at a hotel for the night. They were going to call the police tomorrow—she'd probably be in custody within twenty-four hours. Why not spend the remaining hours of freedom somewhere peaceful and relatively calm? Why torture herself by being around people who hated her?

Swallowing hard, she started to turn. But then she heard a thin, eggshell voice call out from the family room. "Emily? Is that you?"

She froze. It was her mom.

"Emily?" Mrs. Fields called again.

Then there were footsteps. Mrs. Fields appeared in the living room doorway, wearing a pink sweater and jeans.

277

Her hair looked washed. Her face had makeup on it. And—even more bizarre—she was looking at Emily with a faint smile on her face.

Emily tentatively touched her cheeks, wondering if she might be dreaming. "Uh, hi?"

"Hi, honey." Mrs. Fields looked at her bags. "You want help?"

Emily blinked. These were the first words her mom had said to her in more than two weeks. "I wasn't sure if you wanted me home," she squeaked, surprising herself.

Mrs. Fields pressed her lips together. Her shoulders rose up and down, and for a brief second, Emily saw the disappointment gather in the lines on her mother's face and the bags under her eyes. *Here it comes*, she thought. Her mother was going to burst into tears and disappear again.

But then Mrs. Fields stepped forward, her arms outstretched. Before Emily knew what was happening, she'd pulled Emily into a hug. Emily remained ramrod-straight, her arms at her sides, still waiting for the tears ... or a lecture ... or *something* awful. But her mom just rested her head in Emily's hair, breathing in and out steadily.

"I heard there was an explosion on the boat," Mrs. Fields said. "And that you girls almost drowned at sea."

Emily lowered her eyes. "I'm sorry," she said sheepishly.

"I'm just glad you're safe." Mrs. Fields shook Emily's hands.

Emily looked up. "You are?"

Mrs. Fields nodded. "Honey, I've had a lot of time to think. We're going to work through this. We're going to figure out how to be a family again."

Emily pulled away and stared at her mom's face. "Well, *say* something!" Mrs. Fields urged, looking nervous. "That's what you want, isn't it?"

"Of *course* it's what I want," Emily blurted. "I just ... I didn't ever ... I ... " She felt tears welling behind her eyes. "I never thought you'd forgive me," she mumbled, bursting into sobs.

Mrs. Fields collected her in her arms again. "I had a long talk with Father Fleming when you were gone. I know we don't talk about a lot of things. But I hate the idea of you hiding something so big. I've been hard on myself during this time, too, Emily. I feel like I've failed you as a mother."

"Don't say that," Emily blubbered. "It's *my* fault. I should have told you. I was just so ... "

" ... scared," Mrs. Fields finished for her. "I know. Carolyn told us."

Emily drew back. "Carolyn talked to you about it?"

Mrs. Fields nodded. "She feels like she failed you, too. She wants to come home for a long weekend soon to talk things out. This is a reflection on *all* of us, Emily. And if we're ever going to heal, we *all* have to pull together. Don't you think?"

Emily stared at her mom in amazement. "Yes," she whispered. "I really want to be a family, too."

Emily looked around the laundry room with its chicken baskets, old sweatshirts on hooks, and jugs of detergent. She'd never paid much attention to this room, but suddenly it was her favorite place in the world. The possibilities spread out before her. Reconstructing her relationship with her older sister. Making things right with her mom again. Having normal dinners, normal holidays—being a *family*. And being honest with them in the future, not running from them when she had a problem.

Then she remembered: *Tabitha*. But she pushed that aside for the moment, deciding to concentrate on this and only this. For one day, she could have her family back just the way she wanted it. She'd probably never have a moment like this again.

"Come on," Mrs. Fields said, picking up one of Emily's bags and dragging it into the kitchen. "Sit down, I'll make you some tea, and you can tell me all about your trip."

Emily let her mom guide her through the living room and sit her down at the kitchen table. It felt good to watch her fill the teapot with water and place it on the stove. She was about to launch into a description of the ship and the islands they visited, but then an Express Mail envelope caught her eye. *Emily Fields*, said the script in the address window.

She held it up. "What's this?"

Mrs. Fields glanced over her shoulder and smiled. "I don't know. It just came this morning."

Emily ripped open the envelope and pulled out a postcard. When she saw the picture of the Bermuda International Airport on the front, her heart did a flip. The postcard was unsigned, but she knew immediately who it was from. Then she read the date, and her mind stalled. *April 3.* That was two days ago, the day of the explosion on the boat. She pictured Jordan's body leaping from the top deck of the ship, the bubbles in the water, the FBI boats searching the bay. A smile spread across her face. Then she looked down and read the note once more.

Emily: I'm okay. Not going to where we planned, but somewhere even better. We'll find each other someday—that's a promise.

34
The Fun Hasn't Even Begun

The doorbell at Byron's house pealed around 8 A.M. the following morning, and Aria shot up from the couch. The house was empty—Byron was at work, and Meredith had taken baby Lola to a doctor's appointment.

She peered through the window in the door. Hanna, Spencer, and Emily were standing on the porch, grave looks on their faces.

"Thanks for coming," Aria said in a small voice when she pulled the door open.

No one answered. She led them to the den. All three of her friends lined up on the couch facing the TV. They sat with perfect posture, their eyes glazed and red-rimmed, like they were at a funeral. Which, of course, they sort of were.

"Are you sure we should do this?" Spencer blurted.

Everyone exchanged a glance. "I don't want to," Hanna whispered.

"Me neither," Emily said. Her throat bobbed as she swallowed.

Aria perched on the wing chair, feeling just as conflicted. Every moment of this morning had felt like the end of an era. It was the last time she'd ever wake up in her bed. The last time she'd ever brush her teeth in her bathroom. The last time she'd ever kiss Lola without a prison guard standing over her. Would Meredith even *bring* Lola to visit her in prison? A's taunting text haunted her, too: *Will Aria's boyfriend visit her in jail?*

Hanna picked at her nails. Emily stared at a coffee cup she was holding, but couldn't seem to bring herself to drink it. And Spencer kept picking up a magazine, staring at the cover, and then putting it right back down again.

"Maybe we'll get a really kind judge," Emily said. "Maybe someone who understands how scared we were about Real Ali coming back to hurt us."

Spencer scoffed. "No judge will buy that. They'll say everyone knew Real Ali was dead."

Emily wriggled in her seat, either looking like she was about to burst or pee her pants. "Actually, not if we tell the court I left the door open for her the day of the fire."

Everyone's heads shot up. "Ex*cuse* me?" Spencer sputtered.

Emily buried her face in her hands. "I'm sorry. I couldn't just *leave* her on the floor like that. I don't know if she got out, but I did leave the door open."

"But I saw the door," Hanna said. "You shut it."

"No, I didn't."

Aria stared at the ceiling, trying to recall those hot, horrible, frantic moments before the house blew up. She swore she'd looked back and saw that the door was closed tight—or was that just a fabrication in her mind after the fact?

"*God*, Emily," Spencer whispered, her eyes wide.

Hanna ran her hands down the length of her face. "Is this why you're so convinced Real Ali is the one stalking us now?"

"I guess so." Emily fiddled with the coaster on the coffee table. "But I've been thinking about it, and, you guys, maybe it's a good thing. If I bring up how the door was left open and how afraid we were that she'd escaped, maybe the judge will understand our paranoia in Jamaica."

"Or maybe he'll think we're crazy," Hanna snapped.

Aria shook her head. "You should have told us about this before now."

"I know." Emily looked tortured. "And I'm sorry. But would it really have changed anything? We probably would have been even *more* convinced Tabitha was Ali in Jamaica."

"Or we would have gone to the police instead of handling it ourselves," Aria said.

"This might never have happened," Spencer added.

Emily slumped down. "I'm sorry."

"Do you realize what this means?" Aria pushed her fingers through her hair. "Real Ali could be out there! She could be A!"

"That's what I've been trying to tell you," Emily urged. "Ali makes the most sense. She and Tabitha had been such good friends that Tabitha carried her picture in a locket. Maybe *she* was with Tabitha in Jamaica, and maybe the plan had been to push us off the roof, not the other way

284

around. Maybe that was why she was waiting on the sand, taking those pictures. But then, when things went wrong, she'd decided to torture us instead."

"But what about Graham?" Spencer asked. "*He* makes a lot of sense, too. And we're *certain* he's alive."

Aria swallowed hard. "I thought it didn't matter since we were confessing, but I overheard Jeremy and this cop talking yesterday, and Graham's in the hospital."

Hanna squinted. "Why?"

"I don't know. Maybe from the blast. It was unclear."

"Who cares if Graham's in the hospital?" Spencer threw up her hands. "He'll get out eventually. And then he'll tell about everything we did."

"There was something else weird, too," Aria said. "The cop said they identified two figures on the surveillance tape from the boiler room—one was definitely Graham. They couldn't identify the second person, but they thought it was a guy."

Spencer cocked her head. "Do you remember anyone else being down there?"

Aria shook her head. Emily tapped the table. "Maybe they just caught you at a weird angle or something. Or maybe it was a worker just randomly down there the same time you were."

"Maybe," Aria said slowly. Then she shut her eyes. She was so sick of talking about this, going back and forth as to who might be A, letting A torment their lives. She was done.

"We're telling the cops about Tabitha right now," she decided.

"Okay," Emily whispered, widening her eyes at Aria's

285

authoritative tone. Spencer just nodded. Hanna swallowed hard, but then nudged her head toward Aria's cell phone.

"Good." Aria felt electrically charged and a little crazy. She grabbed her phone and looked up the number for Michael Paulson, the man at the FBI in charge of the murder trial. It was a Washington, DC, area code. She punched the numbers on her phone unnecessarily hard.

She pressed the last digit and listened as the line rang. After a moment, someone at the front desk answered. "Can I speak to Michael Paulson, please?" she asked, placing the call on speaker.

"May I ask who's calling?" the woman said in a bored voice.

Aria glanced at her friends, then turned back to the phone. "Someone who has information on the Tabitha Clark murder case."

There was a loaded pause. "Mr. Paulson's at a press conference right now," she said after a moment. "But if it's important, I'll be able to reach him. Can he call you back shortly?"

Aria said that was fine and hung up. She set the phone down on the coffee table, her heart hammering. What was she going to say when the detective called her? How was she going to blurt it out? As soon as she did this, their lives would change. Was she seriously ready for that?

Hanna grabbed for the remote and turned on the TV. "I need some noise," she said. "I can't stand this." A commercial for ice cream cakes popped on the screen. Everyone stared at it absently. Aria wondered if they were all thinking the same thing—they'd probably never have something as frivolous and celebratory as ice cream cake again.

The commercial for ice cream cake ended, and one for Ford trucks came on. Then one for a local pizza parlor, then life insurance. After that, the local news appeared. The weatherman blathered about how it was going to be cloudy today, but there was a high-pressure system moving in tomorrow. "Break out your shorts and T-shirts!" he announced. "It's going to be unseasonably warm!"

"God, does he have to be so cheerful?" Spencer snarled at the screen.

Emily looked desperately at the phone. "Why doesn't he call back? Doesn't he know it's important?"

Hanna cradled a pillow. "There's something I didn't mention about my conversation with Naomi yesterday. Apparently, Real Ali called her when she was back in Rosewood as Courtney and told her everything."

Now it was her everyone stared at. "What do you mean, *everything*?" Aria asked.

"The truth, I guess. Everything that was in that letter she slid under the door at the Poconos. Naomi didn't believe her, though. She thought she was crazy."

Spencer blinked hard. "Why would Ali give away such a big secret?"

Hanna shrugged. "She thought Naomi would take her side. She told me Ali tried to recruit her, just like Mona tried to recruit you, Spencer. Ali said, 'We're going to get those bitches, Naomi.'"

"'*We*'?" Aria blurted.

"That's what she said," Hanna looked at Aria in puzzlement. "What's weird about that?"

287

Aria pushed her hair behind her ear. "I don't know. It just sounded weird for a second, like Ali had a team of people out to get us. But maybe not."

Suddenly, Spencer, who had been looking at her phone, lifted her head. "You know how you said Graham was in the hospital, Aria? Actually, I think he's in a coma."

She turned her phone outward. THE BERMUDA TRIANGLE CRUISE CLAIMS A VICTIM, said the headline of an online story. Aria scanned the text. *Graham Pratt was hospitalized from injuries following the explosion on board the* Splendor of the Seas *Eco Cruise ship. The medical staff in Bermuda says he is in a coma but resting comfortably.*

"Whoa," Aria whispered, her heart pounding hard. A coma? Had he been knocked out from the blast? But why hadn't she seen him lying like an X on the boiler-room floor, unconscious?

The news anchor materialized on the screen with a story about a traffic accident near the Conshohocken Curve, breaking her concentration. Aria grabbed the remote, wanting to put on something else, when the camera turned to a familiar face. Tabitha's blue eyes gleamed. Her smile was sparkly and flirtatious, as though she was keeping a secret. NEW DEVELOPMENTS, read a caption under her photo.

The remote fell from Aria's fingers to the floor. Hanna grabbed her arm and squeezed.

"We just received new information about Tabitha Clark, the teenager who was murdered in Jamaica last year," the blond reporter said. "The medical examiner has finished the autopsy, and he has some surprising results. For more, here's Jennifer Rubenstein."

Emily's face went pale. "Oh my God."

"Here we go," Spencer whispered. "They're going to say Tabitha was pushed."

The picture cut to Michael Paulson, the very man they were waiting for, standing in front of a sea of microphones. A man in a white lab coat stood next to him. Flashbulbs popped.

"After a lengthy examination of Miss Clark's remains," Paulson said, stepping forward, "my team and I have concluded that she was killed by severe trauma to the head. There were multiple blows to her skull, and it appears that she was beaten with a blunt object."

Hanna, who had been covering her eyes with her hands, peeked out. "Wait. *What?*"

Aria cocked her ear toward the TV, certain she'd heard that wrong, too.

"Whoever killed her did so at close range," Paulson went on. "Those are all the findings I can release for now."

The reporters hurled questions, but suddenly one of Paulson's aides tapped his shoulder and pushed a phone toward him. Paulson turned from the camera, mouthed a few terse words to the aide, but then took the phone and put it to his ear.

Aria's phone bleated, and everyone jumped. She looked down at the Caller ID. It was the DC number she had just called. Paulson was still on the TV screen, waiting for her to answer.

Aria widened her eyes at the phone, then at her friends, and then at the television again. TABITHA CLARK KILLED BY HEAD TRAUMA AT CLOSE RANGE, read the caption at the bottom. Slowly, she inched over to the phone and pressed IGNORE. The phone stopped buzzing as the call was sent to voicemail; he didn't leave a message.

Then she muted the TV and turned to the others. Her palms felt prickly. Her head felt like it had detached from the rest of her body.

"I don't understand," she said shakily. "Why didn't the autopsy say her back was broken from the impact of the fall? I mean, blunt-force trauma to the head at close range ... "

" ... isn't something we did," Hanna finished for her. "The fall didn't kill her."

Aria blinked hard. The gears in her brain turned very slowly. "So ... does that mean ... someone *else* killed her?"

On the muted TV, reporters hurled questions at Mr. Clark. Aria attempted a smile. Hanna reached over and squeezed her hand. Spencer and Emily hugged, both of them bursting into tears. A strange mix of feelings flooded over Aria: relief, elation, but also paralyzing fear. Someone else had done this. They were *innocent*. The words were beautiful music in her ears.

And yet her hands were shaking badly and her heart was thudding hard. They'd been about to confess to a crime they didn't commit. Ruin their lives. Destroy their relationships. They'd done it to get A off their backs, but maybe this was exactly what A wanted them to do all along. Because, perhaps, A was Tabitha's real killer. Not them.

"Guys, Graham doesn't make sense as A anymore," she said slowly. "He had no reason to frame us before

290

Jamaica. Whoever is doing this to us is someone we've known for a long, long time."

Everyone exchanged a horrified glance, definitely thinking the same thing at the same time. "Real Ali," Spencer whispered.

"It's got to be." Hanna gulped.

Suddenly, Aria's cell phone bleated. At first, she thought it was the detective calling back, but then she saw the words on the screen. *One new text message.* Her stomach swirled. Any remaining notion that Graham was guilty was gone. People in comas didn't send texts.

Hanna's phone rang next. Spencer's chimed. Emily's let out a low-pitched buzz. Everyone looked at one another, the blood draining from their faces. Then Aria grabbed her phone and pressed READ.

You got me, bitches—I did it. And guess what? You're next. —A

What Happens Next...

Yep, I did it. And I'm only getting started. The rescue crew may have thrown the girls a lifeline, but these liars are still a sinking ship. It's just a matter of time before they go down for good.

Spencer's a little out of breath from chasing Reefer all over the main deck. She may have reeled him back in for now, but nothing with stoners is ever set in stone. If I have anything to say about it, their relationship will crumble before they ever reach the ivy gates of Princeton.

Poor little Hannakins, losing another friend thanks to *moi*. I guess no one ever told her that bridges over troubled water always get burned. Speaking of burns, I hear someone from the ship will be rehabbing in Rosewood's very own burn clinic. And nothing soothes a guilty conscience like a little volunteer work!

The Preppy Thief stole Emily's heart then swan-dived into the sunset, but Jordan's postcard makes it sound like their love story's not over quite yet. Or is it? For Emily, all roads lead back to Ali. And nothing's harder to extinguish than an old flame ...

As for Aria, Tabitha's necklace isn't the only thing she needs to keep buried. If a certain someone finds out about her starry, scary night last summer in Iceland, it'll blow up a whole lot more than a cruise ship.

Enjoy the sunshine while you can, ladies. Tans fade *so* quickly when you're behind bars.

Kisses!

—A

Acknowledgments

Thank you so much to my fantastic team at Alloy Entertainment—Lanie Davis, Sara Shandler, Josh Bank, and Les Morgenstein—for helping so much with *Burned*. There has been a lot of craziness in my life lately, but working with you guys is comforting, nurturing, and definitely comical. Huge kudos to Kari Sutherland and Farrin Jacobs: Your comments and suggestions helped pull this book together. A huge thanks, also, to Kristin Marang, who always creates a great web presence for me when I have no time to do so.

Much love to my family and friends: my parents; my sister, Ali; Kristian the little nut; my cousins Kristen, Colleen, Brian, Greg, and Ryan; and especially thanks to my lovely friend Colleen McGarry, with whom I put on pretend Led Zeppelin concerts, sketched pictures of slithery lizards, danced the night away in our "knitting outfits," took our less-than-enthused kids to the bird aviary, and endured late-night vomiting at that hostel in Galway. You're the best friend someone could ask for. Kisses!